LAUREN MYRACLE

PEACE,

LOVE

&

BABY DUCKS

DUTTON BOOKS

DUTTON BOOKS | A member of Penguin Group (USA) Inc.

Published by the Penguin Group | Penguin Group (USA) Inc., 375 Hudson Street, New York, New York 10014, U.S.A. | Penguin Group (Canada), 90 Eglinton Avenue East, Suite 700, Toronto, Ontario M4P 2Y3, Canada (a division of Pearson Penguin Canada Inc.) | Penguin Books Ltd, 80 Strand, London WC2R 0RL, England | Penguin Ireland, 25 St Stephen's Green, Dublin 2, Ireland (a division of Penguin Books Ltd) | Penguin Group (Australia), 250 Camberwell Road, Camberwell, Victoria 3124, Australia (a division of Pearson Australia Group Pty Ltd) | Penguin Books India Pvt Ltd, 11 Community Centre, Panchsheel Park, New Delhi - 110 017, India | Penguin Group (NZ), 67 Apollo Drive, Rosedale, North Shore 0632, New Zealand (a division of Pearson New Zealand Ltd.) | Penguin Books (South Africa) (Pty) Ltd, 24 Sturdee Avenue, Rosebank, Johannesburg 2196, South Africa | Penguin Books Ltd, Registered Offices: 80 Strand, London WC2R 0RL, England

This book is a work of fiction. Names, characters, places, and incidents are either the product of the author's imagination or are used fictitiously, and any resemblance to actual persons, living or dead, business establishments, events, or locales is entirely coincidental.

The publisher does not have any control over and does not assume any responsibility for author or third-party websites or their content.

Library of Congress Cataloging-in-Publication Data

Myracle, Lauren, date.
Peace, love, and baby ducks / by Lauren Myracle. — 1st ed.
  p. cm.
Summary: Fifteen-year-old Carly's summer volunteer experience makes her feel more real than her life of privilege in Atlanta ever did, but her younger sister starts high school pretending to be what she is not, and both find their relationships suffering.
 ISBN 978-0-525-47743-3
 [1. Sisters—Fiction. 2. Interpersonal relations—Fiction. 3. Individuality—Fiction. 4. Atlanta (Ga.)—Fiction.] I. Title.
PZ7.M9955Pec 2009
[Fic]—dc22   2008034221

Published in the United States by Dutton Books,
a member of Penguin Group (USA) Inc.,
345 Hudson Street, New York, New York 10014
www.penguin.com/youngreaders

Designed by Irene Vandervoort

Printed in USA | First Edition

10 9 8 7 6 5 4 3 2 1

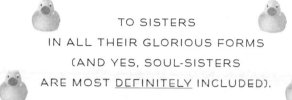

TO SISTERS
IN ALL THEIR GLORIOUS FORMS
(AND YES, SOUL-SISTERS
ARE MOST <u>DEFINITELY</u> INCLUDED).

SISTERS
MAKE THE WORLD
GO ROUND.

"Life is short and we have never too much time for gladdening the hearts of those who are traveling the dark journey with us. Oh, be swift to love, make haste to be kind!"

—HENRI-FRÉDÉRIC AMIEL

PEACE

August 15

Hola, Anna!!!!!
Only one week until I come home—wh-hoo! I can't wait, although there are things I'll miss about the wilds of Tennessee.
It's been *intense,* I tell ya. Every morning we hike thirty minutes
to the ridge of Lookout Mountain where our section of the
trail starts. Then we put in an eight-hour day leveling the
ground and chopping away undergrowth.
    EIGHT HOURS, Anna. Are you getting that?
    Are you fully appreciating the level of actual WORK I've
been doing during this "fun summer enrichment experience"?
Mom would die. Then again, so would you, my little ducky-
wucky.
    JK. LOL. *Enter.* (Heh heh, do I sound like Peyton?)
    But the trail is almost done, thank God, because my boots
are completely trashed. Yesterday I propped them against a
campfire rock and took a picture of them. *No people, just
my work boots,* all broken in and covered with mud. I am so
tough.
    It feels good, though. I mean, it also sucks, because it's
work, and it makes me tired, and sometimes, as I'm heaving a
rock or getting all mucky cutting through the creek, I find myself spacing out and wishing I were at home watching TV Land.
With a big bowl of Doritos. And a Cherry Coke. And maybe ice
cream . . .
    Yes, I fantasize about TV and junk food. Yes, I am *that* girl.
    But—and don't say *oh, there goes Carly, being weird*—
there's a part of me that's been, like, woken up while I've been
here. Like, sometimes I'll be off by myself, with *NO CIVILIZA-
TION AT ALL,* just birds and the creek and the wind rustling
in the trees, and I'll think, *Wow.*

☮ ♥ & 🐥🐥🐥   5

And then I'll wonder if a bear's secretly watching and thinking I look like a Dorito, and I'll come out of my daze.

But I do like it. The stillness.

And you? Been lounging around the pool, sipping daiquiris and eating bonbons? Ah well, we can't all be as studly as me. I have muscles, by the way. Real, live muscles. I'm probably in the best shape I've ever been in, only it's weird, because there aren't any mirrors, so I can't tell for sure. It blows my mind that I've gone for an entire month and a half without seeing myself.

But it feels *real*, Anna. In fact, my goal for sophomore year is to hold on to this realness. Trees, sky, rocks—they're *solid*, you know? (Well, not the sky. But you know what I mean.) Being here makes me realize how fake our Atlanta life can be. Buckhead especially. Holy Redeemer even *more* especially. I don't want to fall back into all that.

You, on the other hand! My little sister who is finally going to be a FRESHMAN!!! You won't be a kid anymore, sweetcakes. Is that freaky or what? We'll see each other in the halls! And during assemblies! And of course in P.E. Since I'm such a stupid generous sister that I waited a *whole year* so I could take it with you! But hey, someone's gotta be there to look after you—especially when it comes time for the swimming unit. It would be a real drag if you drowned.

JK. LOL. *Enter.*

Okay, gotta go, because Park Ranger Chris is tromping down the hill. Park Ranger Chris is forty years old, stares at all the girls' butts, and brings us candy. *Mmm, candy . . .*

Peace out,

Carly

P.S. A water moccasin has taken up residence in the pond by our camp, so I haven't washed my hair in days.

P.P.S. Or bathed.

P.P.P.S. And I probably won't get a chance to until I'm home, so I might be a bit stinky when I first see you. Possibly a lot stinky. Is it a bad sign that I have fungus sprouting all over me?

P.P.P.P.S. CAN'T WAIT TO SEE YOU, SIS! GET THOSE HUGGING ARMS READY!!!

CHAPTER ONE
BACK IN THE ~~SADDLE~~
SWIMMING POOL AGAIN

I'm out by our pool with my sister Anna and my best friend, Peyton. Anna and Peyton are working on their tans; I, on the other hand, am carving a "peace" symbol into a potato. It's not that I'm against reclining on chaise lounges and being a lazy butt, but I feel the need to do something that reminds me of my granola-girl stint on Lookout Mountain. Why? Because being back in Atlanta is weird. Good, but weird.

I'm superskinny, for one thing. I've always been skinnier than Anna, but now I'm model thin. Tiny thin. And I like it. Only wouldn't you know it? While I was off getting skinny, Anna was busy going through her own transformation. Meaning, she grew boobs. Bursting-from-her-bikini, Hooters-esque boobs. During the six weeks I was gone, she went from being "cute little Anna" to the kind of girl guys drool over, and I don't know whether to be jealous or not.

Well, no. I *am* jealous, but I don't want to be. She's my little sister. I love her.

But she looks *really* good.

"Hey, Billy Bob," Peyton says to me from her chaise longue. "Pass me some chew, will ya?"

"Ha ha," I say. Peyton's pretending I'm a redneck because of my farmer's tan, which she finds hilarious. She and Anna are uniformly golden, of course. "The preferred term is *chaw*, and sorry, don't have a pinch to share."

Peyton laughs. Her redneck jokes so far have involved: pickup trucks, deer hunting, Confederate flags, and overalls. Now she's on to chewing tobacco. "Seriously, B.B.—"

"B.B.?"

"For Billy Bob. It's your new nickname."

"No way, that's a horrible nickname."

"It is," Anna agrees from her chaise longue. She's wearing a pink polka-dot bikini that she didn't own before I left. She has cleavage, also un-owned before I left. "It's like a BB gun. You shouldn't call someone a BB gun."

"Unless that someone looks like she owns one," Peyton says.

"Ooo-baby," I hoot. "You take funny pills to get so funny?"

"Seriously, Carly. Your tan I can forgive. Almost. But you have *got* to shave your legs, or I swear I'll call you B.B. till kingdom comes."

"Oh, we're going *there* again," I say. Peyton's been riding me about my legs since she first noticed their hairiness, which was within minutes of joining us by the pool. I've been trying to stay glib—they're my legs, who cares?—but it's getting to me.

"Even rednecks shave their legs," she says.

"Well, girl rednecks," Anna clarifies.

My eyes fly to her. *Is Anna siding with Peyton?*

"Everyone knows you have this driving need to be a *free spirit* or whatever," Peyton says to me. I could really do without her attitude, which is annoyingly patronizing. "Like roughing it in the woods for six weeks when you could have done that sweet internship at the Cloister."

She eyes me meaningfully. She had issues before I left about the fact I turned down the Cloister position, and apparently, she still has issues now. But the only reason she wanted me to work at the Cloister was so she could come ogle the hot rich guys and take advantage of the gourmet dessert bar.

"I didn't want to work at the Cloister," I say. "The Cloister is full of the same overprivileged socialites as Buckhead, only in swimsuits." Buckhead is the part of Atlanta we live in, where everyone has fancy cars, backyard pools, and maids. Yes, maids. And the maids are usually black, and wear crisp white maid uniforms, and it seems so wrong to me. Though Mom's weary response to that is, "Well, do you think they'd rather be jobless?"

"Oh, Carly," Peyton says, adopting a here-we-go-again tone that's scarily similar to Mom's. "What you fail to realize is that while *you* see socialites in swimsuits and think, 'Yuck,' everyone else on the planet thinks, 'Ahhh, the good life. Sure wish *I* were playing shuffleboard and nibbling buttered crackers.'"

"Plus, I was only offered the Cloister job because Dad knows the owner," I say. "I didn't want a *Dad* job. I wanted a *me* job."

"Which you didn't even get paid for," Peyton says dismissively. She sits forward on her chaise longue. "But, Carly, back to your legs. What I'm saying is that—in general—we *accept* your weirdness. Right, Anna?"

"Sometimes," Anna says.

"We accept that you're not into makeup—"

"No, you don't," I say.

"—just as we accept your extremely unnatural aversion to J.Crew. Although I ask you: What's not to like about J.Crew?"

"Besides the brain-numbing overload of pink and lime green? Besides the tiny printed whales?"

Peyton shakes her head, her eyes full of disappointment. "It is very sad that you can't appreciate the beauty of tiny printed whales. But as I said, you march to your own drum." She leans over and plucks my potato from me. She places it peeling-side-down on the flagstone and takes my hands. "Only, sweetie? There comes a point when the drum marching goes too far."

"And you've reached it," Anna says, giggling.

Oh my God, Anna *is* siding with Peyton. I can't believe it. Last night when I first showed Anna my hairy legs, she was impressed, if somewhat horrified.

"Wow," she'd said, tentatively running her hand up my shin. "I could never not shave my legs, even if I wanted to." Then she asked what Roger was going to think, and I told her he wouldn't bat an eye, which is true, because Roger is awesome that way. And also, he's Dutch. Everyone knows that Europeans are cooler than Americans when it comes to hairy legs. For that matter, when it comes to hairy . . . everything.

"Just *swear* you'll shave before Monday," Peyton says. " 'Kay?"

Monday is the day school starts at Holy Redeemer, a "Christian Preparatory School for Girls and Boys."

"No," I tell Peyton, jerking my hands from hers.

"*Carly,*" she says.

"*Peyton,*" I reply.

"It's gross."

"It's not gross. It's natural. My crew leader, Sydney, stopped shaving her legs when she started college. She goes to Wesleyan. She says no one there even notices."

"Yeah, and she probably kisses girls, too."

"*Peyton* . . ."

Why is she being like this? I haven't seen her for six weeks, and instead of reminding me of all the good things about being home, she's doing the exact opposite. "There's no rule that says you have to shave your legs. And there's no rule that says that if you *don't*, you're a lesbian."

Peyton adopts a singsong voice. "If it looks like a lesbo and it smells like a lesbo . . ."

Anna laughs, then claps her hand over her mouth.

For a second I almost wish I were back on Lookout Mountain. I don't *really*, because six weeks of camping out and eating sardines for protein was plenty. But suddenly I don't want to be here, either.

I stare at the pool. My vision blurs, as does the sun-sparkled water.

"Carly?" Anna says uncertainly.

I don't respond.

"I'm *kidding*," Peyton says. "I'm fully, completely kidding, Carly. I know you're not a lesbo."

I roll my eyes, since I've had too many crushes on too many guys for either one of us to think I might be gay. But I'm tempted to tell her that it turns out I *am*, that I spent all summer kissing hairy girls and now I want to kiss *her*.

Only, she would laugh and make *eww* sounds and it would be too depressing. So I don't.

"Carly, what's wrong?" Anna asks.

"Nothing," I say. "It's just . . . hard."

Anna pushes herself up to a sitting position, and if Peyton weren't between us, she'd probably hug me. "What's hard?"

How I am supposed to reply? Of all the thoughts rising to the surface—

Why do people care about labels like "redneck" and "socialite" and "lesbo"?

And why do they care so much about appearances?

And why do I feel scared of drowning in all this fakeness when I've promised *myself I'm going to be more real than that?*

—none of them is worth saying out loud. Also not worth saying is how pathetic it is that I supposedly "march to my own drum," yet one of my biggest rebellions is not liking tiny printed whales. That, and having hairy legs.

I shift my gaze, and my potato comes into focus. Or rather, my half-a-potato. I pick it up and trace the peace symbol I carved into the smooth fleshy part. My next step will be to use it as a stamp to make my potato-print T-shirt.

"Forget it," I say. "Let's talk about something else."

"Okay," Peyton says perkily. "Let's talk about Anna's boobs."

"Hey!" Anna says.

"They're bigger than my head," Peyton goes on.

"They are *not* bigger than your head," Anna protests.

I force a smile. I pour a puddle of blue paint onto a paper plate and dip my potato into it. Then I press the potato onto my soft, white, just-the-right-size T-shirt, which I've laid flat on the flagstone.

"Half my head, then," Peyton says. "Each of your boobs is the size of half my head. If you put them together, they'd equal one entire head."

I lift the potato to reveal a beautiful blue peace sign.

"Nice," Anna says, admiring my artwork.

Peyton thinks Anna's "nice" is in response to the head-boob comment, and she says, "Darn straight it's nice. Your boobs are a blessing from God."

I dip and press, listening as Peyton warns Anna not to be taken in by senior guys who ask her out, but are only interested in one thing.

"No senior guy is going to ask me out," Anna says.

"You never know," Peyton says. "Face it, Anna. You're hot."

"I am not."

"Oh, um, you *are*." Peyton nudges me with her bare foot. "Carly, your sister's hot. In fact, sorry to say it, but she's way hotter than you."

A splot of paint drips onto the flagstone. "I know," I say, pretending her comment doesn't sting.

"I mean, you look great, don't get me wrong. You're like . . . lima-bean girl."

"I think you mean string bean," I say. "I *hope* you mean string bean."

"Lima bean, string bean, whatev. The point is, you're a bean. But our little Anna is . . . a luscious pair of cantaloupes."

"Peyton, shut up," Anna begs.

"Last week?" Peyton says to me. "While you were off being a wild woman up on your mountain? Your charming neighbors"— she jerks her head at the stone wall separating our house from the Millers'—"threw one of their mom's bras into y'all's driveway. They put a rock in each cup and tied the straps together, so they'd stay in. The rocks."

It takes me a second, but then I get it. An over-the-shoulder-boulder-holder—hil*ar*ious.

"What idiots," I say. The Miller boys range in age from eight to twelve, and their names are Larry, Barry, Gary, and Terry. I tell people this, and they're like, *No way*. But it's true.

The oldest, Larry, hasn't even started junior high yet, while the youngest is in third grade, tops.

"What are they doing thinking about bras at their age?" I say.

"They're not thinking about *bras*," Peyton says. "They're thinking about what goes *in* said bras. And yes, it starts early—especially if they have Anna living next door."

"Shut *up*," Anna says.

"So you know what we did?" Peyton goes on.

"What *you* did," Anna says.

"You helped. You're the one who got your dad's jockstrap."

"*Ick*," I say.

"We taped nuts into it—teeny tiny *pea*nuts—and tossed it back over the wall."

"Why?!"

"An under-the-butt-nut-hut. Get it?"

Again, it takes a second, but then I laugh. It breaks up some of the sludge inside me. "Did you make that up?"

"*Peyton* taped the peanuts into it and threw it over the wall," Anna says. "Not me."

"Y'all are crazy."

"But at least we shave our legs," Peyton says.

When I make an indignant sound, she widens her eyes dramatically and delivers her stock Peyton line. "JK! LOL!" She pretends to hit a computer button. "*Enter!*"

I laugh some more. She's so ridiculous.

Peyton rises from her chair and stretches, her sun-streaked blond hair falling down her back. "Swim time, kids," she says. She strolls to the deep end of the pool and dives in.

I glance at Anna, the first full on look I've given her since she sided with Peyton about my legs. "You going in?"

"Nah," she says, because she's not very big on swimming. She *can* swim, she just doesn't like to. Dad used to call her his little ducky, because she had a float shaped like a duck that she always insisted on using. The summer Anna turned four, Dad decided she was too big for her ducky float, and he confiscated it. So Anna decided not to get in the pool, even though the pool guys had just that day pulled the pool cover off and gotten the chlorine levels right and all that. She sat on the steps and refused to get wet, until finally Dad grabbed her under her armpits and lugged her into the deep end. When she started crying, he said impatiently, "You can still be a duck, Anna. Just *paddle.*"

"I am paddling!" she'd whimpered, moving her arms in floppy, pitiful jerks.

"Then paddle harder," was Dad's no-mercy response.

Later, it became a joke between me and Anna. If one of us was struggling with something—homework, the too-tight lid on a jar of pickles, whatever—the other would growl, "Just paddle harder." It was one of those sister jokes that was only amusing to us.

"Come on," I say to Anna now. "It's practically the last day of summer."

"I'd rather work on my tan," Anna says.

I place my potato next to my drying shirt and get to my feet.

Taking her hands and pulling her off her chair, I say, "Up you go, little ducky-wucky."

"I'm not little—and quit calling me that."

"Little duck with big boobs," I say, and with the joke right there in front of me, I keep going without thinking it through. "Hey, I know! Your boobs can be your flotation devices!"

She blushes. And then so do I, because *now* who's being the jerk?

"Sorry," I say quickly.

"It's okay," she replies, just as quick. She swallows.

I point her toward the stairs that lead into the shallow end and get her moving with a push. She wades in waist-high, holding her arms up above the water. She looks back at me.

"Doing great," I encourage. "Paddle harder!"

If Anna were the type to flip me the bird, she would. Since she's not, she scowls. But it turns into a laugh.

Peyton swims over from the deep end, pops up next to Anna, and uses her cupped hands to throw a handful of water at me.

"Hey!" I yelp.

"Get in, you wuss!"

"Wuss? *Wuss*?!" I charge the pool and launch myself into the air, crying, "Cannonball!"

Anna shrieks, and I land with enough precision to know she'll be doused. Then I'm swallowed by the water, my cheeks puffed with air and my arms hugging my hairy shins.

CHAPTER TWO
PEASANTS AND ROYALTY

After Peyton leaves, Anna and I go inside and change out of our swimsuits. Our plans for the rest of the day include back-to-school haircuts, followed by dinner at Slummy Peachtree. Slummy Peachtree is Dad's name for the casual dining area at our country club, the Peachtree Club. The fancy dining room is called the Treetop, and Dad cracks himself up by implying that we're slumming it when we eat in the sunny, pub-style restaurant instead of the fancy-schmancy Treetop.

I select the "Groovy Tunes" playlist on my iPod and peel off my bathing suit. I put on undies, a bra, and my peace shirt, which has dried in the sun. I pair it with a long, flowy skirt which has teeny mirrors sewn along the hem. I twist my hips to make the glass twinkle.

If we were going to the Treetop, I'd be required to wear an actual dress, but at Slummy Peachtree, the attire is casual. Shorts and tank tops aren't allowed, but pretty much everything else is. Another dining option is the Men's Grill, and if we were eating there, I could wear tailored pants, but no jeans. There is no Women's Grill.

Anna comes into my room and flops onto my bed. She's wearing a fitted pink dress. Another of my small rebellions is to never wear a fitted pink dress, ever.

"Fun skirt," she says. "Where'd you get it?"

"At a street fair on our last day in Tennessee," I say. I turn toward her, moving to the music. The song playing is "Almost Cut My Hair" by Crosby, Stills, Nash, and Young—how can I *not* move to the music? I lift my skirt to display my Jesus sandals. "I got these, too."

"You look like a flower child," Anna says.

"And *you* look like a debutante."

"Nuh-uh," she says. "You can't be a deb till after your first year of college."

The song hits the amazingly awesome rock-out part, and I belt out, "I feel like letting my freak flag fly!"

Anna's smile says she likes me, but that she's embarrassed for me.

"Why do you listen to this old stuff?" she asks.

I take a break from my solo. "Sixties music? Because it rocks."

"No. Really."

"Yes, really. How can you not like it?"

"Because it's *old.*"

I shake my head. "Dude, the sixties were all about peace and love and happiness. Woodstock. Social change. Resisting the status quo."

"Never mind," she says. "Forget I asked."

I stride to my iPod and change songs. The opening guitar chords of Neil Young's "Heart of Gold" fill the room, and five beats later, the harmonica part. God, I love the harmonica part. Anna, judging by her expression, does not.

"Listen to the lyrics," I urge.

"Listening," she says. "So?"

"So he's searching for a heart of gold!" I say. "He crossed the ocean for a heart of gold! Don't you want that kind of love?"

"Fergie sings about love, too, you know. And she's still alive."

I lift my eyebrows. With zero inflection, I say, "*The girl can't help it oh baby.*"

She giggles. "You're weird."

"Thank God," I say. I change songs *again* and pull up "Sugar Magnolia" by the Grateful Dead. I return to her and grab her shoulders. "There is no way you can't feel the joy of this song."

"Um . . . not feeling it."

I attempt to make her dance. She turns into a wooden plank.

"Anna! You *have* to like the Grateful Dead. It's the law."

"Oh, riiight." She makes double peace signs with her hands and adopts the voice of a stoner. "I'm Carly. Aren't I so cool?"

"Shut up," I say, laughing. "And, yes. I am, thanks for noticing."

She goes back to my bed and watches as I continue getting ready.

"It must be fun to be so skinny," she says. "Is it?"

"Ehh," I say to downplay it. But yeah, it *is* fun. My arm muscles are firm and lean, and my quads are defined from hiking up the trail every day. Not that anyone can appreciate the fabulous-ness of my quads right this second, since they're hidden beneath my swishy skirt. But I feel stronger in my body than I ever have. I feel *capable.*

Anna reaches over to my bedside table and picks up the framed picture of me standing on top of Lookout Mountain. Yes, I already printed the good ones from my digital camera, and yes, I even framed some. In the one she's looking at, I'm wearing beat-up jeans, my scuffed leather hiking boots, and a sleeveless shirt that shows off my tan arms. I'm leaning on my pickax, and I look downright tough.

Anna has never been that tough.

"Being skinny isn't important," I say. "It's just bodies, you know? Anyway, you're the one who's *hot* all of a sudden."

"Carly!" Dad bellows from the bottom of the staircase. "Anna! Get a move on!"

"We're coming, we're coming!" I call.

Anna clambers off the bed, and we go downstairs to join Mom and Dad. Mom's wearing a linen pantsuit. Dad's decked out in a short-sleeved collared shirt, his idea of dressed down.

He jiggles his keys and says, "Well, daughters, shall we take the Jaguar, which is new, and be treated like royalty? Or shall we take the BMW—an older model, yet a few good years left—and be treated like peasants?"

I groan, imagining what people not in our family would think if they heard Dad's remark. Like if my crew leader, Sydney, heard him being such a tool, or the other volunteers I worked with. One of the guys in our group was from the Appalachians, and he pronounced "wash" like "warsh."

"I don't know many peasants who drive BMWs," I say.

Dad laughs. "The Jaguar it is, then." He punches the "away" code into the security system and hustles us through the door. We have thirty seconds to get out, or the alarm will blare and the people who monitor the system will call to check up on us. Dad will have to give our password, which is "Veuve Clicquot," and in a week, Dad will get a bill for fifty dollars, because we've already gone over our allotted woopsies.

We make it out in time, even though Anna trips on her stacked heel. Dad grabs her to keep her from falling.

"Thanks, Daddy," she says.

He kisses the top of her head. "Guess you're getting a little top-heavy, aren't you?"

Did he really just say that? *Top-heavy?*

Anna turns bright red, so I say, "You just need to get some shoes you can walk in." I show off one of my Jesus sandals. "Like mine."

Dad holds down his thumb and blows air through his teeth in a *sssssssss* of disapproval. It's classic Dad—he frequently gives Anna and me the thumbs-down even when we've in no way asked for his input.

"What's wrong with my sandals?" I retort.

"Come along, girls," Mom says from the front passenger seat. "Time to go."

"If one of my clients saw you in that get-up, he'd think you were in a cult," Dad says.

"Fine, forget it."

He chuckles, oblivious to the fact that he's now hurt *both* his daughters' feelings. Except . . . how can he not know?

As we pull out of the driveway, Anna points at my sandals and whispers, "Cult member!"

I give Anna's stacked heels the thumbs-down and whisper, "*Sssssss!*"

She shoves me. I shove her back. We giggle, and I thank God for giving me a sister. I really do send up a silent prayer of gratitude, because if I were an only child and Dad was my dad? I'd never survive.

CHAPTER THREE
THE COLOR OF CONFORMITY

Ten minutes later, Dad parks in front of Venus Salon, one of several stores in the boutique-y strip mall off West Paces Ferry Road. Toni, the owner, greets us at the door. She's even more hyped up than usual.

"Our expansion is complete!" she exclaims, leading the four of us to the east side of the salon. She gestures at a sun-filled space that used to be a stationery store, but now boasts gleaming chrome salon chairs, silver mirrors, and pale pink walls. "I'm calling it my 'New Talent' wing. All my stylists go through extensive training, you know, and now I have the perfect way to help them make their debut."

"Toni, it's lovely," Mom says. I glance at the stylist who's hard at work behind one of the salon chairs. He's cute—probably gay—with spiky black hair, an eyebrow ring, and dark, almond-shaped eyes. Mediterranean, maybe? He's wearing a black button-down with a flared collar and black pants. I suspect I could learn a lot about style if I had a gay guy pal.

Alas, all the gay guys at Holy Redeemer are still deep, deep in the closet. Either that, or they've transferred to another school. If I were gay, I sure wouldn't want to go to Holy Redeemer, where "the spirit of honoring Christ" includes stocking the nurse's office with informational brochures on Hope for Homosexuals ministries and ex-gay summer camps.

The girl whose hair the stylist is drying is about my age. Her haircut is awesome: short and flippy, with streaks of sky blue mixed in with her blonde layers. *Ooo, I want sky-blue highlights*, I think. Is it possible to do sky blue highlights with dark hair?

"So what do you think?" Toni says to me and Anna. She looks at us expectantly. "My feelings won't be hurt *at all*."

"Sorry, what?" I say.

"At twenty dollars a pop?" Dad says. "Absolutely."

Toni beams. "Terriff." She steers Anna and me farther into the New Talent wing. "Carly, why don't you go first. Anna, you can wait here."

I deduce that we've been bumped from Toni's schedule and placed on the guinea-pig roster. Given that Toni charges seventy dollars per cut, I'm not surprised. While Dad has no problem forking over the big bucks for a new-model Jag, the prospect of "getting a deal," no matter how small, fills him with little-boy glee. "Oh Boy" syrup instead of Aunt Jemima, bought in bulk with his well-used Sam's card. "Wise Owl" cheese curls instead of Cheetos. Dinner for Anna and me from the child's menu, though we're both past twelve.

Though he's not going to be able to pull off that deception anymore, not with Anna. . . . But forget the kids' meals. We're talking hair here, not mac-and-cheese.

"Um, actually . . ." I start.

Toni lifts her eyebrows.

"I'm not sure, you know, that, um . . ." I flounder, because I don't want to hurt the cute stylist's feelings. Not that he's listening. He's shutting off the blow-dryer and giving his client one last hair fluff.

"Beautiful," he says in an accent I can't identify.

The girl smiles.

"Listen, Carly," Dad says. "Unless you're willing to pay the difference, you're getting the bargain matinee."

The girl's getting up, and the stylist is brushing off the chair to prepare for the next client.

"Fine," I say, because (a) I don't have fifty dollars, and (b) what the heck? Maybe it'll be great. Maybe the New Talent guy will be even better than Toni.

"Have fun," Mom says. "I'm going to Sephora. I'll be back in an hour."

Toni ushers me over to the salon chair while Anna and Dad take a seat in the waiting area.

"Carly, this is Kazim," Toni says.

Kazim takes my hand and gives a slight bow. He's even hotter up close. "Pleased to meet you," he says.

"Kazim, I am proud to announce, is as of this moment one of my *premier* stylists," Toni says. "Excellent job with Nicolette, Kazim. Very, very nice."

Kazim flicks the name tag clipped to his shirt, which says *stylist-in-training*. "Does this mean I can finally throw this away?"

Toni laughs. "No, just pass it on to Jerr." She raises her voice. "Jerr, are you ready for your first-ever client?"

Kazim's not cutting my hair? Kazim's going away? I look around for this *Jerr*, my heart pounding.

A chubby girl who looks like she should still be in high school emerges from the back room.

"Am I ever!" Jerr says. Her own hair is long in the front and short in the back, teased up to look like duck fluff.

She bounces over, pumps my hand. "I am so excited, I can't

even tell you. Do you know how boring it is cutting hair on mannequins? I mean, it's all part of the process, life's a journey, I know. But it's going to be *so* different on a real live person." She giggles. "And no, my grandma doesn't count."

Oh no. Jerr scares me—*I want Kazim!*—but how am I supposed to get out of it now? Jerr will think I changed my mind just from seeing her. The fact that it's true doesn't make it any better.

Okay, breathe, I tell myself. *There's no reason Jerr won't be just as fabulous as Kazim, despite her teased hair.* I glance at Anna for reassurance, but Anna's eyes are wide, and she mouths the word *run!*

I glare. *Not* helpful.

Jerr chatters endlessly as she washes my hair, combs out the tangles, and gives me a head massage so rough that I feel like one of those Bozo the Clown punching-bag dolls. I grip the chair for balance.

"Now," she says. "What are we doing today?" She lifts my damp hair. "You have a lot of heaviness here. Should we go shorter? Maybe a bob?"

"Like that girl before me? You could do that?"

"It would look awesome. You want to add some highlights, too?"

My spirits pick up. I glance at Dad to make sure he's not listening—he's not, he's absorbed in his *New York Times*—and say, "I really liked that blue."

"Hmm," Jerr says. "Problem is, your hair's so dark. We'll have to lighten it up first, lift some of that color out. Hey, you know what would be really cute?"

"What?"

"Do a base color underneath, maybe a deep auburn, and then bring the top layer several shades lighter. A honey blond, maybe?"

Me, a blonde? Blond is for Peyton, blond is for Anna. Blond is the color of conformity.

If I had auburn underneath, though, I wouldn't be conforming, since I wouldn't actually *be* a blonde. . . .

"You really think it would look good?"

"Oh my God," Jerr says. "With your brown eyes? A*mazing.*"

Honey blond with auburn underneath. A short flippy bob with fun colors for the first day of school.

Just do it, part of me says. *Do you want to be a free spirit or not?*

The wimpier part of me says, *But do you really want to free your spirit with* Jerr*? Jerr is wearing a miniskirt with holes cut in the front to show her thighs. The pendant hanging from her necklace is a giant rhinestone cherry. You don't like Jerr's own hair, and you want her to radically change yours?*

Then starts the endless back-and-forth of me against me, because I do that. I overanalyze things. I worry that I want the right things for the wrong reasons, or the wrong things for the right reasons, or even—perhaps most often—the wrong things for the wrong reasons.

The wheels in my brain spin like this:

Jerr is . . . kinda redneck.

So you're going to judge her for not being all perfect preppy Buckhead? She's not wearing tiny printed whales, after all. Doesn't that count for anything?

She kinda scares me.

Because you're a big fat weenie, that's why. Because you talk the talk, but you can't walk the walk.

Yeah . . . but getting an un-Holy Roller haircut can hardly be considered social protest.

But it *is* **rebelling against the norm. Isn't something better than nothing?**

I could go on like this for eons, and probably would, except that Jerr cuts off my internal debate by saying, "So whaddaya think?" She can't stop lifting and stroking my hair.

Toni wouldn't have hired her if she wasn't good, I tell myself. So even though the increasingly panicked voice of self-preservation says,

No! Don't do it! You'll regret it!, I throw caution to the wind and say, "Sure, why not?"

Forty-five minutes later, I have the answer to my question. In fact, I have multiple answers to my question.

Why not do a total hair makeover with Jerr? Well, because:

1. the "auburn" underlayer could turn out as bright as a fire engine;
2. the "blond" top layer could end up the color of early-morning urine; and
3. my bangs could end up completely uneven and way too short, as in an entire inch above my eyebrows. And completely uneven. Did I mention completely uneven?

Put them all together, and the answer to "why not?" is BECAUSE JERR IS THE ANTICHRIST AND SHOULD NOT BE ALLOWED NEAR HAIR.

Of course I say none of this because I'm in shock as I stare at my reflection. I am in *shock*, and Jerr needs to go back to beauty school . . . or better yet, Antarctica. Or *I* should go to Antarctica. Maybe the penguins would be nice to me out of a sense of two-toned commiseration.

Who am I kidding? Even the penguins would flap off in squawking terror.

"All done," Jerr chirps, whipping off my cape. "I *love* it. Do you love it?"

I gape at her. Is she *insane*? Like, truly insane, to the degree that she honestly likes what she sees? Or is she attempting to brainwash me while I'm in a state of shock in the hopes that I won't burst into tears until I'm out of the salon?

Mom returns as I'm climbing numbly from the chair. When she

sees me, she blinks in dismay. Anna, whose eyes have grown progressively more alarmed with every step of my "new look," hops up and hurries to her, and there's a quick exchange of whispers. Mom hesitates, then nods. Anna approaches Dad.

"Hey, Daddy?" she says.

He puts down his paper. "Ye-e-ess?" He draws it out as if he's indulging her by giving her his attention. "Isn't it your turn to get your hair cut?"

"Well, um, Mom and I thought maybe we should go on to dinner. And come back another day?"

Dad turns to Mom. "Maureen?"

"The girls are hungry," she says faintly.

Dad's gaze sweeps over me, and his face slackens. "Good Lord."

I fast-walk past him out of the salon, a lump rising in my throat. Anna hurries after me.

"Carly—" she says.

"I look hideous," I say as soon as I'm outside. "You don't need to tell me."

"But . . . why did you . . ."

"I don't want to talk about it," I say fiercely.

Once the four of us are in the car, however, my misery bursts free. "Dad, why did you make me go to her?"

"Me?!" Dad says, as if it's news to him that I hold him responsible.

"My appointment was with Toni," I say. "Toni would never have done . . ." I search for appropriate disaster words. There are none. "*This.*"

"Carly," Mom says, "did you and . . . that *stylist* . . ."

"Jerr," Anna supplies.

"Did you discuss the look you were going for?"

I scowl. *Blame it on me, sure.*

Mom twists in her seat to face me. "It's just . . . it's probably not a good idea to try something so drastic with a new stylist."

"Well, yeah!" I say. I'm floored by the unjustness of it, and I flop back against my seat. If Dad hadn't been such a cheapskate with *my* hair, I would still look like a relatively normal person instead of an escaped mental patient.

Anna's hand snakes across the middle seat to find mine, but I jam both my hands beneath my thighs. What really sucks is that all I wanted was . . . I don't know. To make an outward gesture that said, *Yes. I will hold on to myself. I will not be afraid, and I will not be a clone.*

And look where it got me.

"I didn't want *new talent*," I mutter, my words aimed at Dad. "You *made* me, just like you always do when it comes to saving money. You care more about *deals* than you do about us."

Dad's jaw tightens. "Enough."

"I didn't say anything, Daddy," Anna says in a small voice.

Traitor.

"Carly, your hair isn't as bad as you think," Mom says.

"It really isn't." Anna falters.

I glare at her. She recoils.

"How is this my fault?" she whispers.

"It just is," I snap.

"*Girls*," Dad warns.

I blast hate waves at Anna through pure force of will. Anna can feel it; I know because I can *feel* her feeling it. I'm glad.

CHAPTER FOUR

HOW DO YOU GET A HAIRY-LEGGED
BLONDE OUT OF THE BATHROOM?

At Slummy Peachtree, people stare at me. I can feel them, all the perfect mommies and daddies and little girls in smocked dresses. All the tennis-toned grandmothers with Botox and stylish haircuts that look a heck of a lot better than mine.

Dad tells us we can order anything we want, and I think, *Ooo, such a big man.* Is this his idea of a peace offering?

Anna orders a Diet Coke and the Chinois salad. I order water.

"Very good," our server says. He carefully avoids looking at my hair. "And what to eat?"

"Nothing," I say. "Just water."

Dad exhales through his nose, and I can tell Mom is exasperated. With her eyes, she says, *All right, Carly. If you want to go hungry, you can go hungry.*

Blah, blah, blah, I silently say back to her. I make a face, but only in my head.

The sun slants through the windows, and the muted thump of tennis balls echoes from the courts outside. Mom and Dad discuss where they should take their next vacation: Paris or Italy. Anna glances at me every so often, but leaves me alone. Minutes tick by, and my anger turns into something cold and bleak. I'm a lump on a chair. I'll never be happy again.

Our food comes, and Anna offers to share her salad.

"No, thanks." Sometimes I wonder if I'm manic-depressive and should be on drugs. Sometimes life seems so great, and other times, it just sucks.

I turn to Anna, and her features loosen, as if she's relieved I'm letting her in. "What am I going to do?" I ask. "School starts in three days."

She bites her lip as she looks at my hair. "There's got to be some way to fix it."

"It's piss blond, Anna. My hair is the color of piss."

"Not all of it."

I roll my eyes.

"The red is kind of cool," Anna says tentatively.

Yeah, whatever. "And my bangs? They're grotesque. *I'm* grotesque. I would terrify penguins."

"Your bangs are bad," Anna admits. She tilts her head. "You could even them up, maybe? Turn them into microbangs?"

"I would look so stupid with microbangs. More stupid than usual, even."

"You never look stupid," she says. "This might not be your best-ever haircut—"

I snort.

"—but, Carly, you're still pretty."

"Yeah, right. Pretty like a pee stain."

She lets out a tiny giggle.

Dad turns his head. "You're not still griping about your hair, are you?"

My cheeks burn, because his tone makes me feel *this small.*

"Think of it this way," he says. "You want to be different, right? Well, now you are."

Tears well and overflow, and *dammit*, I don't want him to see me cry. I push back from the table and run for the bathroom.

"Ted," I hear Mom chide.

"What?" Dad says. "She's blowing this way out of proportion."

Screw you, I say in my head. *You're a jerk, and I'm allowed to be upset, and you can't control me. I'm not your puppet.* I reach the ladies' bathroom and stumble inside. Stupid, ugly sobs choke out, and I *hate* it, I hate myself for being so powerless, and I swear to myself that I will never make my kids feel like they're weak for having feelings.

You wanted to be different and now you are, you ridiculous girl who blows things out of proportion.

Anna comes into the bathroom, which is actually an apartment-size lounge with carpet and chairs and spray cans of air freshener. She comes straight to the leather sofa where I'm sitting and wraps her arms around me.

"Why does he do that?" I say. I cry into her shoulder. "Why does he treat me like . . . like . . . a stupid little kid?"

"I don't think he *means* to," she says.

"Well, he does!"

"I know."

"Does he *want* me to hate him? Does he want me to grow up and never have anything to do with my family again?"

A shift in her muscles communicates her distress. "You'd still like *me*."

I take a shuddery breath. I swipe my hand under my nose and say, "Yeah. We could have Thanksgiving together and not invite him."

"Would we invite Mom?"

"She wouldn't come if he didn't."

The ladies' room door swushes open, and there Mom is. My cheeks heat up, wondering if she heard.

"Oh, Carly," Mom says, and I start crying again.

Anna keeps hugging me, and I'm grateful, because Mom stopped hugging me long ago.

"Your dad didn't mean to hurt your feelings," she tells me.

Uh-huh, sure. That's why he made a joke out of my pain.

"He shouldn't have made me switch to *new talent* in the first place," I say through my tears.

"Well . . ." She presses her lips together, and I know she's thinking that Dad may have loaded the gun, but I pulled the trigger.

"I'll take you back to the salon tomorrow," Mom says. "We'll see if Toni can't figure something out."

I keep crying. My throat is so full of tears, it hurts.

"It *is* just hair, Carly."

"I'm not going back to Venus. I'm not going back anywhere where I have to see *Jerr*."

Mom sighs.

"If you looked like this, would you?" I demand.

Mom adjusts her purse. "Anna, let's leave Carly alone for a bit. Let's go eat our dinner, and Carly, you can join us when you're ready."

Anna searches my face. I feel like a ghost with hollow eyes.

"What if I'm never ready?" I say.

"We'll see you at the table," Mom says firmly.

Reluctantly, Anna gets to her feet. My body, where she just was, feels cold.

They leave, and another woman enters. I get up quickly while she's in a stall and go to the sink. I splash my face off and press a fluffy white hand towel to my skin, holding it there until I hear the lady flush, wash her hands, and go out. I lower the towel and gaze at my reflection.

I'm a nightmare. I used to be pretty—or at least acceptable—and now I'm not. Now I'm a ridiculous girl with ridiculous hair.

But Mom, Dad, and Anna are out there *discussing* me. I can't stay in here forever.

I smooth out my peace shirt and adjust my skirt. I lift one leg to tug my sandal strap back into place, and my forearm grazes my shin. My fuzzy, long-haired shin. I make a snap decision that has an angry feel to it, a so-there act of defiance.

Though who am I defying? Myself?

But going to school resembling a pee stain will make me different enough, thanks very much. Tonight I'll take a long bath with one of the "bath bombs" Anna gave me for my birthday, which fizzes and fills the water with glittery stars and hearts. I'll sit and soak, and soak some more. And then I'll dig out my neglected razor and shave.

CHAPTER FIVE
WHY BE A BLONDE WHEN YOU COULD BE A BEIGE?

Peyton sweet-talks her stylist, Frederic, into giving me an emergency appointment the following day, and he manages to make me look marginally better.

I beg him to just redye my hair brown, but he says, "Sorry, sweetheart. Your hair's so overprocessed after what that girl did, I can't even layer color on top. You'd be looking at whole hunks breaking off at the scalp, which is *not* what you want."

No, not what I want. But Frederic "tones the heck-a-doo out of the fried bits," in his words, so now the top layer isn't piss blond as much as just . . . beige. Which is what every girl secretly desires, of course.

Frederic also textures my bangs with some kind of razor, so now they look intentionally short as opposed to "gee, cutting real hair is different from cutting a wig" short.

All of this is something to be thankful for, I guess—just as I'm supposed to appreciate the fact that Dad called Toni from Venus and made a stink about my botched haircut.

"He did it for you," Mom tells me. "He told her, 'My daughter bawled all night, which is unacceptable. I demand my money back.'"

Whoopee, I think. *I look marginally better than freakish, and he gets a refund.*

The next day is Monday, and I wake up as jittery as all get-out. At breakfast, I can't even finish my Pop-Tart, that's how jittery I am. It's not all about me and my hair, either. Quite a few jitters are devoted to Anna, since she's starting high school and high school is scary—especially at Holy Redeemer.

Since Anna's a freshman now, she'll be moving to the upper-school section of Holy Redeemer's campus. The lower school, where we spent our elementary years, is construction-paper adorable. The middle-school building is safe and contained; it was designed for "community building."

The high school, however, is its own intimidating thing: grander and stiffer than the middle school, and not even on the same planet as the elementary school.

"We'll see each other in PE, just remember that," I tell Anna. Last year I didn't sign up for PE on purpose so that this year Anna and I could take it together. Peyton's in the same class as us, too. "Fourth period, 'kay? You just have to make it till fourth period."

"Carly, stop," Anna says as she munches her own Pop-Tart. "You're projecting."

"Sorry, sorry." I exhale. "You, um, look cute. Nice outfit."

"You, too."

"Yeah, whatever." Anna's wearing capris and a white tank top with straps that just barely meet the two-fingers'-width requirement. She looks fantastic. I, on the other hand, opted for jeans and a T-shirt to show how little I care. Not my peace T-shirt, but a yellow one with the Tide laundry-detergent logo on the front. On the back, it says LOADS OF LOVE. It came down to either my Tide shirt or my brown Harajuku shirt, but my Harajuku shirt has a centimeter-long rip at the neck, and it would be just my luck to get written up for a dress-code violation on the very first day.

Also, I'm trying to believe that the yellow color of my Tide shirt makes my hair look brighter.

"If you're worried about your hair, you shouldn't be," Anna says. "You look like an indie-rock chick." She reaches over and snags the rest of my Pop-Tart.

"I think you've had plenty, Anna," Mom says from the sink, where she's washing Dad's breakfast dishes. He and Mom ate already—whole-grain toast, egg whites, coffee—and now Dad's upstairs brushing his teeth and splashing on cologne. "Have a clementine if you're still hungry."

Anna blushes.

"Mom, don't make a big deal out of what we eat," I say. "Don't you know that's how eating disorders start?"

"Neither of you girls has an eating disorder, thank heavens," Mom says.

"Not *yet*," I correct her. "But we might if you keep talking about it."

Dad power-walks into the kitchen, smelling of authority. He tells Anna and me to have a terrific first day of school and kisses each of us on the head. Well, in my case, above the head. Anna gets the real deal, because she's his baby girl and always will be.

"Now if anyone mentions your hair," he says to me, "just give them Jerr's number."

"Uh-huh, sure, Dad."

"Give them *Frederic's* number," Mom corrects. "Ted, stop teasing her."

"She can take it," Dad says.

"No, actually, I can't," I say, and he laughs. Anna's his baby girl, and I'm his ballsy, no-need-for-kisses daughter who is far less ballsy than he thinks.

"Well, I'm off," he says, cruising by the sink and giving Mom a peck on her lips. "Somebody's got to support your mother's extravagant lifestyle, you know."

"Thank goodness," Mom says. "Girls? We should get going, too."

It takes the three of us longer to gather up and leave than it takes Dad, but we're on the road by 7:55. As we drive, I lean my forehead against the window and watch the houses go by. Every house in our neighborhood is a mansion—stately, gorgeous Southern homes that were built way before planned subdivisions came onto the scene.

In Atlanta, where you live is a pretty big deal. There's a saying about it that goes like this: "In Charleston, they ask, 'Who are your people?' In Macon, they ask, 'Where do you go to church?' In Savannah, they ask, 'What do you drink?' But in Atlanta, the only question that matters is, 'Where do you live?'"

Buckhead, where we live, is the best response. The *only* response, Dad would say. Chastain is good, but the public schools have a "diverse" population. Ansley Park is code for "a little on the artsy side"— not a desirable characteristic because the residents of Ansley Park are into recycling and painting their houses fun colors and hanging flags from their porches. Flags decorated with peaches or magnolias, not Gay Pride rainbows, *heaven forbid*. The rainbow flags fly from the porches in Little Five Points.

Madison Miller, a girl in my grade who supposedly tried pot, lives in Little Five Points. In fifth grade, Peyton and I went to Madison's birthday party, and we saw that Madison's mom had a tattoo of a ladybug on her wrist. That was it for Peyton. She wanted out of there. "There's no place like home," she'd whispered to me, clicking the heels of her pretend ruby slippers.

We pull into Holy Redeemer's gated drive. My stomach tightens.

"Okay, I *am* nervous," Anna says from the backseat. I look over my shoulder. She smiles twitchily.

"You can do it," I say. "Just be confident, you know? Walk into a room like you own it, and everyone'll assume you do."

"Oh my God, you just quoted Dad," she says.

"Oh my God, I *did*." I take a moment to process this. "That is so extremely horrifying."

Mom winds past the gymnasium and eases to a stop in front of the high school. "What are you two worried about?" she asks. "Are you worried about boys?"

Oh, Mother, must you? I think. Of course we're worried about boys, but that's not at the top of the list. Not at the top of *my* list, anyway. Not this very second.

"No, Mom. I'm not worried about *boys*," I say. "And honestly, it would be best if you never talked about that with us again."

"If not boys, then what? Is it your hair, Carly?"

"No!" *Yes.*

"Well, there's nothing left. You're an excellent student, you enjoy your teachers . . . and you certainly *can't* be worrying about the Holy Redeemer *girls*."

Uh, yeah. Sure, Mom. The girls at Holy Redeemer all tend to be a certain way: as in rich, Republican, and Christian. And what Mom doesn't get is that that's a bad mix, because it means the halls are filled with super privileged girls who think people deserve what they get in life. According to that logic, they themselves are obviously blessed by Christ Himself, because just look at them. They're perfect.

The fact that they attend Holy Redeemer is bonus proof that they've been handpicked for glory, as Holy Redeemer is the most prestigious prep school in the South. That's why Anna and I go there, not for religion (opiate for the masses, according to Dad) but for the status. Holy Redeemer grads go to Harvard. Princeton. Yale. One day Anna and I are expected to go to Harvard. Princeton. Yale. Except not all three, of course. Unless it's for grad school later down the road.

As a side note: Anna will never go to Harvard, Princeton, or Yale. Anna is not Harvard, Princeton, or Yale material. Neither am

I if I can help it, but I *could* conceivably get in. Anna will end up at a lovely Southern school with a fine-if-not-Ivy-League reputation, like Wake Forest.

As another side note, regarding Holy Redeemer's Christian-ness: I don't know what I think about religion. I am religiously tangled. But while I may not know what I *think*, I do know what I *feel*. Or rather, that I *do* feel.

What, exactly, do I feel? Um . . . something. Something that has a bigness to it, and that involves being authentic instead of stupid and shallow. Like when I'm listening to a totally rock-out gorgeous song, and my soul expands, and I love the whole world and ache to be my very best self—*that's* the feeling I mean. And, well, I call that feeling *God*, though hardly ever out loud.

It's not the same God the other Holy Roller girls believe in. The other Holy Roller girls believe in a God created in their own image.

Mom fails to grasp this distinction; hence, she finds it inconceivable that I'm not jumping with joy at the prospect of reuniting with my (alleged) Holy Roller gal pals.

"Carly, you've known every girl in your class since first grade," she says.

"Exactly."

Her eyes drop to my jeans, then move up the rest of me, taking in my Tide shirt, the necklace I made myself from a piece of twine and a shell, and my earrings, which are dangly miniature doughnuts, complete with strawberry frosting and sprinkles. Her gaze goes a notch higher to my choppy beige bangs before she recalls what she was saying.

"The other Holy Redeemer girls may not be going through such a rebellious phase—"

"Mom, *please*. Laundry detergent is rebellious? Doughnuts are rebellious?"

"—but believe me, you have much more in common with these

girls than you realize. You're creating a network that will last your entire life."

"Should I kill myself now?" I say. "Should I curl into a fetal position in the freezer compartment of our Sub-Zero and never come out?"

Mom leans over and opens my door. "Go on. You, too, Anna. I have a manicure appointment with Kim-Hue, and I don't want to be late."

CHAPTER SIX
SCHOOL OF HARD KNOCKS

The homerooms at Holy Redeemer are segregated by sex so that
we don't go wild and crazy first thing in the morning. Only we do,
anyway. At least the other eleven girls in Ms. MacLean's homeroom
do. I just kind of stand there.

"Wow," Lydia says, checking out my hair. "You look like you're
from New York."

"That's not a compliment, is it?" I say.

"Your earrings are *adorable*, though. Omigod. Little doughnuts."

"Little doughnuts," I agree.

"Do you know how many calories are in a single doughnut?"

"Um . . . a hundred?"

"Two hundred and ninety nine," she says accusingly. "*Sixteen*
grams of fat. A single doughnut hole has fifty-nine calories and
three-point-two grams of fat."

"Yes!" I say, thrusting my fist into the air. "Go, doughnut holes!"

She pulls her eyebrows together. "You're so weird, Carly."

"I'm weird? You're the one who just said 'three-*point-two*,'
Lydia."

"Why is that weird?"

I pause. "Oka-a-ay."

"It's not weird."

When Peyton arrives, she squeals, rushes over, and gives me a hug. She looks awesome with her shiny hair and perfectly white teeth that look like Chiclets. And unlike me, she knows her way around an eyeliner, so her brown eyes look doelike and enormous. She smells good, too. She wears a perfume called Hard Candy that's really yummy.

"Come on, let's sit down," she says, and we drop into adjoining desks. "Did you hear that Madison Miller tried crack cocaine with her cousin in Seattle?"

Madison, as in Little Five Points Madison.

"She did not," I say.

"He bought it on eBay," Peyton says. "Her cousin got sent to rehab, but Madison told her mom she didn't actually snort it or whatever."

"You can buy drugs on eBay?" I ask. Peyton is saving me from being "odd" in front of Lydia and the other girls, and I'm grateful. I'm a little amazed, even. Peyton's so . . . preppy, or peppy, or both these things in her argyle vest, pleated black skirt, and jouncy ponytail. And I'm so incredibly not.

Sometimes I wonder why we're friends. Sometimes I get the itchy feeling of wondering how much longer our relationship will last, because Peyton and I aren't the same girls we were when Mrs. Hopkins assigned us to be homework buddies back in the second grade. Not that I want us to go our own ways. Sometimes I just wonder if—or when—we will.

"So how's Anna?" Peyton asks, after exhausting the subject of Madison and her crack-cocaine addiction. "Price Jensen already told me how hot she is. Isn't that hilarious?"

I'm startled. "Why did Price Jensen tell you how hot my sister is?"

"I don't know, because she is?"

"Price Jensen's a tool," I say.

"He drives a BMW convertible," Peyton says back.

"Half the boys in the junior class drive BMW convertibles."

"But his is black." The bell rings, and she jumps up. "Bye, babe. See you in PE!"

She dashes off, and I'm left feeling like I've just gone through the spin cycle in Mom's front-loading washing machine.

"I don't want guys talking about how hot Anna is," I say to no one. "She's my little sister."

CHAPTER SEVEN

WHEN I GROW UP, I'M MOVING TO SEATTLE

All day long, I get comments on: (a) how awful my hair looks, and, (b) how hot my sister is. I don't get it. Do people not consider the possibility that maybe they're being the tiniest bit insensitive, saying things like, "Omigod, you must have wanted to kill your stylist," and then informing me how incredibly gorgeous Anna is?

"Yes, thanks for that," I say to Chelsea, who's the third person to make the you-must-have-wanted-to-kill-your-stylist remark. "And my stylist has a degenerative nerve disease. It's very sad."

"Oh," Chelsea says, flustered. "God, I'm so sorry." She blinks. "For real, your sister could be a model, though. Did she get a boob job?"

My third-period class is Algebra II. Mr. Jones is putting some fancy formula on the Smart Board when Kylie Ranger leans forward, nods her chin toward the door, and whispers singsong-ily, "Looks like someone has an admirer."

An admirer? Me? I turn my head and see Derek Green. He gives me a "'sup" nod and grins.

No, no, no, I think, getting busy with my notebook. *Do not come over here, Derek Green. Do not sit in the empty chair which is right beside me and which does not need to be filled with—*

"You!" Derek says, sliding into the chair. He points at me to ensure that we both know who he's talking about. "It *is* you, Carly Lauderdale!"

"Hi, Derek," I say. *Go away now, Derek.*

"Love the new look," he drawls.

"Uh-huh, thanks, Derek." I keep our eye contact short and sweet, because Derek is the kind of guy who can take one little eye-to-eye and turn it into a sticky, gooey slime pit. Derek is also the kind of guy who drives home the realization that Patrick Dempsey, say, can carry off the name Derek on *Grey's Anatomy* and make it work, when in reality Derek is and always will be a redneck name for someone who likes guns.

Derek's not technically a redneck, as he lives in Buckhead like the rest of us. (Except for crack-cocaine addict Madison Miller, who's hip enough to live in Little Five Points.) Derek *is* a good ol' boy, though. He'll graduate from Holy Redeemer, go to UGA, live in a frat house with a Confederate flag out front, and then move back to Atlanta to work at his daddy's real estate business. He'll be thirty-five and have a MySpace page that says *Git R Done!* under his profile picture, in which he'll be wearing a Braves baseball cap perched high on his head. Under "favorite activities," he'll list hunting, drinking, and muddin'. That's just my guess.

"So," Derek says. He grins. "Let's talk about your sister."

Ew. "Let's not," I say.

He outlines a female form with his hands. He arches his eyebrows and nods.

I catch sight of a familiar and very welcome form ducking in through the door. "Roger!" I call.

Roger's face lights up, waaaay up high on top of his six-foot-three-inch-tall body. I know his exact height, because we've talked about it. Those three inches mean he can't join the air force, which was his dream ever since he was a little boy and his mom told him they'd be moving to America one day. He has twenty-twenty vision, but his body betrayed him by growing too tall.

"Come sit by me," I say, scooting out of my seat and taking the one next to it.

Roger lumbers over and drops down between me and Derek, who appears confused.

Sorry, Charlie, I tell Derek in my head. To Roger, I say happily, "Hi."

"Hiya, Carly," he says in his deep, oatmeal-y way. Roger's a soph omore like me. He moved here last year from Holland, and his accent makes his words come out gloopy. His last name is Goeltzenleuchter, which I can pronounce perfectly, thanks very much. *Gultz-en-loych-ter.* Most people get it wrong. Actually, most people don't even try.

Roger holds out his hand for a high five. "You're looking good," he says. "Your hair is very colorful."

I touch my palm to his. "Why, thank you."

He gives a slight nod, and I think, not for the first time, that he's like a courtly knight from the olden days . . . an extremely tall, courtly knight who happens to ride a motorcycle (somewhat illegally, but his mom doesn't care) and who has a thing for Japanese samurai movies. I also think, not for the first time, how easy it would be—how great it would be—if I liked him the way he likes me. As in, more than a friend.

Sometimes I even wonder if I should, like, try to like him that way. If it's possible to open yourself up to someone by just saying yes.

But there's something scary about that . . . so I pull my hand away before the touching goes on too long.

"All right, class," Mr. Jones says. "Let's see what you remember from Algebra I."

I turn toward the Smart Board, but my thoughts go elsewhere.

Roger is the one person—for real, the one, single person I've talked to today—who didn't say anything about Anna's new hotness. How sad is that that he's the *only one*? *I'm* the older sister. I'm the one people are supposed to admire, not Anna.

Although is *admire* the right word? Do people *admire* someone's hotness, or *desire* it? I'm not sure I want to be desired for something as superficial as my bra size—although, fine, in Anna's case, it's her plain and undeniable gorgeousness, too. At any rate, I'm busy feeling sorry for myself when a student aide enters the room and delivers a note to Mr. Jones.

Mr. Jones skims it and says, "Carly, you're needed in the headmaster's office."

"I am?"

"No, I just thought it would be fun to mess with you," Mr. Jones says in a deadpan. People titter, and I blush. I get up and grab my backpack.

"Everything okay?" Roger says in his deep voice.

"I don't know." *It's not my hair, is it? Is hideous hair against the dress code?*

"Call me after school. Let me know what's up."

I nod and angle my body to navigate through the row of desks.

"Say 'hey' to your sister for me," Derek whispers as I pass.

In the hall, I pass Madison Miller, who's jamming a Vera Bradley tote into her locker. She doesn't look like a crack addict.

She glances at me and says, "Hey, Carly. You have a good summer?"

"Yeah," I say. I pause, happy to delay my visit to Headmaster Perkins. "You?"

"The best. I am so moving to Seattle for college. That's where I was all summer. Ever been?" When I shake my head, she says, "You've got to go. *So* laid-back—you'd love it."

"Cool."

"People aren't uptight like they are here. Nice bangs, by the way. Very Feist."

"Thanks," I say, cheered by her comment. Feist does know how to rock the short bangs.

"So what class are *you* late to?" she asks.

"Um, none. I got called to the headmaster's office."

She laughs. "On the first day of school? Such a badass."

"That's me, a Holy Roller badass," I say drily.

"Ha. Guess it is an oxymoron, huh?" She shuts her locker and heads down the hall, tossing me an over the shoulder wave. "Later!"

CHAPTER EIGHT
PERCOLATE THIS

In the waiting room outside Headmaster Perkins's office, Anna sits in a leather armchair with her knees pulled up to her chest. My heart rate spikes, and I rush over.

"Anna?" I say. She's been crying. I can see the tearstains. "What happened? Are you okay?"

Anna looks up at me. Her lashes are wet and dark. "I got in trouble during computer science. But it wasn't my fault."

I glance at the secretary, who eyes me over the top of her glasses.

"Your sister was having a hard time calming down," she says. She goes back to her typing. "She wanted you."

"They called Dad," Anna says in a scared voice. "Oh my God, I'm so dead."

I squeeze onto the chair with her. "Anna, tell me what happened."

"This guy, this jerk *Ben*, told me I looked like some actress, and since Mr. Abernathy wasn't there yet, he pulled up her picture on Google."

I try to read her face. True, you're not supposed to use the computers for nonacademic purposes, but surely she didn't get busted just for that. "Who's the actress? Was she ugly or something?"

"No. She was naked."

"What?!"

The secretary lifts her head. I can tell by her expression that she already knows what happened.

"Her name was Tricky Trixie," Anna whispers.

Tricky Trixie?

Ohhh. Comprehension dawns. *My little sister got busted for looking at porn.*

She sniffles. "Ben was all, 'They think their filters can keep me out, but they can *never* keep me out, ha ha ha.'"

"He hacked the filters?"

"And then he was like, 'Want to see that unit on apes and evolution that was blocked last year?' So he pulled that up, too. That's when Mr. Abernathy came in."

"Why didn't you just not look?"

"I did! I tried to escape, but he pulled me back!"

The computer lab is equipped with cushy office chairs on wheels, and I imagine the tug-of-war that must have gone on: Anna paddling her feet to push away from this Ben jerk, and him grabbing Anna's chair and towing her back.

"Did you get in trouble for the evolution or the . . . other thing?"

"Both. Mr. Abernathy pulled up the search history."

"Well, why didn't you tell Mr. Abernathy that it was completely Ben, and you had nothing to do with it?"

"Because Mr. Abernathy, like, snuck up on us, and Ben let go of my chair, and it tipped over backward, and the whole class laughed."

"*Ouch.*"

Her eyes fill with tears.

The door to Headmaster Perkins's inner office opens, and a guy with gelled hair slinks out. Ben, I assume. His mother is with him and looks like a prune. She must be one of those helicopter moms to have gotten here so fast. Bringing up the rear is Headmaster Perkins, otherwise known as the Percolator.

"So . . . they called Dad?" I ask.

"The secretary tried Mom first, but she didn't answer her cell."

Of course she didn't. Mom never answers her cell, because she can never dig it out of her purse in time. "Is he on his way?"

"He was in a meeting. The secretary left a message."

Headmaster Perkins is finishing up with Ben and Ben's mom. Headmaster Perkins is saying, " . . . still responsible for any assignments during the period of his suspension."

Suspension? This is not good. Dad will *not* be happy if one of his daughters gets suspended on the first day—or any day—of school. Dad's daughters don't get suspended, period.

Headmaster Perkins looks our way. His expression is foreboding. "Anna?"

Anna shakily stands up. Ben's mother passes us on her way out and gives Anna a nasty look, like she thinks Anna is an oversexed wench. Anna turns red and crosses her arms over her chest.

"Headmaster Perkins, I need to talk to you," I say. "It's important."

He scans the waiting area. "Where are your parents?"

"Um, my dad's in a meeting. My mom's . . . I don't know. Shopping?"

He glances at his watch. He sighs. "All right. Come along, girls—both of you."

In his office, he listens as I tell Anna's side of the story. He sits behind his humongous desk and drums his fingers, and he's impatient and imposing in the particular way of Southern men who don't expect to be challenged. I'm quite familiar with this type, and

I address him in the tone I know he's most likely to hear. I hold his gaze. I use a confident voice. I throw back my shoulders.

The Percolator turns to Anna when I'm done. "Is what your sister said true?"

"Yes, sir," Anna says.

"Your teacher seems to think you were an equal participant."

"I wasn't. I would *never*."

"Did you tell him that?"

"Um . . . not exactly."

"Why not?"

"I don't know."

"Anna," Headmaster Perkins says, "you can't expect your sister to come to your rescue in situations like this."

"Okay," she whispers, while I think, *Is that what I did? Come to her rescue?*

He stands up. "I'll have Joyce call your father and see if she can catch him before he leaves. But next time, Anna, I want you to come to me yourself." He pauses. "Or rather, I don't want there to *be* a next time. Do you understand?"

"Yes, sir," she says.

"So . . . she's not suspended?" I ask.

"No, you can both return to class."

"Thank you, sir." I surprise myself by sticking out my hand.

He shakes it. I keep my grip firm.

CHAPTER NINE
LITTLE GIRLS DON'T DRINK
BRANDY

Dad is late getting home from work, and Anna and I both think, *Wh-hoo, no confrontation! We escaped the flames!* Anna doesn't *tell* me she thinks that, but she doesn't have to, just as she doesn't have to tell me not to mention Tricky Trixie to Mom. Why burden her with unnecessary information?

But when Dad finally arrives, he summons Anna and me to the living room. It's his favorite room of the house. Fire turned on, snifter of brandy in hand, Mom by his side with a flute of champagne—everything just the way he likes it.

Anna and I perch nervously on the sofa across from them.

"Well, girls, I hear you had an exciting day at school," he says.

Uh-oh.

"Not really," Anna says. I can feel her not looking at me, just as I'm carefully not looking at her.

"That's not what your headmaster reported," Dad says.

Mom is taken aback. "You spoke with Headmaster Perkins, Ted?"

"I did indeed," Dad says.

"You didn't mention anything to me!"

"Well, Maureen, I wanted the girls here when I told you." His tone is stern, but there's something off about it. He takes a sip of his brandy, and I grow suspicious. *Is that a smile he's hiding?*

"When you told me *what?*" Mom asks. She turns to me and Anna. "Girls, did something happen at school?"

Dad holds his hand out like a traffic guard and makes a pre-emptive strike that sounds like *umphh*. This means we're not allowed to talk. This is *his* story—well, he's turning it into his story—and he wants to tell it his way, wringing every ounce of pleasure from it.

"Maureen," he says, "which of your daughters do you think was asked to leave class for looking at porn?"

Mom regards me with dismay. "Carly!"

My mouth opens. "Mom!"

Dad laughs.

"It wasn't *me!*" I say.

She shifts to Anna. "*An*-na?!"

"*Mom!*" Anna makes an indignant sound and turns to Dad. "*Da-a-ad!*"

Dad's laughter swells. He's going to start wheezing soon.

"She wasn't looking at porn," I say. My face heats up, because *porn* is not a word I've ever used in front of Mom and Dad. I hope never to do so again. "Some kid named Ben was."

"And he tipped my chair over," Anna says. "I fell completely backward."

"I didn't hear about that," Dad says, and sure enough, here comes the wheeze. It's a cough wheeze. His face turns red.

"Don't laugh," Anna says. "It really hurt."

"All Headmaster Perkins told me was that you were caught looking at pictures of a naked lady."

"Named Tricky Trixie," I contribute.

Dad goes off again, louder and wheezier. Mom tries not to

laugh, but not very hard. She's part horrified and part tickled, and the tickled part wins out.

"It's not funny," Anna complains.

"Believe me, it is," Dad says, and I have to admit that despite their many other flaws, Mom and Dad aren't uptight about certain things the way most Holy Redeemer parents are. If Anna really had been looking at porn—like, deliberately—it wouldn't be funny. But the fact that she got *falsely* accused of looking at porn on her first day as a freshman at a Christian prep school . . . Now, that *is* funny.

Not to Anna, maybe. But to the rest of us.

Dad pats the cushion beside him.

"Carly, come here," he says.

"Me?" I stand and go over. I sit on the edge of the sofa.

"Headmaster Perkins told me you're the one who bailed Anna out."

"Uh, yeah. I guess." I glance at Anna.

"Well, I think that's terrific," Dad says. "A fine example of sisterly love."

Anna and I groan, and Dad chuckles. Dad is a big fan of the term *sisterly love*, and he works it into the conversation whenever one of us—usually me—is told to do something for the other. Like, if Mom and Dad go out and I have to stay with Anna, I'm told to do it out of sisterly love. Or if Anna can't figure out her homework, I'm expected to help her out of sisterly love. When we were younger, I even had to clean up Anna's room out of sisterly love, which was insanely unfair. But if I complained, Dad would cut me off with his preemptive *umphh* and say, "I don't want to hear it. You two are sisters—it's your job to help each other."

"How did you bail her out, Carly?" Mom asks.

"She talked to Headmaster Perkins for me," Anna tells her before I can. "She explained that I didn't do it."

Mom meets my eyes and smiles. "Oh. Good. I'm proud of you, Carly."

How strange that Headmaster Perkins chided Anna for allowing me to "rescue" her when she should have rescued herself, while Mom and Dad's response is to praise me for it.

"Well . . . thanks." Since I'm here already, I lean over and give first Mom, and then Dad, a brief hug.

"Watch the brandy," Dad says, raising it out of harm's way. But he hugs me back—or rather, he pats me, kind of the way you might pat a dog if you aren't exactly a dog person. Then he sends me and Anna up to bed so that he and Mom can relax in peace.

CHAPTER TEN
SWEET ENOUGH TO EAT

Anna comes to my room after brushing her teeth. She stands in the doorway until I look up from my book, *The Tao of Pooh*.

"Ye-e-essss?" I say.

"Can I sleep in your room?" Anna asks. She's wearing her blue pj's with the cherries all over them. The top is sleeveless with a single cherry on it, and underneath it are the words "SWEET ENOUGH TO EAT!"

"Nice pj's," I remark. *I* bought those pj's first, one day last spring when I went shopping with Peyton. Anna commented on how cute they were, and the next day she came home with the exact same pair.

"Can I?" she presses.

"I guess . . . *if* you stay on your side."

She walks around the bed and slides in. I mark my place in my book, put it down, and turn off the lamp. I wiggle down flat and smush my pillow into the right shape.

"That guy?" she says. "Ben?"

"He's skeevy."

"I know." She pauses. "But, Carly, it was so weird. It was like he was hitting on me or something."

I snort. "Showing a girl porn, always the way to her heart."

She rolls on her side and gazes at me. "You think he wasn't?"

Instead of looking back at her, I stare at the ceiling. I recall all the people—girls and guys alike—who commented on Anna's hotness today. "No, I'm sure he was. But back to exhibit A: skeevy."

"I'm not saying I *like* him, Carly. Gross. I'm just saying it was weird."

I turn so we're facing each other. Her eyes are liquid; her long hair spills over her shoulder. "Guys are going to hit on you sometimes," I tell her, wishing the words came from a nicer place inside me.

"I wouldn't mind having a boyfriend," she says. "*Not* Ben. But . . . you know."

"Yeah, I hear you." In bed, with the lights off, is a good place for this sort of conversation. I have thoughts on the matter, so I share them. "A guy who isn't a player. A guy who likes you for who you are, not how hot you are. Like, a really good friend who happens to be a boy, and who you get to kiss."

"Ex*act*ly."

"And one day I will find this miracle guy, and he will be my love boodle."

Anna giggles. "You cannot call your boyfriend your 'love boodle.'"

"True, because I don't have a boyfriend."

"It's not a very manly nickname."

"I'd call him that *ironically*, obviously. He'd be my ironic love boodle."

"Ahhhh. And how are you going to find your ironic love boodle?"

"Are you talking about me, or are you talking about you?"

"You."

"For real?" I say. "Or do you just want to know how I'm going to find *my* ironic love boodle so you can find *your* ironic love boodle? Because for the record, you are banned from calling anyone love boodle, ever. I claim that nickname, and you don't get to use it. Got it?"

She studies me. "You don't know how you're going to find your ironic love boodle, do you?"

"Well . . . um . . . maybe he has to find me."

"But what if he doesn't?"

"I don't know. No ironic love boodle, I guess."

She tugs the sheet over her bare shoulder, and in the process yanks my section away. I yank it back and give her a look that says, *Watch it, sheet stealer.*

She says, "I think Roger would be a good ironic love boodle."

"For me, or for you?"

"For *you*," she says, as if I've hurt her feelings. "I would never steal Roger!"

"'Steal' him? Anna, you can't *steal* him because I don't *have* him."

"You could if you wanted."

"Yeah, but I don't." I feel the same confusing unease I always do when circling the idea of liking Roger *that way.* "I love Roger, but I don't *love* him love him."

"Why not?"

"What do you mean, 'why not'?"

"What do you mean, 'what do you mean'? I mean, why not?"

I shift, realizing I forgot to call Roger and tell him what happened with Headmaster Perkins. *Oops.*

Then I think back to when I first met Roger, last year when he started at Holy Redeemer. Right away I liked him better than the other Holy Roller guys. Maybe because he wasn't from the South, or even the United States. Maybe because he didn't know how to be anyone other than himself.

"Did I tell you about the time our French class went to Chateau Élan?" I ask Anna. Chateau Élan is a "French" winery a little less than an hour outside of Atlanta. Madame d'Aubigné took us there on a field trip last year. I guess she found it perfectly reasonable to take a class of ten freshmen to learn about wine.

Anna shakes her head.

"Well, Roger and I and two other girls got stuck riding with Eddie Zinsser, who already had his license."

"How could he have his license as a freshman?"

"Because he was sixteen. He was held back."

"Oh. Who'd the other kids go with?"

"Madame d'Aubigné. She has a minivan. So we were on the way to the chateau, and Eddie saw a cop behind us on the highway. We weren't doing anything wrong, but Eddie freaked out, going, 'Oh no! The fuzz is behind us, the fuzz is behind us!'"

"The *fuzz* is behind us?"

"He was trying to be funny. Anyway, Roger told me later that he had a moment of private panic, whipping around and scanning the air for giant balls of fuzz."

Anna frowns.

"*Fuzz*," I repeat. "As in actual dustball-y stuff? Because he'd just moved from Holland. He'd never heard anyone call the police that."

"Because nobody *does* call the police that."

"True. Only Eddie, and actors in cheesy sitcoms."

Anna attempts to claim more sheet. I slap her hand.

"I don't get what this has to do with Roger not being your love boodle," she says.

I sigh, because I don't, either. All I know is that while Roger is sweet and wonderful and sometimes even adorable in his gentle-giant sort of way, he's not boodle material. He's just, well, *Roger*.

"Maybe I should become a nun," I say.

Anna yawns. She rubs her nose with the back of her hand. "You'll find your love boodle," she says. "You just have to paddle harder."

CHAPTER ELEVEN
ONE-WAY TICKET TO HELL

On Friday, we have our first all-school assembly. We'll have these babies every Friday for the rest of eternity—or until the end of high school, whichever comes first—and they will enlighten our souls. Holy Redeemer's all over that, because it is Holy Redeemer's mission to develop not just our minds, not just our bodies, but OUR WHOLE PERSON, soul included.

Today, our lecturer is Dr. al-Fulani, who taught my seventh-grade Bible class. I don't like him.

"Jesus is living water," Dr. al-Fulani is saying. "He satisfies our thirst when we are parched." Dr. al-Fulani is a short, swarthy man, and when he leans forward on the podium, he resembles a troll. "Indeed, it is through the baptism of Christ that we are born anew, wet and dripping like a naked tot."

Snickers ripple through the auditorium. *We're na-ked tots, we're na-ked tots!* They're friendly snickers, though, because when it comes to disliking Dr. al-Fulani, I'm in the minority.

I *used* to like him. I used to like him a lot. On the first day of seventh-grade Bible class, he announced a weakness for Gummi Worms, and I thought he was adorable: a Gummi Worm–eating troll who emerged from the center of the earth and discovered the wonder of sugary candy. Almost every day someone would bring him a bag of Gummi Worms, and he would smile and thank who-ever it was. In a stroke of genius, I once brought him *sour* Gummi Worms, but made no mention that they were different from the normal kind. The whole class erupted in laughter when his face puckered like a clam.

Dr. al-Fulani laughed, too. He shook his finger at me, but he laughed.

Then, two months into the semester, Dr. al-Fulani taught us that according to the Bible, divorce was a sin, and that any person who got divorced would go to hell. Literally.

"But, Dr. al-Fulani, my parents are divorced," Lucy Rothchild had said. Lucy, who had thick ankles and carried boxes of raisins around for snacks. "They got divorced when I was five."

Dr. al-Fulani didn't waver. If anything, he grew more solemn. "I am sorry, Lucy. It is God's law." He went on to explain that divorcés weren't the only ones who would writhe in Satan's flames. Jewish people would go to hell, too, as would Muslims and Buddhists and basically anyone who didn't accept Jesus Christ as their personal savior.

At that moment, I lost all respect for Dr. al-Fulani. Not only was he cruel to Lucy, telling her that her parents were going to fry, but even at twelve, I knew that any God worth His (or Her) salt wouldn't play eenie-meenie-miney-moe like that, tossing people willy-nilly into hell just because they grew up with a different reli-gion, or no religion at all.

Anyway, I don't believe in hell.

Didn't then.

Don't now.

———

After assembly, I find Roger out on the quad and flop down beside him. I lie back on the grass and kick off my sandals. I dig my toes into the freshly mown grass and let out the aggrieved sigh I've been holding throughout Dr. al-Fulani's talk.

Because he's Roger, he understands. "I hear you," he says.

"That man gets my goat," I say.

"Two thousand years earlier, he would have burned your goat."

I snort-laugh. Burnt offerings, sheesh. *Here, God, would you like a slab of charred ram?*

"Why is this school so *weird?*" I say. "Do kids in normal schools get lectured about the state of their souls? Do normal kids get told that they have to do A, B, and C in order to get into heaven?"

"Nope," Roger says, leaning back on his elbows.

"Everybody acts like . . . *la la la, life as usual.* It's like they don't even consider the possibility that Dr. al-Fulani could be wrong. Or that the other Holy Roller teachers could be wrong, or their ministers, or their *parents* . . ."

Roger chuckles.

"What?"

"You know what their religious beliefs are? All those people?"

"*Yes.*" I shove him, knocking his elbow out of place and making him fall.

"Ow."

"Doesn't it bug you?" I say. "*Please* tell me it bugs you."

"Doesn't *what* bug me?"

"I don't know. Just . . . everything."

He lies on his side and props his head on his hand. He gazes at me. "Some things bug me. Not everything."

I blush. I also rip up a handful of grass and throw it at him. And then, because it's still not enough, I reshove him so that he topples onto his back and can't stare at me anymore.

When enough time's gone by, I say, "Maybe it's just . . . you know."

He waits.

"The *transition*. Summer, which was lovely and free, and now school, which isn't. All the God talk. All the pious faces, soaking it in."

"It *is* a Christian school," he points out.

"Don't I know it."

"Half the kids in my row weren't even paying attention during assembly."

I sigh again. He's right, I know he's right. But just because the kids in Roger's row—or mine—weren't paying attention, that doesn't mean they disagreed with Dr. al-Fulani. It just means they didn't feel the need to even think about his message, because they'd already swallowed it hook, line, and sinker.

I pull up more grass, wondering why this twists me up so much. It doesn't twist Anna up. I saw her in the front of the auditorium with her friend Georgia. They were scrunched in close, giggling at something on Georgia's cell phone.

It doesn't twist Roger up, either. He just observes—sometimes chuckles—but mainly does his own thing.

He's my hero that way, the ultimate example of someone who just *is*. Roger is Roger is Roger.

Where does that leave me? Who am I at *my* core, beneath my shifting thoughts and lack of clarity on pretty much everything?

"I don't believe that Jesus is the only way," I say at last. It sounds insanely stupid.

"I don't, either," Roger says.

"You don't?"

"I don't get worked up about it, though."

Coming from anyone else, Roger's remark would sound like a dig at the fact that I *do* get worked up about it. But Roger's just being his laid-back self. All of a sudden I feel lighter.

"So . . . it's okay that I believe in God, but that I don't go around praising Jesus?"

"You can praise Jesus if you want. You can praise Muhammad if you want."

"Or the grass. Can I praise the grass?" I pull up another tuft and sprinkle it on him.

He jerks reflexively, like a dog shaking off water.

"Praise grass," I say.

He looks like he's going to sneeze. "Praise grass."

CHAPTER TWELVE

KIM-HUE LOVES WORKING ON MAUREEN'S FEET

That afternoon, Mom takes Anna and me to get celebratory mani/pedis.

"What are we celebrating?" Anna asks from the backseat of Mom's Beamer.

"The fact that our first week is over, and we survived," I say from the front. One week down—yahoo!

"I just thought it would be a nice treat for you girls," Mom says. She glances at my toes, which are peeking out of my Jesus sandals. They are perhaps a bit grass-stained. "And Carly, your feet could use some attention."

"So true," Anna says. "You know Kim-Hue *loves* working on your feet."

"Shut up," I say. "She loves working on *Mom's* feet, not mine."

"Girls, don't be disrespectful," Mom says, taking a left out of Holy Redeemer's back gate. "Kim-Hue has worked very hard to get where she is. Do you know she used her manicuring money to put her sister through college?"

"Yes, Mom," we chorus. We have heard (and heard and heard) how wonderful Kim-Hue is. How she came to America with her younger sister, Linh, five years ago; how she put Linh through college; how she then brought her parents over from Korea and had them move in with her and her husband.

"*And* she insisted they take the master bedroom!" Mom marvels whenever she trots out that particular nugget of Kim-Hue gold.

"We're not being disrespectful to Kim-Hue," I tell Mom as we drive down Moores Mill. "It's just funny that she says she loves your feet."

"Well, who's to say she doesn't? I keep my feet very clean." She glances at me. "Don't you think she'd rather work on clean feet than filthy feet?"

"*Mom,*" I say.

"Carly has filthy fee-eet," Anna sings.

"Anna is a stu-pid head," I sing back.

Anna flops back against her seat. "Hey, Mom, did you bring us a snack?"

Mom indicates her purse. "Carly, would you please hand your sister a granola bar?"

I fumble in her bag and pull out two foil-wrapped bars. They're not granola bars. They're ninety-calorie Special K cereal bars. I hand one over my shoulder to Anna and drop the other back into Mom's purse.

"Blech," Anna says. "Can we stop by Whole Foods and get monster cookies?"

"I'm afraid we don't have time," Mom says.

That is extremely unlikely, because Whole Foods is five minutes from Cloud Nine. What's more likely is that Mom doesn't want Anna to have a monster cookie. So to call her on it, I say, "By which she means, 'No, you porker. Eat your nice cereal bar and be quiet.'"

Anna kicks my seat.

"Remember when you were the littlest Billy Goat Gruff in Reader's Theater?" I say. "And Georgia said you were too chubby to be the littlest billy goat and you should go on a diet?"

"I was in first grade," Anna says.

"She said you tromped too loud. Remember?"

Anna doesn't respond, and her nonresponse has a bad feeling to it. I peek back at her, and her expression tells me that what I intend as a tease apparently doesn't feel like a tease to Anna.

"You're mean," she says.

"I'm just *kidding*," I say.

"You think I'm fat."

"No, I don't."

"Yeah-huh. That's what you just said."

"Anna," I say impatiently. "You weren't fat then, and you aren't fat now. Right, Mom?"

Mom frowns and keeps her eyes on the road.

"*Mom?*" I prod.

"No, Anna, you're not fat," she says carefully, and I think, *Ah, crap*, because her intonation implies, *But you* could *stand to lose a few.*

What started off as me being punchy has turned into something that's totally ruining the mood.

"You think I need to go on a diet?" Anna says.

Mom hesitates. Mom, who is a size four and who goes to Pilates and yoga and now a new class called Nia, which Peyton's mom persuaded her to try. Peyton's mom is an instructor at Gym Atlanta, where Mom has a membership.

"Mom, tell Anna right now that she doesn't need to go on a diet," I say.

"Carly, I wish you would remember that you're not the parent," Mom says. "And Anna, you *are* slightly heavier than you should be."

"Mom!" Anna cries.

"It's my job to be honest with you," Mom says. "Being overweight is a health issue."

"More like a looking-good-in-clothes issue," I say, trying to redefine who's on whose side here.

"Carly," Mom says sharply. "Do you want me to drop you off at home?"

"Sorry," I mutter. "But, Anna, you're *not* fat. You're beautiful. And I don't know why I brought up that stupid Billy Goat Gruff thing, I just . . ." *You just what?* says a voice in my head. "I didn't mean to hurt your feelings."

We're silent for the rest of the drive, but I continue thinking about bodies and weight and beauty. And boobs. Is it possible that Mom's as startled by Anna's *new figure* as the rest of the planet? Startled by, jealous of, slobberingly interested in . . . whatever. I mean, a single summer went by, and now Anna wears a bigger bra size than Mom does.

Truth: Anna has a different body type from me or Mom.

But also truth: Anna isn't fat. She's curvy, and she has hips. Her body is softer in general than Mom's Nia-sculpted body, or my own strong body, toned by six weeks of grueling physical labor. And turns out—*why look!* Anna's body type is the body type every male on the planet seems wired to notice. And appreciate.

Or maybe it's Anna in particular they appreciate.

But she *isn't* fat.

When we get to Cloud Nine, I apologize to Anna again.

"Seriously, I'm sorry," I say, the two of us falling behind Mom as we walk to the nail salon. "I don't know why I feel compelled to push Mom's buttons."

"It's okay," she says grudgingly. "But I wish you wouldn't talk about things like that." Like being fat, she means.

"Deal," I say, zipping my lips.

But then—*ack*—the topic comes up again as Anna's getting her nails done. This time I'm not the instigator. Kim-Hue is. I'm at the rack of polish, picking out my color, and Mom's on the sofa reading *Southern Living*. Kim-Hue and Anna are chatting about Vitamin Water. Anna's fave is Dragonfruit; Kim-Hue's is Orange-Orange. She's got a twenty-ounce bottle at her station, already half empty. Kim-Hue's husband, however, won't touch the stuff.

"Thanh, all he drinks is Coke," Kim-Hue says. "I tell him, 'Be careful, or you will get fat like Americans.'"

At first Anna doesn't respond. Then, in a lowered voice, she says, "Kim-Hue . . . do you think I'm fat?"

I pretend not to listen.

"You? Never!" Kim-Hue says. "You have very good figure. Not too skinny, like your sister."

Hey! I want to say. But I'm not listening, so I can't.

"She got skinny when she was off on her wilderness adventure," Anna says. "I think she looks good."

Thank you, Anna. I realize my hand has been hovering over the same bottle of polish for a long time. I skim it along the other bottles so it'll look like I'm absorbed in my task.

"Miss Maureen tells me Carly only washed her hair once while she was gone?" Kim-Hue asks. "Is that why it's that color?"

"No, she dyed it, but kind of by accident."

"And she didn't shave her legs?"

"Well, there were snakes in their water hole," Anna says. "But she shaved once she got home."

"Oh, good," Kim-Hue says with what sounds like genuine relief.

"Okay!" I say brightly. I turn and display a bottle of electric-blue polish. "Picked my color!"

Mom lifts her head. "Oh, Carly."

"What?" My face is warm. I go sit by Anna and Kim-Hue so they can't talk about me anymore. I check out Anna's French-manicured toes and say, "Pretty."

Kim-Hue smiles, first at me and then at Anna.

"So different, you two," she says. "But that is the way of sisters, yes?"

CHAPTER THIRTEEN
CONSIDER YOURSELF LUCKY

A month and a half into the semester, we start our swim unit in gym. So far, PE with Anna has proven to be nothing other than "PE with Anna," meaning that it's been fine, and even fun. I haven't felt too terribly jealous over the fact that Anna looks like a Hooters waitress in her gym outfit, while I look like a ten-year-old boy in mine. Holy Redeemer's PE classes are single-sex, like our homerooms, so that helps. Some of the girls in our class do the thing where they point at Anna's chest with their eyeballs and share a snickery look with their friends. But that's to be expected, I guess.

It makes me feel bad for Anna, though. When guys ogle her, they're thinking, *Dude. Sexilicious.* When girls ogle her, they're thinking, *Slut,* which is ridiculous. It's not as if Anna pushed an inflate-o-rama button and made herself swell up.

Would I trade figures with her, if I could? I tell myself I wouldn't . . . but I don't know.

Our PE teacher, Coach Schranker, is hot in a Captain Awesome sort of way, and Peyton thinks she and he would make a cute couple. She's decided that today is the day to make her move. Her logic:

he's going to be seeing her (and the rest of us) in our swimsuits, and if she doesn't snap him up, someone else will. Lydia, perhaps. Or Bad Attitude Cindy, who has even bigger boobs than Anna, and whose pubic hair tufts out of her underwear when we change into our gym uniforms. Although hopefully she's taken care of that ~~little~~ big issue, since today is naked-except-for-small-amounts-of-Lycra day.

I wonder why I think that leg hair on a girl is acceptable (in theory), but not pubes.

There is no way I could wear a bathing suit and have my pubes sticking out.

"Am I hot, or am I hot?" Peyton asks in the locker room. She twists so I can get the full-on effect. Her bathing suit is green and has cutouts along the sides, revealing her tan skin.

"You are hot," I say. The bathing suit I brought for PE is blue and modest. It's got a built-in lining, which is essential, because I have pokey-out-y nipples.

"Hold on," Anna says, coming over from her locker. She's wearing a red one-piece that Mom had to go and buy her just for PE, because no way was she going to wear a bikini to gym class. Not on my watch.

Anna fixes Peyton's strap so that it's no longer twisted and says, "There. Now you're hot."

"Excellent," Peyton says. She lifts her chin. "Let's go."

Grabbing our towels, we exit through the back door of the locker room, which leads to Holy Redeemer's Olympic-size pool. My feet pad against damp tile, and the splish-splash sounds remind me of summer. I would so much rather be sunbathing by our pool with Anna. By the look on Anna's face, so would she.

Peyton, Anna, and I join the rest of our gym class at the end of the pool sectioned off for swimming laps. At the other end are the diving boards. One low and one high, and my stomach tightens when I take in how *high* the high board truly is. I know what's coming with that high board, because it's a Holy Roller tradition. We're going to have to do a *back dive* off it. I don't look at Anna. There are times when I can help her, and times when I can't. This is one of the latter.

When we're all lined up on the edge of the pool, Coach Schranker makes a "swimming-is-important" speech that essentially goes like this: *Everyone needs to know how to swim. Swimming is an essential life skill. If you cannot swim and you fall into a pool, you will drown. It happens every year, especially in California. Any questions?*

"Do we have to go under?" Lydia asks.

"Yes, Lydia, you have to go under," Coach Schranker says.

"But I don't want to get my hair wet. It's bad for my highlights."

Bad Attitude Cindy snickers. Unlike Anna, she *is* wearing a bikini, which is silly since we're going to be swimming laps and—eventually—diving. In fact, I'm surprised it's not against the dress code. Maybe the administration never saw the need to add "no bikinis" to the list of regulations?

A quick glance reveals that Cindy did, however, shave.

"Put olive oil in your hair," Tatiana offers. "That's what French people do."

"Do not get olive oil in this pool," Coach Schranker says.

"Coconut oil works, too, and it smells delish," Tatiana says. She's forgotten to take off her earrings, which are big gold hoops. If she were wearing high heels, she could compete in a beauty pageant.

"I did a mayonnaise treatment last week," Lydia says. "It was revolting."

Coach Schranker blows his whistle. "Girls. There are people who go their whole lives without setting foot in a swimming pool. Do you have any idea how lucky you are to attend a school that has one of the top-ranked swim teams in the country?"

I slouch a little. It's a familiar theme at Holy Redeemer: how lucky we are and how we don't appreciate it. It's true, of course.

I know it's not normal for sixteen-year-olds to receive BMWs on their birthdays, like Bad Attitude Cindy's sister did, nor is it normal to fly to Paris to buy a Freshman Fling dress, as Lydia did last May. But part of me wants to say, *It's not our fault. It's not as if we* chose *this.*

Seemingly out of nowhere, Coach Schranker brings up Holy Redeemer's custodians and cafeteria workers, most of whom are black. Most of Holy Redeemer's students, big surprise, are white. He informs us that by the grace of God and Headmaster Perkins, the custodians and cafeteria workers are given free lessons *in this very pool.*

"Do *they* moan and groan about getting their hair wet?" he says. "No, they do not, and why? Because unlike you girls, they're *grateful* for the chance to improve themselves."

"The lunch ladies do not take swim lessons," Lydia says, as if the concept is ridiculous.

"Yes, Lydia, they do," Coach Schranker says. "Every Thursday evening."

"*Why?*"

"Because they want to learn to swim. Because when they were young, they weren't given the same *opportunities* as you girls."

"They didn't have pools?" Jackie Owens says skeptically. Jackie has a big math brain and loves statistics. She loves challenging people, even teachers, on statements that can't be proven. "Not even public swimming pools, like Garden Hills?"

"Some of them are very afraid of water," Coach Schranker declares.

This "them-ing" is making me fidget. Everyone's sneaking peeks at Vonzelle Coulter, who is one of "them" and attends Holy Redeemer on scholarship. Vonzelle's mom, Chandra, is the head cafeteria lady. In the cafeteria line, white boys in their pink polos jerk their chins at Chandra and say, "'Wuz up, Chandra! That chocolate pee-can pie is off the hook. Yo yo yo, mama!'"

Vonzelle stares straight ahead, her fingers clenched by her sides.

"Anyone who's afraid of water is an idiot," Bad Attitude Cindy says. She gives Coach Schranker a charged look and cocks her hip. "I love getting wet."

There's ducked-head giggling, and also a gasp from Lydia, who is horribly offended. Peyton puts her lips next to my ear and says, "Ho."

Coach Schranker blows his whistle. "Into the pool!"

We screech and squeal into the water. Bad Attitude Cindy is the first to duck under, and she rises from the water with her back arched and her head tilted back. It's a *check-out-my-chest* move, and Coach Schranker does.

He catches me watching and looks away.

CHAPTER FOURTEEN
JUST DO IT

PE is made of suckage. Practicing the crawl and doing the back-stroke aren't too bad (well, for me), but as the days march by, the thought of our required back dive off the high board takes up more and more of my brain space. It is out there and not going away, no matter how much I want it to.

We're allowed to do the possibly-spine-snapping dive anytime we want, as long as it's before the end of the unit. On the final Friday of the three-week session, five girls have yet to meet the re-quirement: me, Peyton, Tatiana, Jackie, and Anna. Today is the day, or we fail—and that means not just the swim unit, but the whole entire PE class. Just another example of the insanity that is Holy Redeemer.

Vonzelle was the first to do her dive. In fact, she did it the day after the swim unit started. Her mouth set in a line, she climbed the ladder, strode to the end, lifted her hands above her head, and just . . . did it. She was amazing. She was fearless. Or maybe she was just determined to show Coach Schranker that not all of "them" are as afraid of water as he suggested.

Her dive behind her, Vonzelle is sitting in the bleachers today. She's in her swimsuit, but working on homework. The other girls who've done the dive play in the shallow water, doing handstands and floating lazily on their backs.

"I'm so nervous," Peyton whispers, huddling next to me and Anna. Holy Redeemer's high-dive extends from an elevated platform, and that's where we are. Tatiana and Jackie are up here, too. "What if I mess up? I don't want Steve to think less of me!"

By Steve, she means Coach Schranker.

I look at her in disbelief, like, *We have to plunge backward to our death, and you're worried what "Steve" is going to think of you?*

Last Monday, Bad Attitude Cindy did her back dive, only she arched her spine instead of falling straight back. She flipped too far over and smacked the water with a slap, and her thighs, when she climbed up the ladder, were purple with broken blood vessels. Anna rushed to the girls' locker room and threw up. She made me promise not to tell.

Coach Schranker blows his whistle. "Who's first? Anna, want to get it over with?"

Anna steps backward to the far edge of the platform. We are so high up, and we're not even over the water yet. "Couldn't I write an extra-credit report?" she asks in a quavery voice. "Please?"

"No extra credit," Coach Schranker says. He scans the line. "Peyton, you ready?"

"Yes," Peyton says. Then she hyperventilates. "JK. LOL. Enter!"

"Peyton, this isn't the time," Coach Schranker says. "Now, come on. Let's see you give it your best shot."

"*Fine,*" Peyton says, stepping onto the board.

"You can do it," I say. From the corner of my eye, I see Anna clenching and unclenching her fingers.

Peyton's breaths are shallow as she takes baby steps to the end of the board. It jiggles under her weight. She makes the mistake of glancing down, then quickly lifts her eyes.

"The longer you wait, the harder it'll be," Coach Schranker says.

Peyton rotates inch by inch until the back of her body faces the pool.

"Now raise your arms," Coach Schranker instructs. "That's right. Hands clasped. Now tilt your head so you're looking at the backs of your hands. *Don't* arch your spine."

"*I'm going to faint.*" I think I hear Anna whisper.

My heart is drumming, and I'm not the one on the end of the board. I feel suddenly like I have to pee, and I vow to go next just to end this torture.

"Go on, Peyton," Coach Schranker says.

She scrunches her face and falls backward, and we hold our breaths as she plummets down, down, down.

And then. . .*splash*. It's over. She did it. She swims up to the surface, and we cheer when her head pops out of the water.

"Way to go," Coach Schranker says. "Now wasn't that easy?"

"No," she says giddily. "It was *awful*."

He laughs. He puts his hands on his hips and looks up. "All right, who's next?"

"I'll go," I say, at the same time as Jackie. We glance at each other.

"Me first," Jackie says. "It is statistically advantageous for me to get it over with."

"And then me," Tatiana says. "Please, Coach Schranker? I'm feeling like it's really important for me to go *now*."

"Get in line, then," Coach Schranker says.

We scramble into place behind the board. I end up second to last. The only person behind me is Anna, who doesn't join the line, but stays put at the back of the platform.

"You're going to be okay," I tell her. "You're psyching yourself out, Anna."

She regards me with round eyes.

"You're not really going to faint, are you?"

She doesn't answer. She's awfully pale.

Jackie goes to the end of the board, turns around, and raises her hands above her head. She threatens to sue if she breaks her neck, then shuts her eyes and falls.

"*Yes*," she says when she surfaces. "Exactly the right angle, exactly the right velocity."

Tatiana doesn't fare so well. Her legs crumple as she begins her dive, and she flails in the air. She lands on her butt, and Coach Schranker winces.

"Ouch," he says. "That's got to hurt."

Tatiana gasps when she comes out. She pauses on the ladder and tugs her bathing suit out of her butt crack.

"I'm okay," she says.

"You sure?" Coach Schranker asks.

She nods as tears stream down her face.

"Shoulda locked your knees," Coach Schranker tells her, shaking his head. "Go on and shower off, then check in with the nurse."

Coach Schranker gazes up at me and Anna. We're the only ones left. "That was because she forgot to lock her knees. Don't do that."

"Gee, thanks," I say under my breath. It's meant to make Anna smile, but she doesn't. She's practically in a comatose state.

"Come on, Carly," Coach Schranker says. He claps. "Let's go."

I hold up a finger. "One sec."

I take three steps to Anna and say, "Anna, you're scaring me. Would you please act like you're alive?"

"*I'm alive*," she whispers. Her lips barely move.

"Hey," I say, touching her arm. "*Hey*. What is it that famous person said? 'It'll all work out in the end, and if it doesn't, that means it's not the end yet'?"

Anna's eyes come briefly into focus. "A famous person said that? Who?"

"I don't know. Someone."

"What does it even mean?" she says. "And what 'end' are they talking about? Death?!"

"Okay, never mind," I say. "But listen. Do you really want to be up here *alone* once I do my dive? You'll be all by yourself. Is that what you want?"

Anna's expression turns remote again, in a glassy-eyed-doll way. She almost imperceptibly shakes her head.

"Go on, then," I say, waving her in front of me. "Don't think about it. Just do it."

Anna approaches the board, but doesn't step onto it. She looks back at me and whispers, "I can't."

"You can," I say.

When Peyton balked, Coach Schranker coddled her. With Anna, he grows curt. "You're wasting time, Anna. Either you go, or let your sister."

Anna takes one step out onto the board, then another, then another. Her movements are stiff and ungraceful.

Good girl, I encourage her silently. *You can do it.*

She reaches the end of the board, and, like Peyton, looks down. It's a mistake. But while Peyton caught herself immediately, Anna keeps looking down, seemingly hypnotized by the water so far away. The girls below cluster together and stare up at her.

"Go for it, Anna," Peyton calls.

Anna doesn't move.

Coach Schranker puts his hands on his hips. "Anna, now."

She still doesn't move.

"I'm going to give you ten seconds. I'm going to count down, starting now. Ten, nine, eight, seven—"

I don't understand what his plan is. Is he going to climb the ladder when he reaches "one"? March down the board and push her off?

That is my sister, I want to say. But what good would it do?

At "three," Anna sinks to a crouch and grips the sides of the board. She's crying now, like Tatiana. She's a crying egg at the end of the board.

"For God's sake," Coach Schranker says.

"Anna . . ." I manage. But I don't know what to do. Should I go out there?

"Come on, Anna," Peyton says.

"Yeah," says Jackie. "The longer you wait, the higher the odds you'll mess up."

The group of them starts up like baby birds: *You can do it, Anna. Don't be scared. Just think how good you'll feel when it's over.* The girls from the shallow end look over at the commotion. So does Vonzelle from the bleachers.

Anna cries harder, and Coach Schranker shakes his head. "Get off the board," he says, disgusted. "You're done. You fail."

I want to tell him he's being a bastard, that he didn't treat Peyton this way or any of the other girls. But he's a teacher, and I'm just me. I don't think a confident voice and a firm handshake is the solution here.

Anyway, I doubt I could pull off either one.

"Get off the *board*, Anna," Coach Schranker says.

Dropping from her crouch to her bottom, Anna scoots backward in small increments, her fingers gripping each edge of the board. Her suit's going to be ruined. When she's back to the front of the board, she twists awkwardly around the way you'd twist on a Sit'n Spin. She steps with trembling legs onto the platform part where I am. She drags her forearm under her nose and doesn't meet my eyes.

"You're up, Carly," Coach Schranker says. "No excuses."

The other girls in the class keep their necks craned. As I step onto the board, Peyton calls, "Come on, Carly. You can do it."

Of course I can, I think angrily.

The board is rough, with points of plaster poking the under-

sides of my feet. It bounces as I approach the end. It's so fragile, this slim, buckling sliver of fiberglass.

I turn around and slide my heels off the edge of the board like I'm supposed to. There is nothing beneath them but air.

Don't look.

I lift my eyes, expecting to see Anna on the platform. But she's gone. Okay, fine. Can't think about it now. I raise my arms above my head and clasp my hands. The board jiggles.

"Let your hands break the water," Coach Schranker says. At least I think he does. I can't breathe normally, and my thoughts have grown slippery-slide-y.

"You're golden, Carly," calls Peyton.

"Don't be scared!" says someone else.

I focus on my hands, on my four visible knuckles. I feel precarious, and I surrender to it.

I fall.

CHAPTER FIFTEEN

BIG SISTERS DON'T TAG ALONG

Anna and I don't talk about what happened in PE, and we don't mention it to Mom when we get home from school. Mom doesn't ask, and I know that Dad, when he gets home from work, won't, either. Other parents might be interested in the fact that their children are plunging backward off twelve-foot-high planks. Other parents might at least be aware of the fact that such plunging goes on at the school to which they fork over twenty thousand dollars a year. Twenty thousand dollars *per child*.

But Mom is oblivious, and for Anna's sake, I guess that's good.

"Girls, your father and I are going to Pricci's tonight with one of your father's clients," Mom says as she arranges the flowers she bought at Whole Foods. "Would either of you like to join us?"

I glance at Anna, who glances at me. It's a *sisters* reflex. Go to Pricci's-of-the-yummy-baked-Brie-appetizer and eat with boring client, or stay at home and fend for ourselves?

Only in this case, the reflex is just that—a reflex. I immediately jerk my eyes away, because I feel like crap for not saving Anna from

Coach Schranker. So instead of deciding together what we want to do, I pretend I'm interested in something on the counter.

"Um . . . sure, I'll go," I say casually. I expect Anna to say "me, too," and I'm already thinking, *Well, at least we'll be in a group. At least it won't be just her and me awkwardly watching TV and hoping* Swimfan *doesn't come on. Or* Jaws. *Or that movie about the surfer girl who almost drowns.*

But Anna doesn't say "me, too." She says, "I don't feel like going out. I'll, um . . . I think I'll call Georgia and maybe go hang at her house."

"But going to Georgia's *would* be going out," I say.

She shrugs.

I open my mouth, then shut it. Who am I to question her plans? It irritates me, though. There's no good reason why. It just does.

"That's fine, as long as you're home by ten," Mom says.

"I'll see if Joe can drop me off," Anna says. Joe is Georgia's college-age brother, who lives at home, goes to Emory, and is pretty darn hot.

"Carly, you could use some freshening up," Mom says. "We'll need to leave in an hour."

My bad mood worsens. I am not a feminine hygiene product, nor am I in need of one.

Mom frowns at my tie-dye with its swirls of red and orange and yellow. "And please, change into something cute."

Up in my room, I try to figure out why I'm so pissed. Then I short-circuit that plan and say, *Screw it.* I've had a crap day. I'm going to have a crap night. Psychoanalyzing myself won't make things better, and anyway, *there was nothing I could do.* Anna failed the dive on her own. *Anna.* And if it feels as if I'm the one who failed her . . . well, so what? There it is. Can't do anything about it now.

I turn on my iPod and spin the dial to a Cat Stevens song called

"If You Want to Sing Out, Sing Out." It's a happy, feel-good song, and I try to push what happened during PE out of my mind.

But I can't stop thinking about Anna, crouched down at the end of the board. The pale backs of her thighs. The way they squished out unattractively because of her position.

Stop it RIGHT NOW.

I fish my cell phone out of my backpack and punch in Peyton's number. Peyton is always good for distraction therapy.

She answers by saying, "Hey, babe, one sec, 'kay? I'm trying something I read about called 'hair plopping.' *One* sec."

"Hair plopping?" I say, but she's gone.

When she returns, she says, "And now we wait."

"For what?"

"If all goes according to plan, I will have smooth, lustrous curls in thirty short minutes."

"Hair plopping," I say again.

"That's right," Peyton affirms.

It's working already, the distraction bit. I sit on my bed. "And hair plopping would be . . . ?"

"I read about it on the Internet," she says. But then, typical Peyton, she doesn't explain the plopping at all. She blabbers about hair extensions instead.

"I want them so bad," she says.

"*Why?*" I ask. "Your hair is already halfway down your back."

"But if I got extensions, I could actually sit on my hair."

"But it wouldn't be *your* hair. It would be someone else's."

"It would be mine once I paid for it."

She asks if I knew that not all hair extensions are made of human hair, and I say, "Gross. No."

I lean against my pillow, and she tells me all I want to know and more about how the best hair extensions come from India, because it's a tradition in India for women to go on a pilgrimage and have their heads shaved to demonstrate that they're not corrupted by vanity.

"And then American women buy that hair to show that they *are* corrupted by vanity?" I say.

"Exactly!" Peyton crows. "The monks at the temple sell the hair to American salons. It's a win-win situation."

"Go, monks!"

"But for now I'm holding off, because I read a post from a woman whose extensions, like, ruined her life. She got into a bar brawl—"

"A bar brawl?"

"And this other woman ripped out huge chunks of her hair. Since the extensions were glued to the woman's real hair, her real hair came out, too, along with pieces of her scalp. Isn't that nasty?"

"Are you thinking you might get into a bar brawl?" I cross my bare feet on my comforter.

"Hey," Peyton says, like *this is no joking matter.* "You never know."

"So," I say, moving on. "Plopping."

"Yes," she says. "I'd never heard of it—"

"Go fig."

"—but it involves washing your hair very nicely and then not drying it at all when you get out of the shower." She giggles. "'Very nicely,' those are the exact words in the instructions. As opposed to washing your hair meanly, I guess."

From down the hall, Mom calls, "Carly? I hope you're getting ready!"

I put my thumb over the microphone part of my cell. "Yes, Mom!"

Meanwhile, Peyton continues her hair-plopping how-to. "So then, with your hair all Rapunzel-y on the towel, you roll the towel into two sausages, kind of. And then you clip them together, and twenty minutes later . . . voilà!"

I've missed a step somewhere, I think.

"I still don't get why it's called hair *plopping*."

"Because you *plop* it against the towel. You plop it and plop it and plop it, and that's how the excess water gets out. You weren't listening, were you?"

"I was!"

"Want me to come over and show you the final result? *If* it looks fabulous, that is."

"I wish," I say. "But I said I'd go out with my mom and dad. Fancy client dinner—wh-hoo."

"Bummer." She pauses. "Is Anna going?"

"No, she's going to Georgia's. At least I think that's her plan."

"Why would someone who lives in Atlanta, Georgia, name their child 'Georgia'?" Peyton asks.

I hear Mom's heels clipping down the hall. I scramble off the bed and hunt for an appropriate blouse.

"Seriously," Peyton goes on. "If they'd lived in Utah, would they have named her 'Utah'?"

"'Utah' would be a horrible name." I pause. "'North Dakota' would also be a horrible name."

"Just plain Dakota is cute."

"For a dog."

Mom raps on my door. "Carly?"

"Almost ready!"

"Know who else is cute?" Peyton says. "Georgia's brother, Jim."

"*Joe.*"

"Joe. Yes. Now, *there's* a name. Manly, broad-shouldered, nice tight butt . . ."

"Names don't have butts."

"But Joe does." She giggles.

"Show me what you're wearing," Mom says, opening the door and peering in. When she sees that I'm still in my tie-dye, she tilts her head and says, "*Carly.*"

"Gotta go," I tell Peyton. "My mom is glowering."

Mom points at my tie-dye and says, "Change."

"She wants me to change," I report to Peyton. "She doesn't like me the way I am."

"I want you downstairs in half an hour," Mom says. She spins on her heel and heads downstairs.

Peyton says, "So, uh, Carly . . ."

I open a drawer and push shirts around. "Yeah?"

"You care if I hang with Anna and Georgia?"

I go still.

"Since you're already doing something," she says. "And since I'm sure Anna could use a friend after the day she had."

"She *has* a friend. And she's going to said friend's house, where she will be loved and stroked and plied with ice cream."

"You know what I mean. That wouldn't bother you, would it?"

I close the drawer. Nothing good in there, anyway. "No, of course not."

I have the fleeting urge to cancel on Mom and Dad and hang out at Georgia's house with Anna and Peyton and possibly cute Joe. But how lame would that be, tagging along with my little sister?

"Have fun with Anna and New Jersey," I say. I snap-shut my phone.

CHAPTER SIXTEEN
BOOBS OVER BRAINS

Dinner with Mom, Dad, and Dad's client proves to be almost as dull as I suspected. The one highlight comes when Dad's client—a hunch-shouldered, sixty-year-old gay man named Bernie Waters—tells a story about how he first knew he "played for the home team."

"The doctor in the delivery room spanked my *bare bottom*, and I twisted around and turned the other cheek," Bernie says. "'*Again*, please,' I said."

Dad guffaws, Mom pretends to be scandalized but can't stop laughing, and Bernie downs the rest of his martini. Maybe the fact that I don't fit in at school *is* to be blamed on my parents. Most Holy Roller parents would find Bernie appalling, not entertaining.

But mainly, the dinner conversation consists of business, business, and more business, which is boring, boring, and more boring.

I wish I'd swallowed my pride and invited myself to Louisiana's house.

———

Anna isn't back by the time we get home, so I go to my room, close my door, and call Roger. I tell him about Bernie, and he laughs. He tells me about how his mom accidentally washed her cell phone along with a load of laundry, and how she's got it in a bag of rice, hoping the rice will draw out the moisture and magically make it work again. I laugh. We shoot the breeze for fifteen minutes or so, and then I get off, wondering why Anna isn't home yet.

When she *does* get home, I hop off my bed and scurry to my window. I'm in time to see Joe's red MG backing out of our drive. He toots the horn as he speeds away.

I call Peyton. I want to be busy when Anna comes upstairs to prevent any mistaken assumptions regarding my possible boredom while she was gone. Plus, I want the scoop.

"Did y'all have fun?" I ask. I walk with my cell to my bedroom door, which I push shut with my foot.

"Omigod, we had a blast," she says. *Not* the response I was hoping for. She tells me about how Joe taught them all to take shots, and when I say, *"What?!,"* she tells me to relax.

"Of apple juice, dummy. We used apple juice."

"That's retarded," I say, and it's a sign of how peeved I am that I would use that word. *Retarded.* I hate it when people use that as an insult.

"We'll be taking shots eventually," Peyton says matter-of-factly. "Might as well learn how."

"Who says we'll be taking shots? *I* won't be taking shots."

She laughs and says, "No, you probably won't."

"Well, I'm glad you had so much fun without me," I say, hating myself even as the words come out. "I'm going to bed now. Bye."

"Don't you want to hear about Joe, and how he hit on your sister?"

I don't hit the hang-up button. I check to make sure that yes, my door is shut, before lowering my voice to say, "Excuse me?"

"He couldn't stop staring at her boobs. That's the only reason he hung out with us. Really, he just wanted to hang out with Anna's boobs."

"Lovely," I say. "She's *fourteen.*"

"So? In India, she'd be married by now."

Why are we talking about India again? Do girls from India really get married at fourteen? And is that before or after they get their hair lopped off?

"Are you obsessed with India or something?" I say at last.

"Yes," she deadpans. "I'm obsessed with India. I'll probably move there after high school—except, wait. No, I won't, because I hear there's poop in their water supply."

When I don't reply, she says, "Carly, he didn't mean anything by it."

"How can you stare at someone's boobs and not mean anything by it?"

"He has a penis. Hence he will stare at boobs. I agree that it's annoying, but it's not worth huffing and puffing about."

Bernie Waters doesn't stare at boobs, I think. What I say is, "who says I'm huffing and puffing?"

Even I can hear how defensive I sound.

"Oh, sweetie," she says, her tone changing. "I'd be jealous, too, if I were you. Heck, I'm jealous, and I'm *not* you. It must suck to have your little sister be the girl guys write about on the bathroom walls. To know she could have any boy she wants just by shaking her ta-tas."

"Wow," I say. I try to come up with an appropriate response. "Her *ta-tas?*"

"I'm just trying to be honest. Would you rather I lied?"

"No." *Yes.*

"But, Carly, you're smarter than she is, so it all balances out. Wouldn't you rather be smart than pretty?"

"Would *you?*"

"We're not talking about me. We're talking about you. And

somewhere in the universe is a guy who would choose brains over boobs." She giggles. "But I don't know where. And it's not Joe. If Anna's boobs had hands, he would have introduced himself and given them a firm shake."

"Thanks for that image," I say sourly.

"You're welcome. And now it's time for my beauty sleep. But, Carly?"

"What?"

She hesitates, then says, "Cut her some slack, you know? Anna's Anna, and you're you. There's nothing either of you can do about it."

Shame squeezes my lungs, because her words bring back the reality of the dive and how Anna couldn't do it, big boobs or not.

But I could.

CHAPTER SEVENTEEN
FULL MOON

Later that night I'm awakened by a thump, or something thump-like. I was asleep, and now I'm awake, and I don't know how I got from one state to the other. I clutch the top of the sheet and listen hard. I don't hear anything.

I glance at the glowing numbers on the clock. It's 2 A.M., which means Mom and Dad have long since gone to bed. Anna, too.

Go back to sleep, I tell myself. *Whatever you heard, it's nothing.*

Sleep doesn't come.

Peyton can fall asleep *like that,* and often does, even in the most exciting part of a movie, or when we're spending the night to-gether and I'm in the middle of telling her something. It can be annoying—but it's a skill I wish I had.

Did Dad turn on the alarm before he went to bed? I'm sure he did. He always does . . .

. . . except when he forgets.

Just a couple of weeks ago, I went downstairs on a Sunday morn-ing and saw the green light glowing on the alarm panel instead of the red. When I pointed it out to Dad and reminded him of all the bad stuff that could have happened, he said, "Carly, relax. We obviously *weren't* murdered in our beds, and why don't you go get my *New York Times* while I make your mother her coffee."

So I went outside and got the paper from the special *New York Times* box under our normal mailbox, and life was sunny and bright. Not a serial murderer in sight.

Bad things *do* happen, though. They do, and no one is immune, and I'm the only one awake in this huge frickin' house which creaks and moans. And just say someone *does* jump out of the shadows, there's a zero percent chance that Dad will come running with a baseball bat to save me. Even if I scream, he won't hear. And why? Because Mom and Dad's master suite is at the opposite end of the hall. A thick wooden door separates their bedroom from their bathroom and walk-in closet, and a second thick wooden door separates their bathroom and walk-in closet from the long hall that leads to Anna's and my wing of the house.

Mom and Dad keep both doors locked throughout the night for "privacy" reasons, and our house is old enough that the locks in question are dead bolts rather than wimpy push buttons. I have a dead bolt on my door, too—so does Anna—but I don't like to use it. Sometimes it sticks, and I have to bang the door with my hip to get it to unlatch. I don't like the idea of being locked *in* a room any more than I like being locked *out*.

I hear another noise. Definitely a thump, coming from outside the house. My body goes rigid.

Last spring, a jogger got raped in our neighborhood.

When I was like, eight, a house was broken into a couple of blocks away, and the lady who was there, but didn't answer the door, was shot in the face. The investigators figured the burglars got scared.

"Carly?"

It's Anna, her voice barely audible from her room across the hall. I push back the covers and don't think, just bound across the cold wood floor to her bedroom. She slides over in her bed, and I scooch in.

"There's somebody out there," she whispers.

"I know," I whisper back.

"Should we get Dad?"

"I don't know. Should we?"

We look at each other. Getting Dad would mean braving the long, dark hall, with both closed doors to negotiate.

There's a plink on Anna's window, and we clutch each other. There are more plinks, followed by boys' laughter.

"Oh, man," Anna says, her demeanor changing.

"The Millers," I say.

I bolt out of her bed in my pj's and march across the room. Anna follows in her T-shirt and undies. I raise the blinds and spot four pale bottoms—four pale *naked* bottoms—gleaming in the light of the moon. They're lined up on the stone wall that separates our houses.

"No *way*," I say. Anna's window is heavy and practically sealed to the rim with paint, but with a grunt, I lift it. Anna and I lean forward.

"We see you!" I yell.

More laughter, and the butts slide off the rock wall. *Ow.* One of the Miller boys pops his head up over the wall and yells, "And we see *you*! Your shirt is see-through, you know!"

Anna and I both glance down. My pajama top is navy blue and completely fine, but Anna's thin shirt is like tissue paper in the moonlight. She gasps and covers herself.

The Miller boy grins. "Your milk shake brings *all* the boys to the yard!" He drops down and disappears with his brothers.

I slam down the window. "What idiots."

Anna goes back to her bed, but doesn't lie down. She sits on the mattress, props her back on the headboard, and pulls the sheets up around her.

I lower the blinds. "Who made the milk-shake comment? Larry?"

"I don't know, and I don't care," Anna says in a voice that says she does.

"God, he's *twelve*. Should a twelve-year-old make comments like that? No."

"Carly, *everyone* makes comments like that," Anna says tightly. "Tonight, Georgia's brother said, 'Whoa, don't knock me over with those things' when I walked past him to get a Coke."

"That's so obnoxious."

"Even Dad says stuff, Carly. It's like . . . so wrong."

I perch on the edge of the mattress. "What has Dad said?"

"Well, he said that top-heavy thing. You were there."

Oh yeah, I think.

"And last weekend he told Mom I was 'bouncing,' and that she should get me a new bra. I was like, 'I can hear you, Dad! I'm right here!'"

"Yuck," I say. Fathers shouldn't notice anyone's boobs except their wives'. No, strike that. Fathers shouldn't notice boobs, period.

Does the same go for sisters?

I decide to change the subject.

"It's late," I say. "Want me to sleep in here?"

"I don't care, whatever."

Her tone is totally lackluster, and I rise. I'm not sticking around if I'm not wanted.

"Wait, I do," she says before I reach the door.

I keep going.

"Carly, I said I do. Come back."

"Chill," I say. I go to my room and return with my iPod, which I plug into Anna's sound dock. I adjust the volume superlow.

"Not your hippie-dippie music," Anna groans.

"Yes, and if you're lucky, you will one day learn to appreciate it." I crawl in beside her, and Cat Stevens's voice wraps around us.

"Hey, Anna?"

"Yeah?"

The darkness is no longer frightening, but simply dark. I can barely make out the cracks in the ceiling. "I'm sorry you had a crappy day." I pause. "In PE."

She's silent.

"Coach Schranker was a jerk," I go on.

She's still silent.

"He was a total jerk, Anna. You did nothing wrong."

"Except not dive," she whispers.

LOVE

CHAPTER EIGHTEEN

THE BOOK OF COLE

Anna can be soooooo slow. It drives me up the wall, as her slowness has a direct impact on me and whether I get to school on time.

Anna's morning routine, as observed from, say, her light fixture:

6:30 A.M. Shrill beeping alarm goes off. Everybody in the house can hear it, everybody but Anna.

6:35 A.M. Extremely cool older sister marches in wearing cherry-themed pj's and punches the off button on Anna's alarm. Extremely cool older sister says, "Anna, *wake up.*"

6:45 A.M. Shrill, fire-alarm-esque alarm blares again. Extremely cool and unlazy older sister strides back in—damp from shower—and shakes the lump under the covers which is Anna. "Get *up*," she says. Takes screaming alarm clock and places it next to Anna's ear. Cranks up volume.

7 A.M. Brisk and efficient mother pops head into room and says, "Anna. It's seven o'clock. Anna? Respond, please. Anna, say something to let me know you hear me." Anna grunts and possibly flails an arm out of the covers.

7:15 A.M. Brisk, efficient, and annoyed mother returns to Anna's room, pulls covers from Anna's body, and says, "Anna. GET UP." Extremely cool, unlazy, and fully dressed sister makes bonus appearance to tell mother that she is enabling her daughter by allowing her to do this every single day. Sister climbs onto bed and shoves Anna from behind until Anna slides into a heap on the floor. Anna makes pitiful sound. Anna regards sister and mother with bleary eyes.

7:30 A.M. Anna dozes while standing in shower. (Light fixture can report this thanks to auditory clues such as drumming water, more drumming water, and no shampooing or other soaping/shaving/washing sounds.)

7:45 A.M. Anna aims blow-dryer at head for a really, really long time.

8 A.M. Anna sighs, looks longingly at bed, and is drawn to it like a moth to the flame. Is *this close* to snuggling back in when extremely fed-up older sister bellows from downstairs that IT IS TIME TO GO AND YOU WILL BE LEFT IF YOU DON'T GET DOWN HERE *NOW*. Which is a lie, as mother-slash-enabler refuses to leave Anna behind, despite encouragement. Light fixture suspects mother of not wanting Anna in house all day, as mother has more important things to do, like catch a rerun of *Law and Order* before heading off to Pilates.

By 8:01, the light fixture is finally left in peace. I am in a state of near apoplexy, however. I can't wait till I get my license and can drive myself to school, because I *will* leave Anna behind, and too bad for her.

"An*na!*" I complain as she sighs and mopes and roots through the pantry for something to eat. "We *have* to go. We're going to be late!"

"Carly's right," Mom says. "Grab a protein bar and let's go."

"I don't want a protein bar," Anna says.

"I have a French essay to turn in," I say to the air. "She'll give me a zero if it's late."

"Wasn't it due yesterday?" Mom asks.

"Yes, but I left it at home. She said she'd give me until this morning."

"Hmm," Mom says, and the message is: *Guess you should have turned it in on time, huh?*

At last, we load up into Mom's BMW and drive to school. Mom drops us off, and I sprint up the outside stairs and into Grady Hall, where the girls' homerooms are. Madame d'Aubigné's room is on the third floor, but Madame d'Aubigné is nowhere to be seen.

"Where's Madame d'Aubigné?" I ask Caitlin, who's in the front row pressing a jewel into the polish on one of her nails.

"She went to the office," Caitlin says.

I jog back down to the first floor.

"Hi," I say to the secretary. The last time we exchanged pleasantries was when Anna was sent here for looking at porn. "Is Madame d'Aubigné here?"

"Have a seat," the secretary says. "She's making some copies."

I hear the *whir-whir-whir* of the Xerox machine. I slip off my backpack and drop into one of the plush leather chairs.

"Are you here to register for the Summer Expo?" asks Jackie Owens from my PE class.

"Huh?" I say. I didn't realize there was anyone else in the office but me, but there Jackie is, sitting primly in a worsted wool skirt. Actually, I have no idea if it's worsted wool. Worsted wool just seems like something Jackie would wear.

"The Summer Expo. Enrichment activities for the summer."

"It's November," I say.

"Which is why it's time to start planning. If you don't, all the good programs get filled."

"Uh, okay."

"You can*not* waste a whole summer," Jackie says. "Summer internships are the kinds of things they'll look for on your college applications."

"I already did one," I say. "This past summer, I volunteered for the Student Conservation Association."

Jackie's not letting this go. She's earnest as she says, "You need to do an enrichment activity *every* summer. One enrichment activity doesn't cut it. Do you realize we'll be seniors in less than *two years?* Do you realize how competitive college admissions are?"

I make an *aaargh* sound and put my head in my hands. I can do this with Jackie because Jackie's not the kind of person who notices when someone makes *aaargh* sounds. At least, not when college admissions are being discussed.

"I'm thinking Vanderbilt, Davidson, and UVA," Jackie says. "Safety: Savannah College. What about you?"

"Gross. Blech. Boring. This is not what I want to talk about."

"The decisions you make now will affect the rest of your life, Carly."

"Anyway, I might not even apply."

"To college?" Jackie laughs. "Yeah, right."

"Maybe I'll take a year off. Maybe I'll get a Eurorail pass and travel around Europe."

"When has anybody from Holy Redeemer not gone straight to college? Can you name one example?"

I don't have to think about it, because no, I can't. Two years ago, Harriet Mackey told her parents she'd sent in her acceptance forms to Kenyon, when in truth she hadn't, that rebel. Her parents didn't find out until the registration check didn't go through. Right away her father called Kenyon and explained the "mistake," and everything got worked out. Peyton, who lives in Harriet's neighborhood, says that whenever Harriet comes home, she says, "I love Kenyon *so much.* I'm having *the* best time."

"So that means I'm not allowed?" I say to Jackie. "I have to go to college straight out of high school just like everybody else?"

"Uh, *yeah*," Jackie says. "If you want to make anything of yourself, you do."

A guy I've never seen before steps into the office. My heart stops, and then it soars back fast and fluttery. Because he's my age (ish), and he's *gorgeous*. Not in a button-down and khakis way, like the majority of the guys at Holy Redeemer, and not in a fake-grunge way or a jock way. He's just. . .

Whew. The air goes out of me.

"Carly. You're staring," Jackie says under her breath. But she is, too.

The guy's got blue eyes, dirty-blond hair, and a faraway expression. He's very James Dean in his jeans and T-shirt, only his jeans fit him a whole lot better than James Dean's ever did. James Dean wore his jeans too high. In those posters of him, they're, like, up to his waist. But this guy wears his jeans just right. They do what good jeans should do, which is make his butt look amazingly, fabulously, adorably *guy*.

"Hey," he says to the secretary. "I'm supposed to check in with Mr. Perkins and get my books." His voice is low-pitched and sure.

"He *dips*," Jackie whispers, jerking her chin at the telltale round outline of a tobacco tin in his jeans pocket. Dipping, in Buckhead, is the equivalent of sneezing all over the salad bar at the Lone Star Steakhouse. It's trashy, it's tacky, and it just isn't done.

"He's beautiful," I whisper back.

"You must be Cole," the secretary says. She stands and smiles. "We're so glad to have you. Come this way, I'll show you to the headmaster's office."

"Yeah, okay," he says.

Jackie straightens her shoulders and says loudly, "So anyway, I think you should really consider the Summer Expo. You could go to D.C. and be part of the mock congress. Or you could do a summer intensive at Fidelity Bank and learn about investment portfolios."

Cole glances at us. His eyes skim over Jackie—I swear they do, they skim right over her—and land on me. I'm filled with unexpected courage, and I try to convey through the air that I am more than I appear.

"I would rather eat my own shoes than learn all about investment portfolios," I say, still holding Cole's gaze.

He grins, and my blood dizzies.

Holy cats, I think I'm falling for this guy. Or rather, I think I already have.

And hard.

CHAPTER NINETEEN

UNLEASH THE BEAST

By my free period, the word has spread: there's a new guy, and he's hot. I feel special because I actually saw him. *And* I know his name. Cole. Cole, Cole, Cole, Cole, Cole.

I tell Peyton about seeing Cole in the office, but I keep our we-are-kindred-souls moment to myself. I do think we might be kindred souls. If I felt a jolt as strong as I did when our eyes locked, then surely he did, too, right? Surely he felt *something*? It would be unfair of the world to give one person a jolt like that and not have it be reciprocated.

During my free, I go to the Hut with Peyton. Lydia tags along. They're hoping for a Cole sighting, and I am, too.

"I'm going to get a Snickers," I say. "You guys want anything?"

"No, thanks," Peyton says.

Lydia shakes her head. "South Beach."

"You sure?"

"I'm sure." She takes in my low-slung jeans. "I don't know how you can eat so much and stay so thin."

"Oh, please." Weight is an issue I refuse to get into with Lydia, because she gets very uptight about it. Like at the blood drive Holy Redeemer held last month, for example. Lydia stood in line and donated her blood and got her Dixie cup of lemonade and short-bread cookie, which she didn't eat. Then, when she found out I *didn't* donate, she got pissed.

"I tried, but they turned me down," I explained.

"What do you mean, they turned you down?" She wasn't pissed *yet*, just baffled. "Do you have AIDS?"

"Yeah, I have AIDS, Lydia."

"You do? Oh my God." Her eyes went glassy, and I could tell she was scrolling through past memories to see if we'd ever shared a needle or sucked each other's blood.

"Lydia, get real. You have to be over a hundred and ten pounds or they won't let you donate."

"Oh," she said. She pressed her lips together. "I'm not over a hundred and ten pounds, and I did it anyway. I just lied."

Uh-huh, right. *Nobody cares what size you are,* I wanted to say, although of course everyone does.

"Did you know that eating refined sugar is linked to Attention Deficit Disorder?" Lydia says now, determined to take all the fun out of my soon-to-be Snickers.

"I'm sorry, what?" I say.

"Attention Deficit Disorder," Lydia repeats.

"I'm sorry, what?"

"*ADD,*" she says, spacing it out slow and loud.

I blink. "Are you talking to *me?*"

"She's being *funny,* Lydia," Peyton says. "Come on, let's go claim a sofa."

The two of them leave, and I fish a crumpled bill out of the bottom pocket of my backpack. It takes two tries to get the machine to accept it. I punch B-6 for a king-size Snickers, and *oh,* the lovely thunk as it hits the tray.

"I'm telling Lydia about Mr. Burnett," Peyton says when I drop down by them. "About how *wacky* he was today."

"Ooo, wacky!" Lydia says, making wacky hands. "I'm so *wacky!*"

Mr. Burnett is our English teacher. As today is Tacky Tie Tuesday, he wore a wide tie with dancing hula girls all over it.

I rip open my Snickers. "I like Mr. Burnett. At least he tries."

"Teachers shouldn't try," Peyton say. "Anyway, he's like fifty years old."

"And he's bald," Lydia says.

"And he's got a beer gut," Peyton says. "He looks like Homer Simpson."

"He shows clips from *Monty Python* skits every Monday," I tell Lydia. "Then on Friday, when he gives us our quizzes, he sticks in a quote from one of the clips. If you get it right, you get extra credit."

"Isn't that *wacky?*" Peyton says. "The reason Carly likes it is because she's *wacky*, too."

Lydia smirks, and I feel the tightness of not wanting Peyton to be such a phony. More and more, I see her pretending to be someone else.

Beside me on the sofa, Peyton watches while I eat my Snickers.

"Break me off a bite, will you?" she says. "Not from the spitty end."

"You said you didn't want anything."

"Just a little. Just one bite."

"I specifically asked," I say, because I hate it when she does this. "I said, 'Does anybody want anything?' And you said no."

Peyton and Lydia share a look.

"It's just a candy bar," Lydia says.

Peyton holds out her hand. I break off a bite from the nonspitty end and reluctantly give it to her. I *asked* if she wanted anything, and she said no.

"Hey," Lydia says, nodding at the door. "Is that him? The new guy?"

I follow her gaze. It *is* him, and he's every bit as gorgeous as I remembered. He pauses to get his bearings, and I'm struck by how . . . *in control* he is. If it were my first day at a new school, I'd be a quivery splat of self-consciousness, and I'd probably be off hiding in the bathroom.

Cole glances around, taking it all in. He doesn't look nervous. He doesn't look eager. He just looks mildly interested.

"Oh my *God*," Peyton says. She pops the bite of Snickers into her mouth and chews like she's on a mission.

"Is he a sophomore?" Lydia says. "Please tell me he's in our grade."

"I don't know," I say.

"But weren't you there when he came to the office?" Peyton says.

"The secretary didn't get out her bullhorn and announce what grade he's in. She just took him to meet Headmaster Perkins."

Cole strolls to the drink machine. He feeds in two dollars and punches the tab for a Monster energy drink.

"Unleash the beast," Lydia murmurs.

He opens his soda, and we can hear the hiss.

"Look how cute he is, popping his top!" Lydia cries, drawing her hand to her chest. "Be still my heart!"

"Can I hold your Monster?" Peyton asks in an innocent school-girl voice.

"Just remember, I saw him first," I say.

"So, what, you own him?" Lydia says.

Yes, I want to say. He tilts his head and swigs his drink. His Adam's apple moves up and down.

"I don't think any of us need to worry," Peyton says, the implication being that he is too crushilicious for all of us. "Especially you, Carly. You're too *wacky*."

The two of them giggle and my feelings are hurt. Peyton makes exaggerated puppy-dog eyes at me and says, "JK. LOL. *Enter*."

"Ha ha," I say.

CHAPTER TWENTY
A LIFE OF FAITH DEMANDS ACTION

I want to meet Cole. I *really* want to meet him. This is my one and only life (as far as I know), and all the time people are telling me to make the most of it.

There's just one problem: when it comes to boys, I'm a wimp. I don't *mean* to be. I just am. All I do is sit wimpily on the steps of Ansley Hall almost every afternoon after school lets out, listening to Cole play his guitar. I'm one of a thousand other girls doing the same thing, but pretending not to. One day in November, I get so wrapped up in how Cole's fingers flit over the strings that I forget to go meet Mom at pickup.

Anna has to come and drag me away. "It's three-forty-five."

"Not yet." I want to stay and gaze at Cole.

"Mom's waiting. I've got a dentist appointment, remember?" She's loud enough that Cole glances over, and I think, *Oh, great. Yes. Of all the things you could overhear me talking about, let's make it the dentist, shall we?*

"Shhh," I say. Several of the other girls nod.

"Come on," she says. "Today's the day I get my teeth whitened. I don't want to miss my appointment."

"Riiiight, because heaven forbid you don't match all the other Barbie dolls with their neon-white teeth." Am I imagining it, or is Cole suppressing a smile?

"You know Dr. Smiley won't hold my time slot," Anna complains.

"Dr. Smiley has halitosis," I say, and I launch into a highly amusing riff on our dentist, whose name really *is* Dr. Smiley. I end with, "Anyway, can you honestly live with yourself if you pay a thousand dollars to get your teeth whitened? You could feed an entire third-world nation for a month with that much money."

A couple of girls giggle, but I don't care about them. I care about Cole, who glances over and grins. Because I'm funny. Because I'm *not* a Barbie doll with bleached white teeth.

I want to meet him—but I'm scared.

I want to meet him.

But I'm scared.

That night, I watch *The Hills* with Anna, and as usual, it's awful and yet addictive. Audrina gets stupid over a guy, and it's so familiar that I feel like shaving my head and wearing a hair shirt for the rest of my days, just to separate myself from the craziness of being a girl and liking a guy and all the senseless, predictable, utterly unoriginal drama that goes along with that.

It's stupid to get stupid over a guy. It's stupid to be such a wimp. I am disgusted with myself, and I decide then and there that I've had enough: IT IS TIME TO BE BOLD. Like Mom and Dad's Starbucks roast, but even bolder.

I get up from the couch and march from the room.

"You're going?" Anna says. I'm surprised she cares, because she's been moody all night, and distant. She hasn't even given her usual commentary on whose clutch she covets and whose shoes are gorgeous, though impractical. Yet now she wants me to stay?

"Sorry, babe," I say. "Larger voices calling."

"But Heidi's about to show up at Vice!"

"Tell her hi for me!"

Upstairs, I open the door to my closet and push through the hangers until I find what I want. Ahhh, yes. Bold, beautiful, and absolutely offbeat. I grab it, hanger and all, and march back down to Anna.

"Anna, prepare thyself." I thrust the hanger in front of me.

The bright colors scream, "Look at me!", and she flinches. She blinks at the shirt existing so boldly on the hanger, then lifts her eyes to my face. Then back at the hanger. She finds her voice and says, "What . . . is it?"

"It's a dashiki." The word is exotic on my tongue. "Don't you love it?"

"No."

"What? Of course you do." I shake the hanger, and together we regard the dashiki's African-esque sunbursts of red, yellow, and orange. We appreciate—okay, fine, *I* appreciate—its flowing triangular sleeves that end in foot-long points that flutter like flags in the wind. It is the insanest, Jimi Hendrix-est, flower-child-est shirt ever.

"Carly?" Anna says.

"Yes?"

"I'm having this very bad worry that you're planning on wearing that thing. Like, in public."

"It's not a thing. It's a shirt, a beautiful shirt, and *yes*, I'm going to wear it. Why wouldn't I?"

She hits "pause" on the TiVo control. "When did you buy it?"

"At the end of the summer," I say. "In Tennessee, at the street fair where I got my Jesus sandals."

"Jesus never wore a tablecloth."

"It's not a *tablecloth*, it's a—" I break off. I give Anna a pained smile. She's being a pill, but I'm not going to let her get to me.

I sit on the sofa and drape the dashiki over the cushion. "Is there something wrong with being different? Is that why you don't think I should wear it?"

"I think you try too hard to be different," Anna says.

"That's ridiculous. There's no *rule* against dashikis. There's no rule saying that just because I'm a girl, I have to wear cute little skirts and tops just so I can fit into the perfect little Holy Redeemer mold."

"Carly, you will never fit the Holy Redeemer mold," Anna says, "so you don't have to worry about that. Although I think it's obnoxious how you're so anti–Holy Redeemer."

"How is that obnoxious? And how did we even get onto this subject? You're not supposed to have opinions."

I mean it as a joke—obviously—but Anna arches her eyebrows. She's *not* supposed to have opinions, though. Unless they agree with mine.

Anna pushes the dashiki away from her. "You want to be *sooo* different from the girls at Holy Redeemer. But you let Holy Redeemer define you just as much as anyone else, just in the opposite way."

"What? You just heard Dr. Phil say something like that when you were watching TV and eating Pop-Tarts."

"Okay," she says in an incredibly annoying I'll-pretend-to-agree-with-you-if-that-makes-you-happy way. "But if you love your dashooki so much—"

"Dashiki," I say, through gritted teeth.

"—then why haven't you ever worn it?" She gestures at my shirt with her chin. "If that eyesore of a shirt is, like, what you're all about, why has it lived in your closet for three months?"

"I'm wearing it tomorrow," I say stonily.

She shrugs. She lifts the remote and reanimates Audrina and

her pals. My jaw falls open, because seriously, since when did she become so obnoxious?

I stand up, swoop my dashiki off the sofa, and say, "I do want to be different, you're right. I want to be someone who thinks for herself, instead of just being some stupid girl who swishes her hair and wears too much makeup and shows off her boobs."

Her cheeks turn red. Her eyes stay glued to the TV, but her arms cross over her chest.

"I'm sorry, but it's true," I say. "I refuse to be part of the herd."

"And how do you think that makes the rest of feel?" Anna says without looking at me. "Huh, Carly?"

I have no idea how things got so out of hand. Heart pounding, I turn and leave.

CHAPTER TWENTY-ONE
WHAT BEE FLEW UP <u>YOUR</u> BELL-BOTTOMS?

Peyton, when I call to vent, is no help.

"Carly, you *do* know why she's mad at you," she states.

"No," I say. I frown. "She's mad at me? She's not allowed to be mad at me."

"You have a lot of rules, Carly. Did you know that?"

My pulse quickens, and I sit cross-legged on my bed with my dashiki in my lap. I grip one of its pointy sleeves as if it's a security blanket.

"It's pretty ironic," she goes on, "since you're all about not wanting rules. Anna and I were just talking about it."

"Excuse me?" *When* were they talking about it? On the phone? Did Anna call Peyton, or did Peyton call Anna?

"Oh, Carly," Peyton says. I hear clacking keyboard sounds, which means she's IMing or e-mailing while she's talking to me. "How you called Anna a Barbie doll on the steps of Ansley Hall? She told me all about it."

"She *is* a Barbie doll," I say. "A Barbie doll is a girl who's cute and sweet and wears matching little outfits, which Anna does." Peyton does, too, for that matter, which fills me with the sudden need to cover my butt. "What's wrong with being a Barbie doll?"

"Nothing. But you mean it as an insult, and you know it. You think *cool chicks* shouldn't care about stuff like that." She says "cool chicks" as derisively as I—supposedly—say "Barbie doll."

"What's going on?" I say. "Are you pissed at me, too?"

"I'm not pissed," Peyton says. "I can see Anna's side, that's all." More clickety-clack sounds. "Sometimes you use her as a punching bag."

"I do not!"

"Sometimes you're like, 'I'm the great and mighty Carly! I can have opinions, but no one else is allowed to! That is the rule!'"

"God, Peyton," I say. "Anna and I *tease* each other. That's what we do. Why am I suddenly Big Bad Carly?"

"You embarrassed her, that's all I'm saying."

"How?!"

"How do you think? First you called her a Barbie doll. Then, based on what she told me, you went on and on about how lame it was that she was getting her teeth bleached."

"I did?" Nothing from Peyton, so I say, "Okay, I did. But I didn't even remember till just now, that's how unimportant it was."

"To you. Not to Anna. You said she could have fed a third-world nation with the money she spent on her bleach job."

"But she went to Dr. Smiley," I say plaintively. "*The Fun Dentist!*" There are cheesy billboards all over the city for Dr. Smiley, the Fun Dentist. "I had no choice but to mock him. It's a—"

Rule, I almost said.

"Uh-huh," Peyton says. She half-laughs. "Like I said, you have a lot of them."

I regroup. I am not the evil person she is making me out to be. "Do you know how much it cost for Anna to sit there while Dr. Smiley zapped her with his special blue-light laser gun? A thousand dollars, Peyton."

"A thousand dollars isn't that much."

"Are you kidding? That missionary lady who spoke at last Friday's assembly said you could feed an Ethiopian orphan for thirty-five cents a day. That means"—I do some messy calculations—"you seriously could feed someone for, like, eight years with a thousand dollars."

"You have money. Are you sponsoring an Ethiopian orphan?"

I exhale through my nose.

"Anyway, extensions cost more than that." Her tone turns reflective. "Hmm, maybe that's what I'll ask for for Christmas."

"What? *No.*"

"See, there you go again. You make people feel bad. You make them feel like they're not good enough."

I have a horrible flash of Dad, who does that all the time. Who accumulates power for himself by taking it from others. But I am not Dad, and anyway, Peyton's the one making me feel like *I'm* not good enough.

I clench my dashiki. "It is ridiculous to spend a thousand dollars to whiten your teeth. Anna could have gotten Crest Whitestrips for ten dollars."

"Nope. Twenty-seven dollars."

I groan.

"If I whiten my teeth, are you going to be mean to me, too?" Peyton asks. "Because I think Anna's teeth look terrific."

"They look the same as before," I lie.

"Loosen up, babe," Peyton says. "You're seriously the most uptight flower child ever. You're, like, a flower child with a bee in your bell-bottoms."

"Bye, Peyton," I say.

I shouldn't have called.

CHAPTER TWENTY-TWO
<u>DAG</u>: DUTCH FOR "HELLO"

That night, I hang my dashiki over the shower rod in my bathroom. It's rumpled from where I clutched it, and my way of ironing things involves not an iron but a sink. I splash water on the offending areas, smooth the creases out, and let whatever it is drip-dry.

"Dewrinkle thyself," I tell my dashiki, waving my fingers up and down. I'm trying to reclaim my sassy-hippie-chick vibe, when in actuality I feel like crying. "Prepare for glory."

When morning comes, I'm a mess. First of all, I'm sleep-addled, because I did that brain-whacked thing at four in the morning where I *thought* my alarm clock went off, and so I got up and took a shower on autopilot, only to finally look at the clock and realize what a spaz I was. So I went back to bed with wet hair, and now it's flat on one side. The top layer is gradually losing its beigeness, though. It's more of a pale gold which could *almost* be called blond. Only it's half flat. Half red, half gold, half poofy, half flat. Oh, and with dark brown roots to add that final, special touch.

It *could* be that I should take a sick day.

But, no. I told Anna I was wearing my dashiki to school today, and I'm not backing down. I will be bold! Fearless! Cole-worthy!

I step into my long skirt and pull the dashiki over my head. I check my reflection in the mirror—*WHOA, THOSE SLEEVES ARE LONG*—then turn away before I can lose my nerve.

"Good heavens," Mom says when I walk into the kitchen. Her expression says, *How did this child spring from my loins?* "Are you wearing that to school?"

"Yes, Mom."

She flounders. "Well, are you going to wear a jacket over it? It's November, you know. Maybe your navy peacoat? The long one we bought at Neiman's?"

"The one *you* bought at Neiman's," I say in a controlled voice. "And no, I will be going jacketless, as it's Atlanta and the temperature's supposed to hit sixty degrees."

"Sixty degrees is chilly, Carly."

My throat goes tight. Sixty degrees is not chilly.

"You better tell Anna to get down here or she'll make us late again," I say.

"Did you check on her when you were up there?"

"Am I my sister's keeper?" I snag a Pop-Tart and head for the back door. "I'll be outside."

All day long, people comment on my dashiki. It's like the day of my hair debut all over again. People are so unoriginal.

"Nice tablecloth," they say, and "Where are my sunglasses?" Also, "Dude, someone's gonna lose an eye if you're not careful." Peyton is embarrassed and walks several feet in front of me when we go to English, and Lydia seems downright offended.

"Uh, Carly?" she says. "We're not in the sixties anymore. Sorry to be the one to tell you."

Some people like my shirt, like Mr. Burnett, who's wearing a tie splattered with huge cows even though it isn't Tacky Tie Tuesday.

And Roger's cool with my fashion choice. He joins me in the cafeteria, since Peyton and Lydia developed an urgent need to spend our lunch period in the library. He sits down, takes in my outfit, and nods, like, *Yeah, okay*, reminding me that Europeans are so much more awesome than Americans. Or at least Roger is.

We chat about random things as we eat, taking frequent breaks to wipe our fingers on the five thousand napkins I grabbed from the dispenser. Today is fried-chicken day—yummy chicken grease!—and I'm happy to be here with Roger, who doesn't care if the sleeves of my dashiki drag in my mashed potatoes.

As I pull off a piece of breast meat with my fingers, Roger looks across the cafeteria and says, "Hey, there's Cole."

My nerves jump. "You know Cole?"

"He's in my Latin class."

"Really? That's cool. Is he nice?"

Roger slants his eyes, and I realize I've made a tactical error. This is *Roger*, who likes me. I can't blabber about Cole around him.

"*Sakkerloot*," Roger says. "Are you one of his groupies?"

"*No*," I say. "I've never even met the guy."

Roger assesses me. He is so calm and steady, my gigantic Roger. I wish he'd quit staring at me, though.

My wish is granted, because he turns toward Cole and raises his voice. "Cole! Over here!"

Cole ambles over, and it's possible I'll disintegrate. He's wearing a leather jacket, and his hair is tousled, and he seems easy in his skin in a way that I constantly strive for but never achieve.

"Hey, man," Cole says to Roger. "What's up?"

Roger jerks his head at me. "My friend wants to meet you. Carly, meet Cole. Cole, Carly."

Heat scorches my face. "Hi," I manage.

"Hey," Cole says, friendly but completely impersonal. If he remembers me from his first day, he fails to show it. And if he remembers his guitar-boy smile from yesterday, he does an extremely good job of pretending he doesn't. He drops into an empty chair, which means that I am essentially done eating, since I can't eat in front of him. My stomach's too knotted.

"So . . . you play the guitar," I say. "I've seen you out on the quad."

"I was in a band in Winston-Salem," Cole says, scratching the back of his neck. "You like music?"

"Uh, yeah. You?"

There's a beat so we can appreciate what an idiot I am.

"No, he just plays the guitar to torture himself," Roger says.

"Thanks, Roger," I say. The look Roger gives me is hard to read.

"What do you listen to?" Cole asks.

I focus back on him, because this one I can handle. "Cat Stevens," I say. "The Grateful Dead. Neil Young. The Doors, even though Jim Morrison was a misogynist."

"You need to listen to some current artists," Roger says, not for the first time.

Cole, however, grows interested. "Neil Young's incredible."

"I know," I say.

"He sounds like he's got a cold," Roger contributes.

"Did you, um, know that it was here in Atlanta that he split off from Crosby, Stills and Nash?" I say. At one point they were Crosby, Stills, Nash and Young. Then Neil Young ditched them, and they turned into Crosby, Stills and Nash. And Neil Young became just plain Neil Young.

"'Funny how some things that start spontaneously end that way,'" Cole quotes. "'Eat a peach. Love, Neil.'"

He knows Neil Young trivia! He *is* a god! I think Roger might roll his eyes, but I can't swear on it because I'm blinded by Cole's god-ness.

He sings a line from a Lynyrd Skynyrd song: "'*I hope Neil Young will remember, a southern man don't need him around anyhow.*'"

His voice is chocolate smoke, and it stirs crazy desire inside me.

I hope what I'm feeling doesn't show. It's way more than just *yay, another sixties-music freak.*

"Enough with the golden oldies," Roger says. "*Sakkerloot.*"

"Saker-what?" Cole says.

"It's Dutch," I say. "He says that as a tribute to his homeland."

"Ah," Cole says. He tears off half his roll, crams it into his mouth, and stands up. His eyes on me, he says, "I gotta run. But catch me later? We can talk about music."

I play it cool and nod.

"*Doie,*" Roger says, saluting.

Cole lifts his eyebrows.

"Dutch for 'good-bye,'" I explain.

"Gotcha," Cole says. He grabs his tray and heads for the conveyor belt, then turns back from a couple feet away. "Oh, and, Carly? Nice dashiki."

CHAPTER TWENTY-THREE
THINGS UNSAID

That afternoon, I tell Anna I'll get a ride home on my own. I say it really nicely, but she looks at me sullenly and says, "Fine. I'll tell Mom."

I ask Roger if he'll take me to Virginia Highlands, and because he's Roger, he says sure. This means riding on the back of his motorcycle, which I'm forbidden to do, since (a) Roger isn't yet sixteen, so he's driving without a license, and (b) motorcycles equal death machines, according to Mom.

But it's for a good cause. Anyway, Roger is an excellent driver and follows all the traffic laws, and he's such a giant that anyone seeing him would assume he's eighteen at least.

He gives me his jacket to wear, which swallows me. His spare helmet creeps down over my eyes, but I can see well enough. I feel the wind on my face. I breathe in the detergent-y smell of Roger's flannel shirt and fantasize about owning my own motorcycle one day. A sweet little cruiser, just my size.

When we reach Virginia Highlands, I try to give Roger his jacket.

"Keep it," he says, and the way he looks at me makes me feel like maybe I look kind of cute in his enormous jacket. "You'll need it for the ride back." He asks if I want company as I shop, and I tell him no. We arrange to meet at Paulo's Gelato, and I go off to explore the boutiques.

I'm looking for something for Anna. A just-because present . . . which in this case is really a just-because-I-was-a-jerk present. Many things tempt me: a custom perfume from Blend, a coolio necklace that I could make for her myself at Atlanta Beads, a set of awesome Hello Kitty stationery from DabberDoo. But all these things are more "me" than Anna. The perfume could possibly work . . . Anna likes perfume. But perfume is pretty personal, and what smells good to me might smell gross to her, like that Shalimar perfume of Mom's that to me smells cloyingly sweet, but which Anna loves.

I end up at Mooncake, which reminds me of a giant dollhouse. It's decorated with old-fashioned hatboxes and shiny ribbons and big bunches of flowers. There's a whole lot of pink. Described in those words, it sounds unappealing, like a grandmother's overstuffed chintz sofa. But it's not like that. It's quirky, like all the stores in Virginia Highlands. Mooncake's take on "quirky" just happens to be especially feminine. And . . . pink.

I pick out a pair of dangly earrings with twinkly crystals at the bottom. They're gorgeous. I put them back and buy a simple pair of seed-pearl earrings that don't dangle at all. They're cute, they're classy, they're totally Anna.

At home, I find her in the TV room curled up on the sofa. She's watching yet another episode of *The Hills*. I start to say something sarcastic, but show great restraint and don't.

"Hey," I say from the doorway. I've got the earrings in a small, gold bag in my pocket.

She gives me a cursory glance, then blows a bubble with her gum. She pulls it back into her mouth and pops it. "Did you *walk* home?" she asks, as if to have done so would have been incredibly lame.

"Roger gave me a ride on his motorcycle. He dropped me off a couple houses down so Mom wouldn't see."

"Oooo," she says. "Such a rebel."

I exhale. She looks ugly with her eyebrows all scowly and her mouth in a frown.

"What's your damage?" I ask.

She snorts. "What's your 'damage'? Omigod, do you have any idea how stupid you sound?"

"Do you have any idea how *bitchy* you sound?"

The word *bitchy* makes my face flush, because despite it all, I'm a Holy Roller. Holy Rollers don't use words like *bitchy*.

"Well, maybe I wouldn't be such a *bitch* if you were the slightest bit nice to me," Anna says, which is ludicrous, because I am nice to her almost all the time.

My jaw tightens and I'm probably going to get a migraine and it's all her fault. I pull the gold bag out of my pocket and hurl it at her. "I got these for you. Hope you like them."

The bag lands in her lap. Her hand goes instinctively to it, as does her gaze. When she lifts her head, her expression is scared.

Good, I think. *Jerk. Loser. Bitch.*

Of course it's my eyes that well with tears. I turn on my heel and stride away before she can see.

CHAPTER TWENTY-FOUR
DUCKY-WUCKY

Ten minutes later comes the knock on my door.

"Come in," I say from my bed, where I've been staring at the ceiling and telling myself that I am always right and Anna is always wrong. And maybe that's not true, but this time it is.

Anna opens the door. "You busy?"

"No," I say. "Just staring at the ceiling, wondering why you've been acting like such a brat recently."

The tension in the room intensifies. I can feel it. It's so strange how you can *feel* things like that.

"I love my earrings," she says with a decent amount of control. "They're beautiful."

I swivel my head. She's got the earrings on, and yeah, they look good.

"I got them to say sorry for making fun of Dr. Smiley yesterday," I say.

She hesitates, then sits on the edge of my bed. "You didn't make fun of Dr. Smiley. You made fun of me."

Same difference, I want to say. But I don't, because it's not. I sigh and let my eyes go back to the ceiling cracks. "Anna . . ."

"What?"

I don't like the way I feel inside. I don't like the messiness of having to work things out. "I can't believe we're having a fight about *teeth.*"

"I can't, either," she says, and not in a let's-giggle-and-make-nice way. The implication is more, *Yeah, it's ridiculous, and I personally think* you're *ridiculous.*

"Well, I'm sorry," I say. "You could have just told me you were upset, though."

She makes a sarcastic *pfff.* "Yeah, we're real good at that."

We're quiet.

She sits. I try to find a place inside of me that's free of coiled-up resistance.

"But come on," I finally say. I try to take the accusation out of my tone. "Don't you think it's silly to stay mad at me for that one remark?"

"You didn't just make fun of my teeth. You made fun of my makeup and my clothes, too." She plays with a strand of her hair. "That's not why I was mad today, though. Not the only reason."

"Then why did you bite my head off when I came to say hi and give you a present?"

She looks at me from under her lashes.

I raise my eyebrows.

"Some guy called me a whale," she says in a low voice.

"What?! That's absurd. Who?"

"Tony D'Abrezzio. In math."

"Well, he's an idiot," I say. "You're not a whale, Anna."

"He was sitting behind me. Jake Knudson was next to him, and Tony goes, 'Hey, Knudson, check out Lauderdale's butt. *Whale tail.*'" The "whale tail" part she stretches out in a bitter singsong.

"Anna—"

"Why does everyone care about my body so much? Why do they think they can say anything they want about it?"

"He wasn't calling you a whale," I tell her.

"Uh, yeah, he was. If my butt's a whale tail, then I'm the whale."

"Were you wearing a thong?"

"Maybe," she says defensively. "So?"

So thongs are dumb, I think. *Thongs are butt floss.* But she already knows my opinion on thongs—an opinion Mom and I share, which means that Anna's been going off on her own to buy sexy underwear. This alone freaks me out, but I've got bigger fish to fry.

"Visualize with me, please. If you were sitting in your chair, and Tony was behind you, and your thong was showing above your jeans . . ."

Comprehension fails to dawn on her face.

"Muffin tops?" I try. "Whale tails? Camel toes?"

Her brown eyes stay confused. How do I know these terms and she doesn't, when she's the one wearing size 36-C bras and thongs?

"All right, sister-to-sister time," I say. "A muffin top is that bit of belly that ploofs out over your jeans."

Anna sits forward and looks down at the overflow of flab formed by her waistband.

"Ugh," she says, sitting back and covering her stomach with her hands.

"Camel toes: when a girl wears her jeans too tight and they go up too high in the front. Um, in her delicate feminine area."

I let her envision it. When she does, she goes, "Ew!"

"I've never seen you with camel toes, so don't worry," I say.

"Wouldn't that *hurt?*"

"I'd sure think so. But I think that about thongs, too."

She turns her imagination skills to thongs. I see her processing the way a plainly visible thong would make a *Y* above the waist of too-low jeans.

"Ohhhh," she says. "So a whale tail . . ."

" . . . has nothing to do with being fat," I finish.

"Ew," she says again.

The mood in the room is lighter than it was five minutes ago. It's amazing. We twist to our sides so we're facing each other on my bed.

"You're not fat, Anna. You *should*, however, stop wearing thongs."

"Yeah, only you don't get to tell me that."

"I do, too, because I'm your big sister and that's my job. I have to shower you with sisterly love, which sometimes means telling you the hard truth about things." I poke her. "Because you're my ducky-wucky."

"Please don't call me that."

"I have to. It would be so sad if I didn't."

"Sad for who?"

I pause. Are we still happy, or are we tumbling back down the hill? I swear, it used to be so easy with Anna. These days, I never know what to expect.

"Sad for me," I say carefully. "But sad for you, too"—I make my voice poor-little-me-ish—"because don't you *want* to be my ducky-wucky?"

"No," she says.

I find her toes with mine so that we're touching. I have the slippery sense of losing something. "Why not?"

"Would you want to be called ducky-wucky?"

"Sure, why not? It's cute. It's . . . ducky-ish."

"Which is great, only I don't want to be ducky-ish."

"Anna," I say. "Nicknames mean you love somebody. Do you not . . . am I not allowed to love you anymore?"

"Carly . . ."

"You're my little sister," I say. To my horror, my voice wavers.

"I have a whole life you don't know about," she says.

"I'm not saying I *own* you. I'm just saying you're my little sister."

"I wish you'd stop calling me that, too. 'Little' sister. I'm bigger than you, Carly."

"Oh, sure, rub it in."

She maintains a level gaze.

"Fine. *Younger* sister—can you live with that?"

She exhales as if I'm exasperating her, which in turn exasperates me.

"Listen, Anna, I *am* older than you," I state. "That's just the way it is. I'm older than you, and I'll *always* be older than you." I pause. "Unless I die. Then you'd be older."

"Not till fourteen months after," she says. "I'd have to catch up with you before I could pass you."

"Okay, you're missing a key point here: I'd be *dead*."

Grudgingly, she laughs. "But, Carly . . ." Our toes are still touching. "Yes, I'm your sister. But I don't want that to be *all* I am."

"It's not all you are. It never has been."

"Sometimes it feels like it."

I swallow.

"So will you quit calling me ducky-wucky?"

Stop looking at me like that, I think. I feel as if I'm drowning—or if not drowning, then as if I'm keeping my head above water, but just barely. Which is silly. Nothing bad is happening here. Anna is safe. I'm safe. We'll always be sisters.

"I'll try," I say. "But I might forget sometimes. Okay, ducky-wucky?"

Her smile is sad. It tells me I've disappointed her. She sits up, and my toes miss her toes.

She slides off the bed. "I'm going to go finish my show."

"Wait." I push myself up, and the sleeve of my dashiki gets caught under my butt. I tug it free. "Are we good, you and me?"

She smiles, but it's woven through with a thread of *lonely*. "Thanks for the earrings. I love them."

CHAPTER TWENTY-FIVE
SOUP CANS AND STOCKINGS

Rumor has it that at public schools—insert exaggerated shivers of horror—students aren't allowed to have Secret Santas. *Or* sing Christmas carols, *or* deck the halls with boughs of holly, or do anything Christmas-y *at all*, since Christmas is a Christian holiday and public schools aren't allowed to have religion. My cousin Frances, who lives in South Carolina and goes to public school, says that instead of Christmas break, they have winter break, and instead of Christmas parties, they have "holiday" parties.

Although she says they still make those candy-cane reindeer, and what's up with that? As any good Holy Roller can tell you, candy canes represent shepherds' staffs, as in the shepherds who followed the star to see Jesus. And, sorry, but that's Christmas all the way, baby.

At Holy Redeemer, we most certainly do have Secret Santas and Christmas carols and boughs of holly, and I love it. I love it all. Yes, the world is filled with sadness, and yes, Holy Redeemer is whacked-out in oh-so-many ways. But Christmas—the *real* Christmas, what it's supposed to be—is an example of what I feel when

I think about God. Christmas is a time to believe that, deep down, people are good.

Trista Van Houser, for example, is being very good. She's making a Service Council announcement during homeroom, because Trista is big into community service. I grudgingly admire her for it, because Trista is super-rich even by Holy Redeemer standards, and she doesn't *have* to do community service at all. She could float around a pool all day in a five-star Hawaiian resort. Or jet off to New York and shop at Barneys, just for the heck of it. Every fall she does exactly that when her daddy takes her shopping for a new school wardrobe.

Today Trista is wearing a cream-colored silk shirt tucked into a short suede skirt. As she talks, she alternates between playing with her gold charm bracelet and finger-combing her streaky blond hair. She's here to remind us to make Christmas stockings for needy families.

"I mean, y'all," she entreats, "this is serious. I could just cry when I think how I'd feel if I woke up Christmas morning and didn't have any presents to open."

I'm a little surprised she cares. Guess it's a reminder that I'm not as good a judge of character as I like to think I am.

"We all need to bring in one stocking apiece, and it needs to be full," she continues. "Just put in some soup cans or something, that's what I'm telling all the homerooms."

Then again, yes I am.

That doesn't mean that Christmas equals hypocrisy, though. It is complicated living in my head, because it's so easy to make fun of Christianity (and Christian fluff-fluff heads like Trista), and yet I do believe in something bigger. I do, I do.

Trista runs her tongue over her teeth. "Now, today is Tuesday, and the deadline is this Friday. You can bring in more stockings after that, but they won't count for class-spirit points, and we've just *got* to beat the juniors. So don't forget, 'kay?" She waves as she leaves the room. "Y'all have a good one!"

Oh, Trista, I think. She's not a *bad* person. She just lives in her own little world, where soup equals good Christmas fun for needy children.

In my head, I play a movie of Trista on Christmas morning. She trots downstairs in her BCBG pajamas, peers beneath the branches of her fourteen-foot Christmas tree, and exclaims in delight when she spots a can of Campbell's cream of asparagus tied with a bright red bow.

During my free period, I see that Trista has set up a Service Council table in the foyer of Butler Hall. Chatting with Trista, his thumbs hooked through his belt loops, is Cole. His shirt is gray with black letters, and it says I Live in My Own Little World. But It's Okay, They Know Me Here.

Now, that's just plain weird, I think, stopping short.

Peyton rams into me. "Ow," she says, even though it's my heel that gets stepped on. Then Lydia rams into Peyton. She says "ow," too.

"Sorry," I say. The weirdness isn't that Cole is talking to Trista (though he should STOP RIGHT NOW). The weirdness is that just this morning I was thinking about how Trista lives in *her* own little world—and now here Cole is, proclaiming the same sentiment on his T-shirt. But he's being ironic, of course. Even if he wasn't, it wouldn't matter, because Cole living in his own world is a whole different ball of wax from Trista living in her own world. Trista's world is shallow. Cole's world is sexy and deep and full of texture.

Cole and I have developed a . . . *thing* over the last month, which makes it painful to see him chatting up Trista. Admittedly, what Cole and I have isn't a *thing* thing. It's more of a *riff* thing. It started out with quizzing each other on old song lyrics, and it grew into goofy exchanges of sixties speak. *Far out. What a trip. Neato. Keen.*

I think Cole is keen. I also think that a riff thing is better than nothing. A riff thing could, one day, turn into a *thing* thing.

"Stop drooling," Peyton says. Peyton thinks the odds of our riff thing turning into a thing thing are low to the point of zilch.

I blush.

"Yeah," Lydia says, prodding my back with her knuckles. "I'm in the middle of a *story*."

I feel like a mule being herded along. I also wonder why, if Peyton and Lydia are my friends, I don't always like the way I feel when I'm with them.

We reach a bench and sit down.

"*I* think he's sexually starved," Lydia says, referring to her math teacher, Mr. Owens. "Because why just the girls and not the boys, huh? Somebody could sue him for discrimination. Somebody *should* sue him for discrimination!"

"Is there another way for the guys to earn points?" Peyton asks.

I listen, but my attention is on Cole, who's still talking to Trista.

"No," Lydia says. "He was just, 'If you get your picture taken with Santa, I'll give you extra credit. But you have to be sitting in his lap.'"

"Then he didn't say the guys *couldn't* do it," Peyton says.

Lydia makes an offended sound. "Oh, right, like some guy is going to plop down in Santa's lap."

Usually I'm entertained by stories about Mr. Owens—and Lydia has a lot of them—but Cole is now laughing at something Trista said. I wish Trista wasn't so pretty. I wish somebody would go over there and remind Cole that prettiness isn't everything, and that girls who are quirky and smart and appreciate good music are ultimately far more appealing.

I get to my feet.

"Where are you going?" Lydia demands.

"Where do you think?" Peyton says. She uses her eyes to point across the room.

"*Oh*," Lydia says. "Good luck."

They snicker, and I press my lips together.

"Give him a kiss for me," Peyton calls.

Shut up, I say in my head. I swallow and try to push that negative energy out. Peyton and Lydia? Unimportant. Cole? Important. *Smile. Be confident. Be chill.*

"Hi," I say to Trista when I reach her table. I glance at Cole as if I'm just now noticing him. "Hey, Cole."

"Carly, my man," he says.

I grin. "Peace, brother."

Trista looks confused, and it takes away a bit of the Peyton/Lydia sting. *See?* I tell them mentally. *He does like me.*

"Still trying to get those stockings filled?" I ask Trista. I keep my tone neutral, since I don't yet know where Cole stands. Stockings: dumb or good?

"Now I'm signing up volunteers to do the actual deliveries," Trista says. "We have two drivers, and each driver can take four passengers. Chuck *might* be able to take more if his Hummer's out of the shop, but he won't know until the very day."

I glance at Cole. He gives no hint of his position.

"Uh. . .where exactly are you delivering them to?" I ask.

"To the poor people. We've got a list."

Surely Cole is scoffing by now. A *list*? Of the poor people? Except he says to me, "You should come. It's going to be cool."

Trista's pen hovers. "Can I put you down?"

"Uh . . . when is it?"

"Next Thursday night."

"Um, okay." I feel flustered, but I tell myself not to. Poor people. Stockings. It's all good.

"Terriff," Trista says.

Cole nods his approval in his slow, easy way, and Christmas spirit fills me up and lifts me to the sky. Or rather, the ceiling, where I bob, balloon-like, and smile down at all the oh-so-human humans.

CHAPTER TWENTY-SIX

PASHMINA IS SO LAST YEAR

That weekend, I tell Mom about the service project and explain that I need to go shopping. She immediately gets fired up and suggests we go right away. Anna comes, too. Dad stays home to watch the football game.

All I want is something cute to wear when we deliver stockings, but I make the mistake of mentioning Trista Van Houser, and Mom loses all perspective. At Neiman's, she strides to the cocktail-dress section and pulls out a black silk dress with bows. A salesclerk named Joy nods approvingly.

"*Very* Chanel," Joy tells us. "*So* precious and darling."

"Mom, you're insane," I say. *How little does she know me that she'd think a Chanel cocktail dress is what I wanted to go shopping for?* "I'm not going to a dance. It's a charity thing."

"Ooo, charity balls," Joy says. "Such fun. The question is, what to wear with?" She rubs the fabric of the skirt. "You *could* do a pashmina scarf, but I really think we've seen the end of that trend."

"Oh no!" Mom exclaims. "I *love* my pashmina scarf. Are you telling me I can't wear it anymore?"

I make eyes at Anna. She makes them back.

"What you want is a capelet," Joy says. "A fur capelet, like something that belonged to your grandmama."

"A capelet," Mom muses. "My grandmother *did* have a capelet, come to think of it. Although I don't know that she called it that. Isn't it funny how fashions truly do come around again?"

"Mo-o-m," I say.

Anna smirks. I pinch her, and she yelps.

"Anna, inside voice," Mom scolds, as if Anna is five.

"Capelets, capelets, capelets," Joy says, drumming her fingers on the dress rack. "We don't have any—but maybe you could find one at a thrift store?"

"Now that's an idea," Mom says as if she's genuinely considering trucking us off to Goodwill. She hates Goodwill. The smell gives her a headache, and she doesn't like the homeless men who congregate outside.

"Just make sure it doesn't have fleas," Joy says with a tinkly laugh.

All right, then.

"Mom, we're delivering stockings," I say firmly. "People will be wearing *jeans.*"

"Jeans," Mom repeats, meaning, *Then why in the world did we go shopping?*

"Who are you delivering stockings to?" Joy asks.

"The poor people," I hear myself say.

Joy puts her hand over her heart. "Oh, *honey.*"

"They do some wonderful service projects at Holy Redeemer," Mom tells her. "They work hard to encourage altruism."

"Hmm," Joy says. "Perhaps a crisp, tailored blouse and wide-leg pants? Navy, perhaps? Or"—she brightens—"of course! We just received the most *darling* Marc Jacobs cherry-print tie blouse." She splays her hands as if seeing it on Broadway. "Doesn't that just *scream* Candy Striper?"

I step back. I'm getting the sinking-in-mire feeling that accompanies shopping with Mom, which is why I never want to go shopping with Mom.

Anna touches Mom's arm. "Hey, Mom?"

Mom seems surprised to see her. "Yes, Anna?"

"I'm taking Carly to Urban Outfitters. I'll make sure she gets something cute, 'kay? You do some shopping of your own, and we'll meet you back here."

"Oh," Mom says.

Anna smiles pleasantly. Taking my cue from her, I paste on a pleasant smile as well. Anna is just *better* in this world of mannequins and brand names.

Mom's gaze drifts to the couture section. "Well . . ."

"We just put out our new Armani," Joy says.

"I *love* Armani," Mom says. "The styles are classic, and the fit is good. I find myself wearing my Armani pieces year after year."

Joy nods. "I agree. You *always* feel well dressed in Armani." She goes for the kill. "Have you seen the holiday collection?"

Mom reaches into her purse and extracts her Platinum Visa. "Here," she says, handing it to Anna. "No more than a hundred dollars."

I start to protest—why is Anna in charge of the credit card?—but bite it back. Pleasant smile, pleasant smile.

"Can I buy an outfit, too?" Anna says, widening her brown eyes.

"I suppose," Mom says.

"Thanks, Mom, you're the best," she says, and gives Mom a hug.

I kind of lift my hand in a wave—I'm *waving* at my mom?—and add, "Yeah, thanks."

Anna grabs my arm and fast-walks me out of Neiman's. "Run, run, before the Candy Stripers attack!"

I giggle. Oh my *God*, it's good to get out of Neiman's.

At Urban Outfitters, Anna plays the role of personal stylist, plucking tanks and tees and jeans and cargo pants from the racks.

She shoves me and a heaping pile of clothes into one of the cloth-curtained dressing rooms and gets comfy in the armchair outside.

"Show me everything," she orders.

"Yes, ma'am." I love Urban Outfitters, even though I technically shouldn't, since it's pretty much a rich girl's Salvation Army. It pretends to be *of the people*, but really it's a mass-market pit of conspicuous consumption. Only at Salvation Army, there are so many ugly clothes mixed in with the good stuff, and it's a crapshoot whether anything will be in your size. At Urban Outfitters, the funky peasant skirts are available in sizes zero through twelve, and the grunge-hip bomber jackets are perfectly distressed without actually falling apart or smelling like mothballs.

They don't have capelets, though. Bummer.

Anna gives the thumbs-up to a soft white camisole with lace around the edge. I try it with a pair of baggy brown trousers, and Anna gives a Dad-style *ssssss* and a big thumbs-down.

"What?" I say. I snagged the brown trousers from the rack when Anna wasn't watching.

"They make you look like Granddad," Anna says.

Ugh. They do. I make a face at her for being right and go back behind the curtain.

I try on a pair of black cords (thumbs-medium), an Indian-print skirt (thumbs-down and a command to stop sneaking in unapproved articles), and some wide-leg railroad stripe pants (thumbs-*way*-down) before lighting on a pair of beat-up jeans with frayed cuffs, a frayed waistband, and a pink patch on the upper left thigh. The patch is shaped like a heart, and it's stitched on with red thread in a handmade-seeming way.

In standing-up position, they're perfect. I kind of think they might even look . . . well . . . sexy. I step outside into the main area and look at Anna hopefully.

"Hmm," she says, tapping her lip. "A bit folksy, but then, you like folksy. Squat test, please."

I turn around and squat.

"No whale tail," Anna proclaims.

I stand. "Duh, because I don't wear thongs. But no visible butt crack?"

"You're covered, babe." She thrusts out her thumb. "*Big* thumbs-up."

So I get the white cami and the heart jeans, and I have enough left over to throw in a red-and-black-checked lumberjack hoodie. It's snug and fun and makes me happy, even though it earns an eye roll from Anna.

For herself, she picks out a Free People miniskirt printed with a pattern called Forbidden Fruit.

I snort. "Like *that's* not suggestive."

She twirls in front of the mirror, revealing winter-pale thighs. "But fabulous, yeah?"

"Yeah," I admit. "Not fabulous for me, but fabulous for you."

"Well, I didn't pick it out for you, did I?"

She pairs it with a fake-vintage T-shirt that says Meet Me on the Moon. I resist fake-vintage T-shirts on principle, but . . . *aww*. Anna's is so sweet. There's another shirt on the rack with the words Protesting Is So Hot Right Now printed across the front, and she grabs that one, too.

"No way," I say, taking it from her and putting it back. "Copying my sixties vibe."

"Like I'd want to." Her hand hovers, then swoops to the rack. "This one, then. Do you love it, or do you love it?"

It's a baby-blue hockey shirt with the slogan Love Is Color-Blind. The graphic shows three overly precious toddlers with chubby cheeks and little pug noses and teardrop-shaped eyes. One's white, one's Asian, and one's black. They're all wearing button-flap pj's, and for some reason they're on a scooter. Oh, and there's a butterfly.

It's hideously, cheesily wonderful.

"I love it," I admit. Curse her for spotting it first. "But if you get it, you have to put back the 'Meet Me on the Moon' one."

"Says who?" Anna asks.

"Says our hundred-dollar limit."

"Oh, please. Like Mom will know or care. You think *she's* sticking to a hundred-dollar limit?"

With the Armani holiday collection bowing and curtsying in front of her? *No.* But my going shopping for a feed-the-poor-people outfit is a lame enough move already. I am a big ball of hypocrisy and contradiction, but I'm not going to make it worse by going crazy with Mom's Visa.

"Sorry, Charlie," I say, taking the "Meet Me at the Moon" shirt from Anna's hand and placing it back on the rack. Anna pouts, but I stay firm. I even resist the "No Nukes" shirt calling to me from among the hangers.

At the register, Anna signs Mom's name on the credit-card slip and grandly pronounces, "We will wear these pieces year after year."

"Absolutely," I agree. "I *always* feel well dressed in Urban Outfitters."

CHAPTER TWENTY-SEVEN
SANTA'S LITTLE HELPERS

On the evening of the Service Council project, Mom drops me off in the boys'-school parking lot. I'm decked out in my new jeans and camisole and lumberjack hoodie, and I'm reminding myself that despite my new duds, I'm still just me. I don't want to get self-conscious about wearing a new outfit, because when I get self-conscious, I grow stiff and hold myself weird.

"Have fun!" Mom calls, pulling away.

I feel immediately out of place and think, *Ack, why did I do this?*

Then I get stern and tell myself, *Hush. You're helping the poor.*

Trista's already here, along with Chuck, a junior named Owen, and Lydia. Since when did Lydia sign up to do this? They're loading the back of Chuck's Hummer, and as Chuck heaves in an armful of stockings, he says, "Christ, there's a lot of these suckers."

"Please don't take the Lord's name in vain," Lydia says.

I don't see Cole. Where is Cole? There are a couple of other sophomore girls, including Vonzelle from my PE class. But no Cole.

Vonzelle lifts her hand, and I go over.

"Hey," I say.

"Hey," she replies. We've never hung out together, so it's a little awkward. Side by side, we watch the people who know what they're doing.

A few minutes later, Pete pulls up, and with him is my beautiful Cole. My heart leaps. Cole spots me and grins. He climbs out of Pete's Volvo and saunters over.

"Groovy," he says, fingering the collar of my lumberjack jacket. I'm so glad I came. So so *so* glad.

"You're looking pretty psychedelic yourself," I reply, though he's not. He's wearing jeans and a white T-shirt; nothing psychedelic about that. But I'm running out of sixties words.

Cole chuckles, and Trista clears her throat. She's watching us with a funny expression.

"Okay!" she says. "Scotty, you come with me and Pete. You, too, Cole. And Chuck, you take Owen, Lydia, Kendra, Vonzelle, and Carly. All right?"

I get a hot feeling in my stomach. I want to protest.

"I'm glad we get to be together," Vonzelle says to me. "I don't know any of these people."

I turn to her. "Uh . . . yeah."

Vonzelle senses my lack of enthusiasm. I can see it in the way her mouth flattens. But my disappointment has nothing to do with being put in the same car as her. It has to do with *not* being put in the same car as Cole. Why do I have the feeling that Trista split us up on purpose?

"Dudes, let's motor," Chuck says.

"You've got your list of addresses?" Trista asks.

"Affirmative."

I watch Cole head back over to Pete's Volvo. Pete's car is a two-door, so Cole opens the passenger-side door and yanks the seat lever. The front seat flies forward, and Cole steps back to let Trista climb in. *What a gentleman*, I think sourly. He climbs in after her,

and the two of them are alone in the completely un-roomy back-seat.

I dig my fingernails into my palms.

Chuck toots the horn. "What's the holdup?"

My face heats up, and I hurry over. Owen's in the front passenger seat, Lydia and Kendra are in the first row of backseats, and Vonzelle is alone in the second row of seats. I scooch in and join her.

She looks away.

The first house we go to is in Cabbage Town. I've heard of Cabbage Town, but it's a part of Atlanta I've never been to. The houses are small and crowded, and there are a lot of mom-and-pop liquor stores. We pass a billboard advertising Dark and Lovely Hair Relaxer, and Chuck punches Owen's shoulder.

"Need some hair relaxer, dude?"

"Shit, dude, I'll relax *her*," Owen replies, meaning the billboard model who is dark-skinned and voluptuous. He lowers his voice to a put-on growl. "I like my women black, like my coffee."

Chuck laughs, and I'm mortified. I feel Vonzelle stiffen beside me, and I don't know what to do. Challenge them? Tell them they're being jerks? They're juniors. They don't even know my name.

"Y'all, hush," Lydia says.

Owen twists around from the front seat and says, "Excuse me?"

Lydia jerks her eyes at Vonzelle, and Owen says, "Oh, sorry. My bad."

Chuck cracks up more.

"Dude," Owen says, as if reprimanding him. But he doesn't care. Neither of them cares. They're too busy being hilarious.

"They're idiots," Lydia says to Vonzelle. "Ignore them."

"Oh, I will," Vonzelle says.

I try to make eye contact with her, to say without words that they *are* idiots, and that honestly, I'm fine being in the same group as she is. There were just other factors at play.

She holds her spine straight and stares out the window.

Every house we go to, the families are black. Maybe I should have expected it, but I didn't. It makes me fidget.

One little boy we visit is named Terrell. "Like the football player," he tells us, but I don't know who he's talking about since I don't know football. He grins hugely when Lydia gives him his stocking.

"For me?" he asks. "The whole thing?"

"Don't you open it now, Terrell," says an older woman I'm guessing is his grandmom. She's sitting in an armchair with a McDonald's bag on her lap. The air smells like french fries. "You save it, you hear?"

"Well, y'all have a merry Christmas," Lydia says. She pats Terrell's head. "Blessings to you, cutie."

"What do you say?" prods Terrell's grandmom.

"Thank you," Terrell recites, his smile lighting up the room.

Back in the Hummer, Lydia goes on about Terrell and how adorable he was.

"He is going to be a heartbreaker one day," she says. "I just wanted to wrap him up and take him home with me." She launches into a story about some friends of her parents who adopted a little black boy who was just as adorable as Terrell, only at first the parents didn't know how to deal with his hair.

"Because you can't just wash it, right, Vonzelle?" she says. "You have to use, like, oils and stuff. Right?"

I look at Vonzelle apologetically, but Vonzelle appears unruffled.

"Not for an infant," she says. "For an infant, plain old baby shampoo is good—just not more than once a week."

"Okay," Lydia says. "I mean, I probably won't adopt a black baby, but you never know." She fishes through one of the undelivered stockings and pulls out a Hershey's Kiss. "You know who's really adorable? Those Chinese babies. Although my mom has this *other* friend who adopted a little Chinese baby—"

"Your mom sure has a lot of friends who've adopted babies," I say.

"—and this is *really* awful: she came home without the roof of her mouth."

"*What?*" Kendra says.

"I know," Lydia says. "The orphanage people said she was fine, everyone said she was fine, and then the parents got her and found out the whole top of her mouth was missing. She had to have, like, five zillion surgeries."

That is absolutely awful, to be without the roof of a mouth. I want Lydia to stop talking about it, and she does, only to move on to African orphans and how they're left in their cribs for hours on end.

The streetlights cast shadows on Lydia's face as she twists in her seat to include me and Vonzelle in the conversation.

"They don't even have crib mattresses," she says. "Just wooden boards. But if you sponsor one of those babies, you get to name it."

You get to name it? I'm horrified, and I'm also having one of those out-of-body moments where I can't believe I'm actually participating—by simple virtue of existing—in this conversation.

"That's cool," Kendra says. "Kind of like how you can buy a star and name it. I wish someone would name a star for me."

"But you know what's really awful?" Lydia goes on. "And, like, I feel *terrible* for feeling this way?"

"What?" Kendra says.

"Even though it's not their fault—those pagan babies, I mean— I would never adopt one, because they'd be so messed up by the time you got them. Like, with attachment disorder and stuff."

Those pagan babies?! Oh my God. I'm going to break out in hives. I do not and do not look at Vonzelle.

"I've never thought about that," Kendra says.

Lydia nods. "But I totally admire the people who do—or who

adopt black babies or Chinese babies or *any* little orphan babies. It's so Christian of them."

Oh, no no no no no. I *hate* it when people say "that's so Christian of them" or "that's so Christian of you" or any sentence where the word "Christian" is thrown in to mean *the way you should be.* See, that is *not* the type of Christian I am.

Also, Lydia's making out like all those babies are broken or something. She's lumping them together in one big broken pile.

We keep passing hair-relaxer billboards, and billboards for malt liquor, and I feel massively uncomfortable with this whole outing— and especially how I accidentally made Vonzelle feel bad. So out of the blue I say, "You know, some people say Jesus was black."

"I'm sorry, what?" Lydia says.

"Because of where he was born. The people there are black, not white."

I'm not on solid footing here, because I can't remember what country I'm talking about. Palestine? But in sixth grade, our Bible teacher showed us images of Jesus from around the world, and in one of the pictures, he was black. Her response, when the class guffawed, was something along the lines of "Now, children, let's keep our tolerant hats on. A black Jesus may seem silly to us, but love comes in all shapes and colors."

Lydia does not have her tolerant hat on, nor is she wearing a "Love Is Color-Blind" shirt from Urban Outfitters.

"That's ridiculous," she says. "Baby Jesus was not black."

"You don't know that," I say. Fragments of the lesson come back to me. "He was born in the Middle East, right? And there's Bible verses about how his hair was like wool and his feet shone like bronze."

I'm fairly impressed with myself for pulling all this out of my brain. I think I deserve a pat on the back.

Instead, I get a peeved look from Lydia, who says, "Bronze isn't black."

"Bronze isn't *white*," I retort.

"Obviously, he had a tan," Lydia says haughtily. "They didn't have sunscreen back then."

I look at her like she's crazy. And then, one beat later, I laugh, because it's actually the perfect comeback. Vonzelle presses her knuckles to her mouth to hide her smile, and a second later, Lydia laughs, too. Every so often she reminds me that she's not completely irredeemable.

"Well, they *didn't*," she insists.

Kendra looks put out. "It's *possible* he had an olive complexion," she says, "but unlikely, because he had blue eyes. Blue-eyed people are usually fair. But it doesn't matter where he was born, because God made Jesus in His own image, remember?"

"And God's *white?*" I say incredulously. I've got the giggles now for real, and so does Vonzelle.

Kendra looks at me like, *Well, duh.*

This makes Vonzelle and me laugh harder.

Lydia doesn't get why, because she thinks God is white, too. I can see it on her face.

CHAPTER TWENTY-EIGHT

WHITE BOYS DON'T GIVE NOOGIES
(TO ME)

After we drop off our final stocking, we get on I-20 and head back into familiar territory. Vonzelle and I talk. The floodgates have been loosed or whatever, and chatting now comes easily.

"So what's up with your sister?" she asks.

"What do you mean?"

"With PE. With Coach Wanker."

I gave a loud *ha* and tell her that's the most brilliant nickname ever. "All this time, I've been calling him Captain Awesome. Not as good, is it?"

"Why does she keep coming to class?" Vonzelle says. "If I were her, and I knew I'd failed, I'd go to the library and at least get some work done."

"Huh," I say, because this is a twist I haven't considered. Why *does* Anna keep coming to PE? "It's not fair that just because she failed the dive, she fails the whole class."

"The Wanker's a sadist," Vonzelle says.

"And a racist," I add, recalling his "those people" speech. Immediately I wish I'd kept my mouth shut. Just when things were going well, I have to lead us back into treacherous waters?

"A sadist *and* a racist," Vonzelle says. She doesn't seem terribly troubled, and I wonder if she doesn't care. Although, no, because she was the first in our class to do the back dive off the high dive. The way she climbed the ladder and marched to the end of the board and just *did* it?

She cares.

"Did she ask if she could try again?" Vonzelle asks.

"Uh . . . he said no," I say. Didn't he? On that particular day in class, he made it clear that Anna was done, finished, *you fail, get off the board.* But now I'm wondering why Anna didn't push it further. I'm also wondering if a failing grade for fall semester equals a failing grade for the whole year, because PE is a yearlong class.

Vonzelle purses her lips. "*Mmm,*" she says disapprovingly. "What'd your parents say?"

"She never told them."

"She never *told* them? Well, they're going to find out soon enough, aren't they?"

"Crap," I say, because Anna's grades are already a sore spot. Even my occasional A-minuses earn a disapproving arch of Dad's eyebrows. Last week I brought home a math test I got a ninety-eight on, and his response was, "What happened to the other two points?"

Vonzelle tilts her head, as if she's willing to hear more if I'm willing to share. But we're almost back at school, and she doesn't pursue it.

When we pull into Holy Redeemer's parking lot, Pete's Volvo is already there. Pete, Cole, and Trista are outside the car, leaning against it. I sit up and finger-brush my hair.

"Hey, guys," Pete says as we spill from Chuck's Hummer. "How'd it go?"

"Good times," Chuck says. "You?"

"Awesome," Pete says. "We made those little kids' day."

"I know," Lydia says. "I was like, '*This* is what Christmas is about, giving those kids something to rejoice in.'"

Trista beams. Her expression says, *Yes, and I made it happen.*

I roll my eyes.

"What?" she says, zeroing in on me.

"Nothing." I'm startled she noticed.

"You rolled your eyes. Do you not think it's important, what we did?"

"No, I do, it's just—"

"Just what?" Trista says. Her earrings are tiny bells. They jingle as she puts her hands on her hips.

My eyes go to Cole, who's regarding me as if he wants to know, too. Vonzelle is also listening.

"It *was* good," I say slowly. I think of Terrell and how he practically vibrated off the floor. But true Christmas spirit shouldn't involve taking credit, should it? Especially if you're a fancy prep-school kid who has more than enough already?

"Shouldn't we have given the stockings to the grown-ups, though?" I say. "Like . . . in private?"

Trista is put out. "The adults don't get stockings. They get hams, but not until later."

"No," I say. "I mean, we could have given the kids' stockings to their parents or grandparents or whoever, and then *they* could have put them out on Christmas morning."

"I don't get it," Trista says.

"Oh," Cole says. "Because of Santa Claus. You're right, Carls."

"But we *are* Santa Claus," Trista says.

Cole hooks his arm around her and gives her a noogie, and she giggles.

"What? We are!"

I smile, but my smile is wooden and awful. Trista likes Cole, and Cole likes her back. There it is. Undeniable.

"Come on," Vonzelle says, taking my arm and leading me to the curb. She sits, and I lower myself dumbly beside her. *The guys I like never like me back. Why? Am I not good enough? Will I never be good enough?*

"So is that why you didn't want to ride with me?" Vonzelle says. She motions with her chin to indicate Cole and Trista.

"I didn't *not* want to ride with you," I say.

"That's what I'm saying. You weren't like, '*Ew*, Vonzelle.' You were, 'Ooo, what's-his-name.'"

"Cole," I say. I haven't even admitted it to Peyton, the extent of my crush. But, yeah.

Vonzelle props her head in her hands. "Pretty cute for a white boy."

I glance at her. "Pretty unavailable, too."

Trista glances at the curb where Vonzelle and I are sitting. She nestles against Cole's chest and gives me a he's-mine look from under a swoop of blond hair.

"Did you see that?" I say, astounded.

"I sure did."

"For real—the look she gave me." I've never been given a look like that before, a look that so blatantly said *hands off.*

"Guess she's afraid you're the other woman," Vonzelle says.

"Seriously?"

Vonzelle snorts. "For a white girl, you sure are dumb."

"Can we stop with the black/white thing?" I say. "We're all just people. We're not that different, okay?"

Her gaze floats over my hippie jeans and lumberjack hoodie. "And here I thought you *wanted* to be different, always wearing your crazy clothes."

I'm not sure whether to be offended or not. "You think my clothes are crazy?"

"Heck yeah, 'cause you're a crazy honky. Crazy honkies wear crazy honky clothes."

"You just called me a honky," I say. I'm shocked, but kind of delighted.

"I go to a honky school, don't I? I think I know a honky when I see one."

"Shut up. I'm not a honky."

"Oh, I'm sorry, but you are."

"Nuh-uh. Lydia can be the honky. Or Trista! Trista can be the honky!" I say it more loudly than I intend, and Trista swivels her head.

You did not just say what I think you did, her expression says.

"Oh, crud," I say.

Vonzelle cracks up. "Keep calling people names, and Santa's going to bring you a lump of coal."

It takes me a second, but I get it. A lump of *coal* . . . a lump of *Cole?* Clever girl, that Vonzelle.

"I wish," I say.

She grins and leans back on her palms. "Or not. Word around town is that the best honkies are getting big ole cans of Campbell's cream of Jesus."

CHAPTER TWENTY-NINE

WHO CARES WHAT BRAND YOUR JEANS ARE IF YOU DON'T HAVE A BUTT?

The next day, I fill Peyton in about the Trista/Cole situation. She's disgusted.

"*Trista?*" she says as we file into the auditorium for our Friday-morning assembly.

"Yes, but hush," I say. Lydia is behind us. I don't want her knowing I care.

Peyton scooches into a row. "Oh, that is just sad," she whispers. "But maybe they were just flirting. Maybe it won't stick."

I jerk my chin at Cole, who's ten rows in front of us. Trista is sitting beside him. Cole leans his head toward hers and says something into her ear, and she smiles up at him in a sweet, scrunched-nose kind of way.

"Dang," Peyton says. "It stuck."

The assembly starts, and for the first ten minutes it's all *Yay, Christmas! Yay, Christmas break! And here are the five thousand things you need to do before the end of the day, like clean out your lockers and turn in your final papers and, oh yeah, be really really super grateful that Jesus was born all those years ago so He could die for your sins!*

Miss Potter, head of administration, has lots of announcements. Peyton and I switch to written communication.

She needs a DYE JOB!!! Peyton scribbles on a notepad, meaning Trista.

Does she? Her hair looks good to me. Maybe it's not perfectly *plopped* like Peyton's, but *shiny*, *bouncy*, and *blond* would be annoyingly appropriate adjectives to describe it.

Maybe I need a dye job, I write back. *And not from Jerr.*

Maybe Trista needs to go to Jerr, Peyton writes. *She needs to be taken DOWN.*

I get inspired and sketch a line drawing of Peyton that looks like "What's Her Face" from *Teen Girl Squad,* an extremely funny Web cartoon about high-school girls. The characters say things like, "Hey, gals! Let's go get ready to LOOK SO GOOD!"

I draw Peyton with stick arms, swoopy hair, and a cute little swimsuit with cutouts. I draw me next to her. I take the role of the Ugly One, so I give myself a dumpy one-piece. Behind us, I sketch a swimming pool.

Peyton tries to peek, but I shoo her away.

"Patience, young grasshopper," I say.

Next I draw Trista, who of course gets to be Cheerleader. *Boo.* She gets perky pigtails, empty circle eyes, and a wide-open smile that looks manic. Oh, and a bikini. Since I'm in control of my pen, I employ artistic license and add a necklace with a huge, sparkly cross. Cheerleaders for Christ!

Now it's time for speech bubbles. I crib from the cartoon, but add my own touches. First I make Peyton say, "I like boys!"

"Not *my* boy," Trista says.

In the next frame, I draw a giant squid coming out of the pool, wrapping its tentacles around Trista and pulling her under.

"Uh-oh . . ." my cartoon Peyton says.

"Let's go to Starbucks!" says Ugly Girl, who is really me.

"Yeah!" Peyton says. *"I love coffee!!!!!"*

At the bottom, in big letters: THE END.

I hand Peyton the notebook. She chortles. A teacher behind us leans forward and hisses, "Girls. You need to be listening."

Peyton faces forward and pretends to pay rapt attention to Headmaster Perkins, who's taken over from Miss Potter. Headmaster Perkins introduces today's speaker, a man in a wheelchair named Sergeant Franco. The Percolator tells us that Sergeant Franco was a paratrooper in the Iraq war (Operation Enduring Freedom), and he jumped out of a plane, and his parachute didn't open all the way. Big-time suckage.

So now Sergeant Franco has no legs, and his face is a misshapen, reconstructed mess. If you saw him on the street, you'd think, *oh my God* and look away. But because he's our assembly speaker, we have to look at him.

At first, I'm still distracted by Cole and Trista. But when the Percolator gives Sergeant Franco the mike and takes a seat at the back of the stage, I find myself drawn into Sergeant Franco's talk.

"I'm no longer imprisoned by ego," he tells us happily. His speech is slurred because when he landed, he bit off a chunk of his tongue. "Are my sunglasses the right brand? Who cares! Am I wearing the right jeans? Doesn't matter! I've got nothing to put in them!"

On the other side of Peyton, Lydia harrumphs. "Just because he's in a wheelchair doesn't mean he shouldn't care about how he looks," she whispers.

"Almost every part of my body is gone, damaged, or fake," Sergeant Franco says. "I have to clean my stumps to prevent infection, and I wear a colostomy bag to collect intestinal waste."

"Eww," Lydia says.

Judging by Headmaster Perkins's expression, he feels the same way. Likewise, Miss Potter. I get the sense that Sergeant Franco is not what they expected.

"I know some of you find that unpleasant," Sergeant Franco

says, "and that's okay. You see, that's the gift I've been given: I see our earthly existence for what it is. Our bodies are impermanent. Beauty is impermanent. Every single one of us will die."

"He's kind of being supernegative," Peyton whispers.

"I know," Lydia whispers back. "Like, since he's ugly, he wants to rub it in that everyone else is going to be ugly one day, too."

I lean over. "That is *not* what he's saying."

"Anyway, they're doing so much these days with laser surgery and chemical peels and stuff," Lydia goes on.

"My mom says there's no reason not to look good all the way into your sixties," Peyton replies.

Grrrrr. Ten minutes ago, Peyton was fun, but in the blink of Sergeant Franco's wounded eye, she's gone all Lydia on me.

I angle my body away from them and focus on Sergeant Franco. I feel like it matters, what he's saying. Like, two minutes ago I was moaning and groaning about my stupid problems, and now here Sergeant Franco is, reminding me that there are more important things to care about than crushes and jealousies and dye jobs.

"Does realizing that 'this, too, shall pass' mean life has no purpose?" Sergeant Franco asks. "No, exactly the opposite. It allows me to look past the surface, that's all."

My heart beats faster, because I want my life to have purpose. I really do. I want to look *past* the surface . . . and maybe if I had Sergeant Franco wheeling along beside me every minute of my life, I could.

"One way I connect with what's real is through music," he says.

Yes! I think. *Me, too!*

He rolls his wheelchair over to a grand piano that's been set up on stage. He plays a few bars of "Joyful, Joyful, We Adore Thee."

"Now, I've never had any formal training," he says. "People ask if I play by ear, and I tell them indeed I do." He reaches up to his ear, *pulls it off,* and bangs it on the keys.

There's a collective gasp, and Lydia puts her hand over her

mouth. I'm shocked, too—but then I laugh. Other people join in. I recognize Roger's distinctive chortle.

"Play by ear," Sergeant Franco repeats, grinning. He twists his head so we can see the nub of his own ear, a flesh-colored melted marshmallow. "The parachute cord ripped it off. But thanks to modern medicine"—he screws back on his prosthetic ear— "ta-da!"

"That is seriously sick," Lydia mutters.

Sergeant Franco closes his eyes. "Let us pray," he says. "Merciful God, thank You for music. May we forever be Your song."

CHAPTER THIRTY

RIPPLE IN STILL WATER

Our report cards arrive three days into break. When Dad sees Anna's, he erupts.

"Anna!" he bellows from downstairs, and Anna, who's been hiding out in my room, glances at me fearfully. We know without discussion what Dad's anger is about, because we saw the twin Holy Redeemer envelopes on the kitchen counter this afternoon.

"Just tell him how scary it was," I say, meaning the back dive off the high dive.

"He won't care," Anna says.

"Well, tell him you'll go to Coach Schranker and beg to do it over."

"But that would be a lie. No way am I going to Coach Schranker and begging for *anything*."

"Because you don't want to ask, or because you don't want to do the dive?"

"Both."

"You're going to have to do it eventually. If not now, then next year when you're forced to take PE again." As I say it, I'm struck once more by the insanity of basing an entire year's grade on one terrifying plunge off the high dive. I am *not* sending my kids to private school.

Anna gnaws on her thumbnail.

"*Anna!* Get down here!"

She scrambles to her feet. Her face is pale.

"Good luck," I say. "Be strong."

"I don't like being yelled at," she says in a trembly voice.

"The longer you wait, the worse it's going to be."

She breathes out a puff of air, gives a skittish nod, and goes to face the music—

which is loud

and angry

and cruel, in my opinion. Not Sergeant Franco's kind of music at all.

I hear Dad's rant from my room, even when I close the door. Even when I turn up the volume on my sound dock. I'm listening to "Ripple" by the Grateful Dead. It's so lovely and pure that I wish I could pipe it into Dad's heart.

He would hate it, though. How sad it must be to be him and not have the ears to hear its beauty. Not that I've played it for him . . . and I won't, because I won't let him take it away from me.

"But, Daddy," I hear Anna say, her voice traveling to my room through our house's ancient heating system.

More yelling. Dad's face is red, I know it. And Anna's, by now, is tearstained.

I concentrate on falling into the music, and I realize that instead of piping it into Dad's soul, I should pipe it into Anna's. So I sing along with Jerry Garcia and send the words as best I can to my sister, who is being made to feel smaller and smaller for something she's already been made to feel worthless for.

"If I knew the way," I sing, "I would take you home."

CHAPTER THIRTY-ONE
P.S.

My report card shows a column of A's, all with excellent posture.
They receive no mention.

CHAPTER THIRTY-TWO
IN THE BEGINNING

Christmas day is lovely, though Grandmother Lauderdale gives me and Anna socks. The lady is batty. She's a millionaire—Granddad Lauderdale, who died several years ago, was a real estate mogul—but because Dad isn't her "real" son, she treats him and his offspring as *less than*. The reason Dad isn't her real son is that Dad's mom (Granddad Lauderdale's first wife) died of cancer. She died when Dad was five, which makes me sad whenever I think about it.

Anyway, after marrying Granddad, Grandmother Lauderdale gave birth to two more sons. They are the chosen ones. Their kids get Wii's and stock in Coca-Cola.

Whatever.

It does give me some insight into Dad, however. Like, why he works so hard to be successful. It must have sucked to grow up with a stepmom whose love was definitely conditional.

I, on the other hand, give my loved ones a flock of ducks. Through the Heifer Project! It's so cool! I buy the ducks in honor of Mom, Dad, and Anna (meaning, their names get put on a special gift card), but the ducks won't really come live with us. They'll go to a family in China and do the following amazing things:

—add protein to their owners' diet by providing their owners with eggs;
—put money in their owners' pockets by laying bonus eggs that the owners can sell;
—make the owners' crops do better, because duck poo is a good fertilizer. Go, poo!

Oh, and I give Peyton a hen. I wanted to give her a water buffalo, but it cost too much. Still, I am quite pleased with myself and think, *So there, Little Miss Did-You-Sponsor-an-Ethiopian-Orphan?*

Peyton e-mails me after receiving the e-card which says a hen has been donated in her name. *Ha ha,* she writes. *But cool. I'll give ya that. Only next time throw in a diamond tennis bracelet, too, would ya? For me. Not the hen.* ☺ ☺ ☺

For the record, I *do* supplement Anna's ducky gift with a pair of supercute ducky earrings from Curiosities. I buy myself a pair, too, so we can be ducky twins, and so I'm not being Grandmother-esque with the whole lame-present thing. Ducks aren't lame, but, as with socks, Anna doesn't truly get to *enjoy* them. Jewelry, Anna can enjoy.

So, Christmas day is good. So is New Year's. Mom makes corn bread and black-eyed peas, the traditional Southern meal for a year filled with good luck.

And then it's time to go back to school.

I hope the peas and corn bread work.

For our first all-school assembly of the new semester, Headmaster Perkins has arranged for a fancy theology dude to lecture us about Intelligent Design. Our homeroom teacher informs us of this first thing in the morning, and she's quite excited. Because he's famous! And from Yale! And after Fancy Dude's lecture, we'll be put in breakout groups to further explore the ideas he presents!

I groan, because I hate breakout groups. Plus, I believe in evolution.

Roger catches me before I enter the auditorium, and his expression suggests that he's as unthrilled about Intelligent Design as I am.

"Hold up," he says, grabbing my arm. I look down. His hand is so big that his fingers wrap all the way around me. He follows my gaze and lets go abruptly. "I'm ditching. Want to join me?"

"You're ditching?"

"Not the whole day, just the assembly. I'm not in the mood for *because the Bible says so.*"

"Are you ever?" I say, equally demoralized. But to sneak away and not attend? I've never in my life cut class before. I'm such a goody-goody, even though I don't want to be.

"You've got to decide quick," Roger says. "Cole's waiting behind the building."

"Cole's coming? Cole's ditching?"

The way Roger looks at me makes me shrivel.

"He's not going to dump Trista for you," he says.

"I know," I say, my cheeks burning.

"But you wish he would. You like him."

"No, I don't. It's just . . ."

"Just what?"

I jut my chin, because Roger doesn't get to decide who I like and who I don't. "He has soulful eyes, that's all."

Roger assesses me. I exercise great self-control and don't fidget.

"Coming or staying?" he says.

I glance at the rapidly filling auditorium. I glance outside, where Cole waits, unseen.

"Coming," I say, and just like that, the flip inside me is switched. I follow Roger, thrilled to be breaking the rules.

I can tell by Cole's expression that he's surprised to see me. Surprised and impressed. And, why look: Trista isn't behind the building with him, because Trista isn't cutting.

I am not Trista.

I stand a little taller.

"Come on," Cole says, pushing off the wall. He leads us into the wooded area south of Butler Hall, and I admire his stride. It's self-assured and purposeful, yet not the strut of a Holy Roller striding to a Harvard interview with thrown-back shoulders and a power tie.

We pick our way over roots and under branches. In the distance, I catch occasional glimpses of the JV tennis courts. My T-shirt snags on a branch, and Roger, who's bringing up the rear, reaches around and frees me.

At last we reach a clearing.

"Here we are," Cole says. He grins at me and Roger, and I tingle with the awareness of being part of his group.

I'm one of the cool kids, I think. How bizarre.

We sit, and Cole reaches into the inner pocket of his leather jacket. I'm worried he's going to pull out a joint or something, but he withdraws his iPod. It's black, with a set of small headphones wrapped around it. He rests it on his thigh.

"So. Carly. Have you seen the light?" he asks.

I wrinkle my brow. "What do you mean? Because of cutting assembly?"

He laughs. "No. I mean have you looked around at our glorious world recently? Because anyone with eyes can see that it was designed by a magnificent Creator."

Ohhh. We're skipping assembly in order to make fun of assembly.

"Here's my question," I say, although in fact it's not my question. It's Ms. Anders's question, posed during first period biology. "The argument for Intelligent Design is that the world is so perfect, it must have been designed intentionally, right? By a designer. But if you go with that logic, who designed the designer?"

"Exactly," Cole says, shaking his head at all the dummies who think otherwise. But me, he approves of. I glow.

"Friday-morning assemblies are a waste," he goes on. "Jamming Christianity down my throat is going to do nothing but reinforce how ludicrous Christianity is." He leans back on his elbows. "Let's kill people in the name of Christ! Anyone up for a good stoning?"

I giggle.

Roger raises his eyebrows. "There's more to Christianity than that."

Cole hits his head. "Of course. There's the gay bashing and the Bible-thumping, what was I thinking? And the self-righteous smugness of knowing nonbelievers will be smited." He grins at me. "Smote? Smoted? What's the past tense of *smite?*"

Smitten, I think, but am smart enough not to say.

"How is saying that all Christians are fools different from Christians saying all non-Christians are fools?" Roger asks mildly.

Cole turns to him. The expression in his eyes is this close to incredulous. "You a believer, man?"

Roger grunts. He's looking at me, not Cole, and it makes me uncomfortable. I pick up a stick and trace lines in the dirt.

"You think Buddhism's a crock, too?" Roger says. "Islam? Rastafarianism?"

Cole laughs. He adopts a Jamaican accent and says, "*No way, mon. Rastas bad like yaz. Rastas smoke da ganja, mon.*"

I don't even know what that means. It sounds slightly sexy and slightly . . . well, stupid.

"If you grew up in Jamaica and went to a Rasatafarian school, would you think Rastafarianism was a crock?" Roger asks.

Cole squints, like maybe Roger's getting on his nerves. "Have I slighted your faith, buddy? 'Cause if so, I'm sorry." He pauses. "But do you *really* believe there's some big daddy in the sky doling out punishments and rewards?" He laughs again, but this time, there's an edge to it. "Shit, man. Do you believe in *angels*?"

Roger remains calm. "Not necessarily."

"Then what do you believe in?"

"That having a knee-jerk reaction against something is as bad as blindly accepting it. That people need to think for themselves."

"Oh, come on," I say, feeling the need to lighten the mood. There's something scary about where this is heading. "Where's the fun in that?"

"Most people don't *know* what they think," Cole challenges. It's cock-of-the-walk time all of a sudden, a face-off between Cole and Roger.

"Then they need to figure it out," Roger says.

My heart pounds. I admire Roger for not backing down, but I'm pissed at him for the very same thing. Because I feel like it has to do with me, somehow—the fact that he's pushing the issue.

"That's a nice idea in theory," Cole says. "But most people aren't capable of that—present company excluded, of course."

"Of course," Roger says drily.

Cole turns to me. His blue eyes pierce me with their intensity. "Carly, you're a smart girl. Do *you* believe in God?"

I balk, because *this* is the scary thing I didn't want. I didn't know it till now, but it is. Because not only do I *believe* in God; I *feel* Him. Or Her. Because God's, like, not a *man*. Not a woman, either. Just . . . God. But I'm so accustomed to scoffing at the blindly accepting Holy Rollers—just like Cole's doing—that it's terrifying to know this about myself. And to care. And to not want my own personal feeling of God-ness to be mocked by someone else I care about.

Namely, Cole.

So I don't answer, but look at my lap instead. My eyes fill with tears, because I feel as if I've betrayed myself by being too wimpy to claim my beliefs. As if I've betrayed God.

"People don't all have to believe the same thing," Roger says in his deep voice. He shifts slightly, so that his long leg grazes mine. He keeps it there, solid as a rock. "Think how boring it would be if they did."

"I don't have to think about it," Cole says. "Thanks to Holy Redeemer, I'm living it."

I need to say something in order to reclaim my dignity. And it can't come out shaky. I take a deep breath and say, "Hey now, buddy. We're not boring."

"Present company excluded, of course," Cole says for the second time today. "Enough philosophizing. Let's listen to some music."

He turns on his iPod and stretches out on the ground, and Roger and I follow suit. Since there are two earbuds and three of us, we form a three-pointed star, our heads touching and our legs pointing in different directions.

Roger gets his own earbud. Cole and I share.

Cole scrolls to the song he wants: Emerson, Lake & Palmer's "From the Beginning." I know this song, because Emerson, Lake & Palmer are a rock group from the sixties. I can't help but wonder if Cole picked this song for me.

The song starts off with a guitar solo that's slow and haunting, and then the lyrics kick in: "You see it's all clear, you were meant to be here . . . from the beginning."

BABY
DUCKS

CHAPTER THIRTY-THREE
JED CLAMPETT KICKS
WONDER WOMAN'S BUTT

These days, Vonzelle and I eat lunch together pretty much every day. If Peyton cares, she doesn't say so. She sits with Lydia, and they paint each other's nails. Anna has early lunch with the other freshmen; I don't know who she sits with. Alaska, probably.

Vonzelle and I chat about a wide spectrum of fascinating topics: Coke versus Pepsi, arm huggies, the proper technique for applying lip gloss. Also, Hello Kitty and Hello Kitty's lesser-known buddy, Tenorikuma, who appears to be a bear/raccoon hybrid and who enjoys a good marshmallow latte. Who doesn't?

Often, Roger joins us. He makes droll Dutch remarks and states that in his opinion, too much lip gloss makes a girl looks sticky.

"You got a problem with sticky?" I ask him on the day of lip-gloss conversation, wagging my half-eaten egg roll in a menacing fashion.

"Not on the right girl," he says, looking pointedly at my lips. His expression is of the you-have-something-in-your-teeth variety, so I use the back of my spoon to check my reflection.

"Ha ha," I say. I wipe the sweet-and-sour sauce off my mouth, then wad up my napkin and lob it at him.

Then we switch to a better topic: classic TV sitcoms. I coax Vonzelle and Roger into ranking theme songs, and I sing a snippet of *The Brady Bunch* theme to inspire them.

"More of your olden-days obsession?" Roger says.

"*Olden days?*" I say. "Roger. *The Brady Bunch* is hardly from the olden days."

"Which one was the middle sister?" Vonzelle asks. "Jan? She bugs me."

"No, no, no," I say. "Jan's misunderstood, that's all."

"Jan's a whiner," Vonzelle says.

"She's an acquired taste," I concede. "The theme song, however? Brilliant."

"Old music, old TV shows, more old music," Roger says.

"Not 'old' music," I correct him. "*Classic* music. Flower-power music."

"Is that an acquired taste, too?" Vonzelle asks. "'Cause I've yet to acquire it."

Roger chuckles.

I huff.

"My question is this," he says. I take a glug of milk, eyeing him from above the carton. "Why is yesterday better than today?"

The milk spurts out as I laugh. "Ooo, deep-ness. Why *is* yesterday better than today?"

"It's not."

"Tell that to the head honchos at *Nick at Nite* and *TV Land*."

"You romanticize the sixties," Roger states.

"No, I don't."

Roger clears his throat. "My point—"

"You have a point? Yay! A point!"

"—is that life is what you make it. Saying, 'Everything was so much better *then*' is running away from reality."

"But what if things *were* better then?"

"What if they were? You can't go back in time."

Huh, I think.

"You can have your 'acquired tastes,'" he says. "That's fine. That's what makes you Carly."

"Thanks," I say sarcastically.

"But you have to live in the present. You have to take the old and make it new—that's my point."

"Yeah, yeah, yeah," I say. "Back to theme songs. I think I'm going to have to go with *Wonder Woman*, because it's so patriotic." I belt out a sampling of the lyrics. "In her satin tights, fighting for her rights, and the ol' red, white, and blue-oo-ooo!"

"That lady who played Wonder Woman . . . what was her name?" Vonzelle asks.

"Lynda Carter," I supply.

"I used to think she had a really big butt," Vonzelle says. "But now that I'm older and wiser, I don't actually think she did."

"I *know*," I say excitedly, because I've thought the exact same thing. "It's not that she had a big butt. It's just how high up those star-spangled undies of hers came."

"Like granny panties," Vonzelle agrees.

"Which is worse: granny panties or thong?" I ask. I don't think Vonzelle wears thongs, but we've never actually discussed it.

"Granny panties," Vonzelle says with no hesitation.

Hmm. I don't want thongs winning, so I say, "Granny panties or peekaboo thong?"

She laughs. "Carly!"

Roger rubs his temple. "Peekaboo thong?" he repeats in his deep, Dutch-accented voice.

Vonzelle and I crack up.

"Just be glad you're a boy," Vonzelle tells him.

"Back to theme songs," he says. "Can we return to theme songs?"

"I thought that was living in the past," I say.

"I'd rather live in the past than discuss ladies' underwear."

Vonzelle props her chin in her hand and considers him. "You are a rare breed, Roger. Not many guys could say that and mean it."

"But you do, and that's why we love you," I say. "Now, give us your best."

He contemplates. "I don't know many ancient American sit-coms. But I'm going to have to go with . . . what's that one called? With the rich white guy who adopts two black kids?"

"*Diff'rent Strokes*," I say, "and no way." I'm familiar with the show—chubby-cheeked Arnold, big brother Willis, white sister whose name I don't remember—but I can't even call up the theme song, which says it all right there. "*Wonder Woman* kicks *Diff'rent Strokes*' butt any day."

"Y'all are both wrong," Vonzelle informs us.

I whip my head toward her. "Wha'choo talkin' 'bout, Vonzelle?"

Roger laughs. I grin, feeling clever.

"The best theme song ever . . ." Vonzelle says, letting her sentence hang in the air.

"Ye-e-e-s?"

She starts singing the theme song to *The Beverly Hillbillies*, and I groan in defeat. *The Beverly Hillbillies* theme song is toe-tapping, banjo-strumming great.

". . . then one day he was shootin' at some food," Vonzelle croons, "and up from the ground came a-bubblin' crude."

I have no choice but to join in. "Oil that is," I say in a slick TV-host voice. "Black gold, Texas tea."

Roger raises his eyebrows.

Vonzelle moves on to verse two. As she nears the end, I think quick, scrambling for the last spoken bits. Do I know them?

"So they loaded up their truck and moved to Beverly," Vonzelle sings, giving me the nod.

"Hills, that is," I say. "Swimmin' pools, movie stars."

Together we bring it home: "The Beverly Hillbillies!"

Roger claps, and so do a few other kids. One guy boos, but we don't care about him.

"That is one rocking theme song," I say, flushed and happy.

"Apparently," Roger says. "And yet I must ask: Who are these Beverly Hillbillies of whom you speak?"

He says it all old-fashioned-ly and Dutch-accented-y, and I giggle.

"Just the coolest hillbillies ever." I pause. "Do you know what a hillbilly is?"

He shakes his head.

"A hillbilly is someone who . . . lives in the hills," I say. "Like, with overalls and rifles and potbellied stoves."

"And smushed brown felt hats," Vonzelle says. "That's what Jed Clampett wore."

"Good ol' Jed Clampett," I say fondly. To Roger, I say, "Jed was the hillbilly dad on the show. He was all grizzled."

"But with kind eyes," Vonzelle says.

"And one day he fired his rifle into a swamp and discovered oil," I say. "Voilà! Instant millionaire!"

"Ah," Roger says.

"*So* he moves to Beverly Hills along with Granny—who does indeed wear granny panties—and Jethro and Elly Mae."

"Jethro's all brawny and dumb, and Elly Mae is a buxom farm girl in short shorts," Vonzelle says.

"And the show is made of awesomeness, and so is the theme song." I'm struck with a brilliant idea. "Ooo, ooo, we should make a video!"

Vonzelle laughs.

"Seriously!" I say, bouncing. I turn to Roger. "You'd be our film guy, wouldn't you? We could post it on YouTube!"

Vonzelle chokes on her ham. "Carly, we are not posting the two of us singing the theme song to *The Beverly Hillbillies* on YouTube."

I widen my eyes as if she's confused. "No, we are. It'll be our one-hit wonder."

"You're crazy."

"Four o'clock? *Chez moi?*" I glance from Vonzelle to Roger, nodding encouragingly.

"I'm free," Roger says.

"Fine," Vonzelle says at last. "But we are *not* posting it on YouTube."

CHAPTER THIRTY-FOUR
WHAT A WAY TO GO

At home after school, I scurry around like mad before Vonzelle and Roger arrive. There are several excellent props I want to gather. Plus, I've got to find the video camera.

"What are you doing?" Anna asks.

"Nothing," I say as I rummage through the downstairs coat closet.

"Yes, you are," she says. "What are you looking for?"

"*Nothing,*" I say. "I'm looking for the camcorder. Do you know where it is?"

"Why do you want the camcorder?"

"I just do. Vonzelle and Roger are coming over, and we need it."

She trails me to the living room. "For what?"

"We just *do.*" I squat and start going through the bottom drawer of the armoire where the Christmas ornaments are stored.

"Are you making a video?"

"Anna, I don't have time for this. They're going to be here in twenty minutes." I spot the camera beneath a box of red glass bulbs. *Aha!*

"Well, can I be in it?" Anna asks. I almost knock her over when I stand up. She stumbles back.

"No," I say. "I love you, but go away."

"'I love you, but go away'?"

"Yes. Go. A. *Way.*"

Her eyes darken, and I feel bad. She and I haven't spent a lot of time together since the day at Urban Outfitters. In fact, for the last couple of weeks she's seemed kind of . . . *off.* Like, moody. Like, a return to the *Hills* watching scowler of yore.

I overheard her talking to South Dakota last night, and it sounded like they were fighting. I meant to ask Anna about it, but I forgot.

But it's not my job to *always* take care of her, is it? I'm allowed to have fun with my friends without her. I'm allowed to be just *Carly,* and not *Carly, sister of (superhot) Anna.* Especially when video making is involved. Especially when images are to be captured on film.

"Tonight let's watch TV together," I say. "Okay?"

Anna regards me sullenly. "Are you trying to buy me off?"

"Or not," I say, because if she's going to have an attitude, forget it. Sisterly love is a two-way street.

"Fine," she says, and turns on her heel.

Behind her back, I pretend to strangle her. Then I return to the task at hand. I check off items on a mental list:

—Camcorder. Check.

—Batteries. Check.

—Anna's toddler-sized red plastic car from when she was three, the one she could putter around in by using her feet. Check.

—Computer printout of my revised theme-song lyrics with hilarious references to Buckhead and power ties. *Heh heh heh,* I think. *This is going to make history, baby.* Check, check, check.

Only one item left to acquire, so I trot upstairs to find Mom. Anna's in her room listening to music, but her door is open, and she peeks out when she hears my footsteps. She's like a puppy at the pound, wanting me to suddenly change my mind and say, *Oh, why not. You can sleep at the foot of my bed* and *be in my movie!*

I stride past her down the hall. "Hey, Mom," I call. "Can I borrow your leather hat from Australia?"

Mom bought a gorgeous leather hat when she and Dad went down under for a "luxury safari" through the Australian outback. It looks like a high-end version of Jed Clampett's crumpled felt hat, and supposedly Nicole Kidman has one just like it.

Mom doesn't respond. She's not in the bedroom, so I try her extra-spacious bathroom, where I spot her sitting on the upholstered stool in front of her vanity.

"Hey, Mom?"

She turns toward me from her mirror, and I gasp. There is a miniature plunger stuck to her eyeball.

"*Mom!* What the . . . ?!"

Mom starts laughing, and it makes me doubt her sanity, because *there is a miniature plunger sticking out of her eye.*

"Carly, thank goodness," she says.

"What *is* that?"

"It's what I use to take out my contacts. I'm so glad you're here so you can pull it out for me."

"Exsqueeze me?"

She can't stop laughing.

"Quit laughing!" I tell her.

"I forgot I'd already taken *out* my contacts. That's the problem."

"So it's stuck to your actual *eye?*" I might vomit, especially if I don't quit thinking about the swimmy texture of the human eye. *Stop thinking about the swimmy texture of the human eye. Stop it right now.*

"I'm afraid to pull too hard on it. I don't want my eyeball popping out."

"So you want *me* to do it?"

"If you can just wiggle it enough to break the suction . . ."

"*Ew. Mom!*"

"Carly, please."

I make a growly sound. Then glare at her. I step closer and gingerly grasp the tiny plunger's handle between my thumb and forefinger. When I pull, there's resistance, and Mom's head comes toward me. My toes curl. I release the handle.

"You didn't get it," Mom informs me.

"Yes, Mom, thanks," I say, as the fact that she still has a stick jutting from her eye hasn't escaped me. "Why did you buy that thing?"

"To make taking my contacts out easier."

"Uh-huh. And how's that working for you?"

She laughs, and I marvel at how differently we see the world. She sees it as an unending parade of fancy dinners and manicures and daylong shopping excursions spent in the part of Neiman's dedicated to "The Woman Who Has Everything." Her contact-lens remover would be found in this department, as would her gold-plated Miss Army Knife with its perfume-bottle attachment and pullout pillbox.

At least she finds it amusing, the whole foreign-object-embedded-in-cornea thing.

"How long has it been stuck?" I ask her. "Why didn't you call Anna to come help you?" Anna's music is audible from here, so Mom surely knows Anna's upstairs.

"Oh, I don't know," Mom says. "You're more suited for this sort of thing. Anna would be . . . squeamish."

"*I* am squeamish, Mom. I am right here in front of you being squeamish."

"Well, perhaps. But you can push past it."

"And Anna can't?" I'm indignant and pleased, both. I *am* the stronger sister. Even Mom knows it.

She turns serious—or at least, as serious as one can be with a miniature plunger protruding from one's eye. "You know, I'm a little worried about Anna, Carly. Does she seem . . . depressed to you?"

I groan. I'm glad I'm the stronger sister, but just because I am doesn't mean I want to have a let's-talk-about-poor-sad-Anna chat. Not right now. "I don't think she needs to be on antidepressants, if that's what you mean." I fidget. "I've kind of got to go, Mom. I've got people coming over."

Mom holds open her plungified eye with her thumb and fore-finger. "All right, try again. I'll keep my hand here just in case."

"In case what? Your *eyeball* pops out?"

"Go ahead and pull."

With *extreme* squeamishness, I grab the handle again. I tug, and there is a *splop*, wet and awful. I lean on the bathroom counter and hand the miniature plunger to Mom. I don't look at it. I hope never to look at it again.

"*Much* better," Mom says. "Thank you, Carly."

I'm light-headed. I need to regroup before Vonzelle and Roger arrive.

"Sweetie, did you need something?" Mom calls as I veer un-steadily out of her bathroom.

"No, I'm good."

"You sure?"

"I'm positive." That Australian leather hat? Mine. I earned it.

CHAPTER THIRTY-FIVE

THE BALLAD OF TED CLAMPETT

"I don't understand," Vonzelle says. "Why am I getting into a toy car?"

She's not, actually, which is why I push on her shoulders to make her scrunch down. "'Cause you're Granny," I say, urging her into the passenger seat of the red plastic Cozy Coupe. "Good girl. There you go."

"I don't want to be Granny," she complains. "I want to be Elly Mae."

"But Granny's funnier."

"But Elly Mae's hotter." She reflects. "You know who should actually be Elly Mae?"

"*No*," I say.

"Anna. Anna would make a perfect Elly Mae."

Maybe so, but I don't *want* Anna to be Elly Mae. I don't want her looking all sexy-farm-girl on top of the Cozy Coupe, especially with Roger manning the video camera. A prickle in my chest tells me I'm being—selfish, but aren't I allowed to be selfish sometimes?

I love you, but go away.

Pushing past my guilt, I say, "Fine, Vonzelle, you can be Elly Mae. But that means you have to sit on top of the car, like Elly Mae sits on top of Jed's rattletrap truck."

"Oh, sure, now you tell me," Vonzelle says from her cramped position within the Cozy Coupe. She swings her feet out of the plastic car and plants them on the floor, but she's unable to free her hips from the narrow door. When she attempts to rise, the Cozy Coupe rises with her, attached to her bottom like a big, red turtle shell.

"You seem to be stuck there, toots," I say.

"Would you help me, please?"

"Sure, sure, of course." I hold out my hand so she can grab it. "Why'd you get in there anyway? That was kind of silly, don't you think?"

She tries to shove me, but the plastic car attached to her butt throws her off balance. And even with me pulling on her, she stays stuck.

"Get me out of here!" she cries.

Roger puts down the camera, walks behind her, and grabs the Cozy Coupe. One good yank, and she's free.

"*Thank* you," she says to him as she rubs her butt.

"No problem," I say. "However, you've wasted precious time, so let's away to the powder room, shall we? I've rethought my vision. That's where our art film should begin."

"Art film?" Roger says.

"Grab the iPod and the camera."

I lead them to the downstairs bathroom, where I position myself squarely in front of the gleaming toilet. I cock my Australian hat, hitch both thumbs through my belt loops, and nod at Roger. "'The Buckhead Hillbillies,' take one. Vonzelle, you're just backup in this first scene. Your moment of glory comes in verse two."

She scans the page. "Oh, *Carly*, nuh-uh." She giggles. "You've *got* to change the name."

"Sorry, can't." I nod at Roger. "Three, two, one . . ."

"Action," Roger says. He lifts the video camera, then reaches over to my iPod and hits the play button. The instrumental version of "The Ballad of Jed Clampett" song blares through my mini-speaker, and I squat up and down to the beat, knees splayed.

"Come and listen to a story 'bout a man named Ted. Not a lick of money, barely kept his family fed." I hunker down on the toilet, though of course I keep my pants on. "Then one day he was sitting on the ca-a-a-a-n! And out of his butt came a bubbling plan."

Vonzelle's having a hard time keeping it together. "Law school, that is. Clever lies, power ties."

I rise and link arms with Vonzelle. Roger keeps the camera trained on us as we skip back to the den, singing the second verse. I catch a glimpse of Anna at the top of the staircase, watching from behind the wrought-iron railing, but I'm in character and the show must go on.

"Well, the next thing you know, ol' Ted's a millionaire. Got himself a Realtor and moved away from there. Decided Atlanta, Georgy, was the place he ought to be-e-e-e-e! So he loaded up his truck and moved to West Wesley."

"Buckhead, that is," Vonzelle says. "Country clubs, folks to snub."

I nod to indicate that it's rattletrap-truck time, and she hops on top of the Cozy Coupe and strikes a sex-kitten pose.

"The Buckhead Hillbillies!" we cry. I fling my arms out wide and accidentally whack Vonzelle, who topples off the Cozy Coupe and lands with a thunk.

"*Ow!*" she says, laughing.

"Cut!" I yell.

Roger lowers the camera. "*Sakkerloot.*"

"That was *so* fun," I say, flushed and riding high. I glance at the door to the den, half expecting to see Anna. I tell myself that if I do, I'll invite her in.

Roger chuckles, and my eyes go to him. The way he's looking at me makes me both nervous and pleased. Nervous, because what I see in his eyes is pretty darn appreciative. Pleased for the very same reason.

I go over to him and say, "Let's see what you got, bucko. Get over here, V."

Vonzelle picks herself up from the floor and joins us. We watch our video, and I couldn't be more delighted. The toilet, the rattletrap truck, Vonzelle falling off the rattletrap truck . . .

We are *artistes*. It is a masterpiece.

"Just promise you won't show it to your dad," Vonzelle says. "*Ever*."

"Duh," I say.

"And you *can't* post it on YouTube."

I grin, first at her and then at Roger. I feel the thrill of triumph as I say, "And just in case you missed it? *That* is called taking something old and making it new."

CHAPTER THIRTY-SIX
Y'ALL COME BACK NOW, Y'HEAR?

After Vonzelle and Roger leave, I make some improvements to our video. I just want to spice it up a bit, make it even funnier. I'm buzzing with the thrill of creating something, and also with the thrill of entertaining my buds. It's addictive, getting attention. Addictive and exhilarating.

I grab my camera—not the video camera, just my plain old digital one—and go around the house taking pictures of all the pretentious crap Dad has accumulated over the years. His Rémy Martin brandy. The Steinway baby grand piano, which no one in the family knows how to play. The Waterford chandelier, which I, on occasion, have been made to clean—crystal by crystal.

I also snap shots of Dad's Italian suits and ties and an awesome close-up of his handcrafted French wingtips, shoes which took seven months to make and involved some French shoemaker making a cast of Dad's feet so the shoes would fit exactly right. That same shoemaker sewed the seams of the shoes with a pig's bristle instead of a needle. Dad bragged about it when the shoes arrived, and he passed them around so that Mom, Anna, and I could appreciate them. I clapped, as I recall.

After I've collected an impressive collection of yes-my-father-really-is-this-pretentious photos, I upload them onto my MacBook Air. Then comes the chortle-making part: making a video montage. First I download a picture of Jed Clampett, the grizzled mountain man who finds the bubbling crude. The image I choose shows Jed wearing a tattered jacket and his ever-present, beat-up brown felt hat. He's gripping a double-barreled shotgun.

I photoshop out Jed's face, but leave the mountain-man hat. Then I select a picture of Dad from one of my iPhoto albums, trim the image, and stick Dad's head on top of Jed's scruffy body.

Oh, man, I think, because my Ted Clampett is PERFECT. The pasted-in head is from a photo Mom took at the Peachtree Club one day last summer, when she and Dad were watching Anna and me play tennis. One of us must have gotten smacked by the tennis ball—probably me—because Dad's face is split by a grin. He's pre-wheeze, but just barely.

Dad's grin, coupled with Jed's hat, coat, and double-barreled shotgun? I hate to boast, but it's pure genius.

Next I find a pirated *Beverly Hillbillies* episode on YouTube and download a sample of Jed Clampett's thick country accent. Then I go to VoiceDub.com, plug the snippet in, and voilà! I can type in any phrase I want, and *Ted Clampett* will say it in *Jed Clampett's* backwoods drawl.

After due consideration, I go with the following gems:

Git yer mitts off my handcrafted wingtips!

Just 'cause I cain't play the piano don't mean I ain't got no ed-ja-ma-ca-tion.

And the clincher:

Y'all come back now, y'hear?

Now it's time to roll up my sleeves and put it all together. Thank you, Mr. Abernathy, for teaching me about computers, even though you did accuse my sister of being a pervert. And thank you, Mom and Dad, for my state-of-the-art laptop, which will enable me to share my exposé of wealth and pretension with the masses.

The final product is a seamless blend of Roger's original footage, shots of Dad's fancy shoes and fancier piano, and animated clips of my gun-toting Ted Clampett sharing down-home wisdom. And, fine, it's not really seamless—I have a hard time getting Dad's jaw to open and shut so it looks like he's really talking—but it's pretty frickin' great.

I name my masterpiece "The Ballad of Ted Clampett," and I post it to YouTube, even though I know Vonzelle will freak. It would be criminal not to share such brilliance with the world.

And anyway: Dad's never going to see it unless (a) he has a closet fascination with old sitcom theme remixes; (b) knows how to troll for such remixes on YouTube; and (c) knows what YouTube is. I would bet my last silver dollar that he meets none of those criteria.

And even if he DOES see it . . . it's a farce! A satire! It's *art as social commentary*, and you can't argue with art.

I hit the upload button and forward Vonzelle and Roger the link. I want to call them and tell them to check their darn e-mail, but I don't. Far more fun for them to find it themselves.

CHAPTER THIRTY-SEVEN

LOVE THE SINNER, HATE THE SIN

Monday at school, I'm a grouchy black rain cloud. Why? Because despite all logic and probability, Dad *did* see the Ted Clampett video. He wouldn't have, and he *shouldn't* have, except for the tiny little detail of Anna "accidentally" showing him.

"Anna claims she didn't mean to get me in trouble, but she knew exactly what she was doing," I tell Vonzelle before first period. We're leaning against a row of lockers. "She was like, 'Oh, Dad, you've got to see this, you're going to think it's hysterical.'"

"But she had to know he wouldn't," Vonzelle says.

I hold my hands palms up, like *duh.*

"Then why did she do it?"

"Because I was supposed to watch TV with her, and I forgot. Isn't that such a crime? Wasn't she totally right to screw with me just because I didn't watch *The Hills* with her?"

"So did your dad totally flip?"

I twist around so that my shoulder blades press against the locker. "I don't know. Sort of. He said it was offensive."

What Dad actually said was, "How could you be so *stupid?* Is it your *goal* to offend every single person in Buckhead?!" And so on. Red splotches mottled his cheeks, and his jaw kept twitching as if he couldn't control his face muscles. It pretty much scared the daylights out of me.

"I can kind of see his point," Vonzelle says tentatively.

"No you can't," I say. "And you know why? Because *you* have a sense of humor. If I put your face on Jed Clampett's body, would you be all, 'What if my clients see? Did you think of *that,* you idiot?'"

"Is that what he's worried about? His clients?"

"Isn't that the most ridiculous thing you've ever heard? Like his clients are really going to comb the Internet for *Beverly Hillbillies* re-mixes." I pause, because I made the same wrong assumption about Dad. "I take that back. Maybe Anna'll send a bulletin to his entire law firm, and everyone will make fun of Dad for being so material-istic, boo hoo hoo. And I'll be the one who gets the blame, because of course innocent little Anna had nothing to do with it."

Vonzelle bites her lip, and her expression makes me itch. It's not a full-out wow-you're-kind-of-being-a-witch expression, but it does make me worry that she's feeling bad for Dad—or, just as un-acceptable, for Anna. I only want her feeling bad for me.

"Anna tried to apologize this morning," I say, to show I can be fair. "But I was like, 'Whatever.' And then Dad came downstairs and laid into me *again.* He only quit when Tracy showed up, and only then because he didn't want to air out our dirty laundry, I guess."

"Who's Tracy?"

Oops. I didn't mean to mention Tracy. "She's the cleaning lady, kind of. She's white."

Vonzelle looks at me funny. But Tracy *is* white.

Down the hall, a girl bursts into tears. Vonzelle and I turn to-ward the sound.

"Oh my God, it's Trista," I say. Trista's crying, and Lydia is patting her shoulders and saying stuff. I can't make out all the words, but the ones I do catch send thoughts of Dad and Anna right out of my mind.

Cole, I hear Trista say. And *last night*, and *broken.*

I look at Vonzelle, a new emotion taking up space in my chest. "Broken? As in broken up?"

"Nuh-uh, no," Vonzelle says, because she doesn't like Cole the way I do. She doesn't think *I* should like Cole the way I do. "Don't go there, Carly. Finish telling me about your dad."

"There's nothing more to tell. He's a jerk. Story over."

"But did you take it down? The video?"

"No way, he's not the boss of me." My gaze travels back to Trista. I have to find out what happened.

"So what's he going to do?" Vonzelle says. "Is he going to ground you?"

"Dad doesn't ground us," I say distractedly. "He fines us."

"He *fines* you?" When I don't respond, she pokes me. "Hey. Hey!"

Lydia hugs Trista and says something comforting like, "I'm here for you, I'm on your side." At this particular moment, however, she's *leaving* Trista's side.

"We'll talk at lunch," I say to Vonzelle. "Hopefully, I'll have Trista-and-Cole details to share."

"Carly!" she complains.

"*Gotta-go-bye*," I say, running it together like one big word. And then I'm off, dashing down the hall to catch up with Lydia.

The rumors: Cole cheated on Trista, Cole broke up with Trista, Trista broke up with Cole. If Cole *did* cheat on Trista, no one knows with whom, although there's speculation that it was with a girl from another school. No one thinks Trista cheated on Cole.

"If he *did* step out on her, she should dump him," Lydia says, standing by Vonzelle's and my table at lunch.

"I agree," I say.

"And if he stepped out on her and *lied* about it, that's two sins," she goes on.

"She should dump him twice."

"I'm going to the chapel to pray for her. You two want to come?"

"That's all right," I say.

"I'll say a prayer for Cole, too," Lydia says. "Love the sinner, hate the sin."

I nod, and she strides off.

"I do love the sinner," I confess to Vonzelle.

"I know you do, and *you* know you shouldn't," Vonzelle says. Today is spaghetti day, and she twirls a noodle around her fork. "I bet Cole did cheat on Trista. Is that the kind of boy you want?"

"Well . . . I agree that cheating is bad."

She snorts.

"But if he's, like, tempted to cheat on her—which is bad! bad, bad, bad!—then doesn't that mean she isn't right for him?"

"No. It means *he's* no good."

"But he *is* good. He's smart and gorgeous and . . . and . . ."

"A complete player who can bend any girl to his will with a single smoldering look?"

"Not what I was going to say, though he does smolder. You're right. What *I* was going to say is that he gets it, you know?"

She rips off a bite of garlic bread. "What does he 'get,' Carly?"

"I don't know. Stuff."

I think of the way he looks at me sometimes, with his smoldering eyes that see right through me. *He gets it that I'm special.*

"He thinks for himself," I say defensively.

"So?" Vonzelle says. "Other guys think for themselves. He's just the only one who happens to be so amazingly hot—"

"See! You admitted it!"

"—that even girls who should know better get sucked in." She leans back from the table. "*Every* girl gets sucked in."

"Except you," I say, to call her out on her superiority complex.

She's unfazed. "Even Lydia goes noodle-y around him. Yes, she's on Trista's side, but I've seen her buy Cole those Monster drinks at the student center."

"That's embarrassing."

"Even Jackie Owens acts like he's God's gift to Holy Redeemer," Vonzelle says.

I believe her for a nanosecond, and I'm alarmed, because Jackie has announced frequently and without provocation that there will be no boys for her until spring semester of senior year, when she will assumedly have her admission letter to Harvard tucked safely in her bra. If it's true that *Jackie* is susceptible to Cole's charms . . .

Then I realize that Vonzelle is yanking my chain.

"Ha ha. Jackie doesn't care about Cole. All she cares about is her big math brain."

"She does his algebra homework for him, did you know that?"

Oh God. No, I did not.

"She needs to stop that," I say, primarily to myself.

Vonzelle cocks her head. The message in her brown eyes is not a pleasant one.

"Well, those girls don't count, because unlike Jackie and Lydia, I don't have to bribe Cole to like me," I say. I regard her imploringly. "Don't you get it? Cole's my ironic love boodle."

"No, he's not."

"He *could* be."

"Carly . . ." She sighs. "I can see his appeal. I'm not blind. But I can also see that he's just . . . He's not there yet. He's not *real.*"

That's silly. Cole's the most real person I know.

"Who *is* real, if he's not?" I demand. Then, because I know whose name she's going to throw out, I quickly say, "Never mind."

She shakes her head like she's sick and tired of this conversation. Well, I am, too. Vonzelle doesn't know Cole the way I do. She doesn't get that I could be the one to *make* him real.

"Wake up, Carly," she says. "Wouldn't it be amazing if for once the right girl ended up with the right guy?"

"*Yes*," I say.

We stare at each other. Neither of us gives in.

CHAPTER THIRTY-EIGHT
REAL GIRLS WEAR SNEAKERS

Cole and Trista don't break up.

"Told you," Vonzelle says after several days of me saying, "Wait, just give it time." While she wouldn't be Vonzelle if she *didn't* say that, it's not what I want to hear.

I almost want to talk to Peyton about it, because Peyton would be mean to Trista with me. She'd definitely understand my Cole lust. Except for me, it's more than lust, which is why I don't track Peyton down. I don't want to cheapen my feelings. I know in my gut that I'm perfect for Cole. I'd appreciate him far more than Trista *or* Cheater Girl X . . . if Cheater Girl X even exists.

Bad Attitude Cindy thinks Cheater Girl X exists. I overhear her talking to Lydia about it at Lydia's locker. She calls Cheater Girl X a ho, and I briefly think, *But . . . Cole's the one with the girlfriend. He's the one who's cheating.*

I also think, horribly, *I'd cheat with him.* I seriously can't imagine how anyone wouldn't, and while it's not Cole's fault that he's brilliant and talented and gorgeous and intense, I do realize that he milks it sometimes.

Despite Vonzelle's opinion, I am capable of seeing Cole's flaws. I just see *past* them, that's all.

After lunch on Thursday, I spot Cole and Roger out on the lawn. Just the two of them, no Trista. Cole's playing his guitar.

Vonzelle notices and huffs. She says, "Go on. Go get it out of your system—and then take a look at the boy sitting next to him and say, 'Oh. Roger. *There* you are.'"

"If you like Roger so much, *you* go say, 'Oh, there you are,'" I tell her.

"Can't, he's into someone else." She narrows her eyes meaningfully. "Now go."

I start toward them, then hesitate at the edge of the quad. Roger sees me and says, "Hey, Carly!"

He beckons, and I feel important being called over by Roger and, by proxy, Cole. I'm aware of people noticing.

"Hey," I say, dropping down next to them. Well, next to Roger, because I don't want to overstep. I don't know where Cole's at with the whole Trista thing—like, if he's brooding or whatever—and I'm not about to ask. I don't want to be *that girl*, the one who cares about relationship drama like every other girl on the planet.

Cole acknowledges me with a nod. He keeps playing his guitar, and when he gets to the end of one song, he starts another. It's "Trouble," by Cat Stevens. Cole gazes off into the distance as he strums the opening chords. He *is* brooding. I can see it in the tension of his jaw. I want to reach across the universe and let him know it's okay, he's not alone.

He starts to sing, and my heart wells with something so raw and aching that I can't put a name to it. It's such a sad song. Sad and beautiful, both. A lump rises in my throat.

He turns and looks at me, still playing. He gazes straight into my eyes. "You're eating my heart away," he sings, "and there's nothing much left of me."

The connection between the two of us pulses in the air. Part of me feels self-conscious in front of Roger, but I do not look away and I will not look away. I will hold Cole's gaze as long as he wants me to. I will hold his gaze forever.

"Heads up, bro," Roger says, and Cole stops playing. His eyes move from me to the girl taking mincing steps through the grass to get to us. It's Trista. She's wearing a black knit dress, black tights, and chunky black heels. On her, even black looks adorable.

She's not happy, though. She has circles under her eyes, and her fine features seem unusually fragile. Her highlighted hair gleams in the sun, but she's wrecked. I can't lie to myself and say she isn't.

I feel Roger's gaze on me, and I know how foolish and stupid I must seem, watching Cole and Trista so intently. But I can't help it. I have to know.

"Hey, baby," Cole says. Maybe he's trying to act self-assured, but I can hear his uncertainty.

"Can we talk?" Trista says.

"Yeah, let's talk." He slides his guitar in its case, clips the locks, and stands.

They go off together. Trista stumbles in her chunky heels, and Cole catches her arm.

I shift my gaze to my beat-up black Rocket Dogs without the laces.

"Yours are cooler," Roger says.

"Huh?"

"Your shoes."

"My shoes," I repeat dumbly. My vision blurs.

"Yeah. Much."

The eyelets on my sneakers swim in the sun.

CHAPTER THIRTY-NINE

NOTHING IS MORE TACKY THAN BEING TACKY

I spend the weekend wondering how Cole could look at me the way he did, and then get up and call Trista "baby" and walk away with her without a backward glance. I don't get it. I. Just. Don't. Get. It.

Anna hovers about shooting plaintive looks, but I ignore her. What does she have to be plaintive about? Is her plaintiveness supposed to be on *my* behalf, like she feels bad for me that I'm not Cole-worthy? Given that she *is* Cole-worthy—maybe not Anna herself, but girls like her—her sympathy means little.

"Do you want to watch *Gilmore Girls?*" she asks, slipping into my room while I'm lying lumpishly on my bed. "They're having a marathon."

"No."

"Do you want me to, um, give you a manicure?"

Oh, sure, like having pretty pink nails is going to make Cole realize what a mistake he's made. "Thanks for the offer, but no."

She sighs. She's all sad-eyed and beseeching and *I'm trying here, can't you see?* "Well . . . do you want to go to the mall?"

"No, I don't want to go to the mall. Thank you, but *no*." I gaze at the ceiling. "Ask Hawaii, why don't you? You two can try on clothes and be beautiful together."

"What's that supposed to mean?"

"Nothing," I groan. I'm persecuted by her mere presence.

"Fine," she says in a small voice. She lingers in my doorway (is she waiting for me to dismiss her?), then finally turns and leaves. She doesn't call California, though. She goes to her room and closes her door, and I feel a twinge of shame. It's not fair to be mad at Anna for being gorgeous. But it's also not fair that she *is* gorgeous, and that she lives in the same house with me and reminds me every single minute that I'm not.

If Trista got a horrible swelling-up disease, now that would be fair. And a flaky scalp—a *really* flaky scalp. *Our Lady of Perpetual Dandruff*, people would call her.

With the whole stupidness of appearance taken out of the equation, Cole would see things differently. He would look past his frickin' hormones and see *me*.

On Monday, Cole gives Trista his leather jacket to wear, because she's cold. She stays cold all day, even in the cafeteria and the halls, and his beat-up leather jacket looks so wrong and horrible paired with her Ann Taylor skirt and sweet white blouse that I want to puke.

That afternoon, I sit in the sunporch and drown my sorrows in a Cherry Coke. Only my sorrows refuse to drown. After a while Anna wanders into the room, and I think, *Again?* Can't she see that another pretty face is not what I need?

Obviously not, because she takes a seat in the lime-green armchair that's a twin to the lime-green armchair I'm in. Between the chairs is a lamp that's turned on by pulling a gold ball on the end of a gold chain. When Anna was little, she loved pulling that ball. She thinks I don't remember stuff like that since I'm only one year older, but I do.

"What's up?" she says.

I turn my head and look at her.

"I'm sorry Cole and Trista are still together," she says. She hesitates. "Although I think Roger's better for you, anyway."

I can't believe her. "Did I *ask* if you thought Roger was better for me? I don't think I did."

She pushes out her next words in a rapid stream. "And I'm sorry I told Dad about your YouTube video."

Uh-huh, I think. *And here we have it: the real reason for all your unasked-for attention.* She couldn't care less about my pain; she just wants forgiveness for being a crap sister.

"Didn't see you handing over your allowance on Saturday," I say. "Or offering to split it with me, since Dad kept mine because of you."

"How is it because of me? You're the one who *made* the video. Not me."

"But you're the one who thought it would be fun to rat me out. You wanted me to get yelled at, and I did. So be happy. You won."

Her voice goes little-girlie. "You said you would watch TV with me. And make popcorn."

"So because I forgot, you punished me? That's pathetic."

She swallows. "You forget about me a lot."

"Oh, please."

"You do," she whispers. "Ever since you started hanging out with Vonzelle."

I bang down my Coke. "What, you don't like Vonzelle? What's wrong with Vonzelle? I *love* Vonzelle!"

Anna presses the back of her scalp against the upholstered chair. "There's nothing *wrong* with her," she says as if it's *so* much work to get the words out. "She's fine."

"She's '*fine*'?"

She swivels her head. "Peyton's noticed it, too. She's like, 'Carly's too good for us now. Carly just wants to hang out with her *new* friend.'"

"That's absurd," I say. My heart pounds. "Peyton hangs out with other people. She and Lydia are, like, best buds these days. And you've got your own friends."

"We used to hang out together, though," Anna says. "You and me and Peyton. But now it's like . . ."

"Like what?"

Anna's expression is defensive, as if she knows I'm not going to like what she's about to say. "Vonzelle was never our friend before. Was never *your* friend before. But all of a sudden you've dumped us for her just because she's *different*." She says it bitterly. "And as everyone knows, being different is all you care about."

I'm sweaty all of a sudden. I feel my pulse way down low in my stomach.

"I can't believe you," I say. "Oh my God, Anna, you're a racist. *You*."

Anna's flustered. "What?"

"You think I'm friends with Vonzelle because she's *black*? You think she's . . . my new funky shirt or something?" My skin and cells and blood vessels are freaking out. I'm, like, shaking.

Is *Vonzelle my new funky shirt?*

Anna gapes at me. "I can't believe you would think that."

"I can't believe *you* would think that."

"I don't." She keeps staring at me. "*God*, Carly."

We fall into a standoff. I blink first, but force myself to keep looking at her, and say, "Then what do you mean, 'different'? How is she different?"

"She's different because . . ."

I lift my eyebrows.

"Because she makes silly videos," Anna says. "Because everything either one of you says is so funny, and you get each other's jokes, and you, like, play off each other. And she's not a Barbie doll, and she doesn't care what people think."

I blink some more. My breaths come quick.

"She's different from *me*, Carly," Anna says. "*That's* what I meant."

My cheeks burn. There's really no way to make this come out in my favor. "Well . . . fine."

She shakes her head like she's disgusted by me. But she doesn't get to be disgusted by me. I decide the best strategy is to turn the conversation back to her.

"Anyway, you're like that with your friends. You have inside jokes, too."

"Not really."

I roll my eyes.

"I don't because I don't *have* any friends. Not the you-and-Vonzelle kind."

"What about Oklahoma? Don't you do stuff with her anymore?"

She shrugs.

"Did y'all have a fight?"

"I'm not mad at her, but she's mad at me." She bites her lip, then mumbles something that starts off, "She thinks I . . ." and ends in unintelligible syllables.

"She thinks you what?"

Her head lolls back to its center position. She gazes at the ceiling. "She's jealous. I don't know. It's all awful and weird." She's trying not to cry . . . and the answer of *why* clicks in my brain.

"*Oh.* Georgia's going out with that guy Kip, right?"

Anna nods.

I blow out a breath of air. "And Kip thinks you're cute, or whatever."

Anna doesn't deny it. She just stares at the ceiling. I study her profile, and my gut clenches, because she gets more beautiful every day. Even with moodiness etched across her features, she's beautiful.

I'm jealous, and I'm her big sister, who should be above such things. Of course Idaho is jealous, too.

"It's not like I told him to," Anna says defensively.

"Duh."

"I don't like him like that. I totally don't! But apparently Kip made some comment to Georgia . . ." Her sentence trickles off. "Whatever. Who cares. It's stupid."

Knowledge of the world's suckiness presses in on me like a dense gray mist, and I feel bad for acting like such a jerk. Who's the crap sister? *I'm* the crap sister.

"I hate life," Anna says to the room in general.

"No you don't."

"Yeah, I pretty much do."

I'm silent for a couple of seconds. Then I say, "All right, fine. I do, too."

She half laughs, and the mist lifts. Not a lot, but enough that I can breathe again. How weird to think that you can drown in all the muck inside of you. You can literally *drown*, unless someone pulls you out.

"So . . . are you ever going to take it down?" Anna asks. "The video?"

"No. Dad can fine me all he wants—that doesn't mean I'm his puppet."

She changes positions, unfolding her legs from beneath her and extending one of them toward me. She puts her foot on my lap. "Who made up the lyrics?"

"Me."

She nods, like that's what she expected. "It's funny, the parts with the actual singing. Well, the whole thing is funny, but . . ."

I look at her sharply. She better not say, " . . . but I feel sorry for Dad" or anything like that.

She doesn't. She smiles ruefully.

We hear Mom's heels clicking on the floor. Anna drops her foot from my leg, and we both straighten our postures.

Mom steps into the sunporch, looking fit and stylish in gray pants and a burnt-orange cashmere sweater. "Girls, I'm off to pick up the dry cleaning," she says. "Tracy will be here if you need any-thing—she's upstairs doing the ironing. Oh, and she'll be baby-sitting the two of you next weekend, so you know."

"*Baby*sitting us?" Anna says, aghast.

I'm more than aghast. I'm appalled. Why in the world does Mom think we need a babysitter? And just say there's some legiti-mate reason, why in the world would she pick *Tracy*?

"Your father won tickets to New York on eBay," Mom explains. "We'll be gone both Friday and Saturday nights, and you need a grown-up in the house."

"No we don't," Anna says.

"And Tracy's not a grown-up," I say.

"She's twenty-one," Mom says. "Don't give me a hard time, girls." She glances toward the hall and lowers her voice. "Your father is set on going. Two first-class tickets plus accommodations at the Ritz-Carlton—he says it's too good to pass up."

Bleh, I think, because Tracy's not my favorite. She smokes, for one thing, and for another, she doesn't seem to like me. I always feel self-conscious around her, like she blames me for living in the nice house she gets paid to clean.

Then I think, *However* . . .

There *are* pluses to this situation, like, to name the biggest one, *no Dad*.

Mom adjusts her purse. "I've got to run if I'm going to have din-ner on the table when your father gets home. I'll be back soon."

She strides out of the room, and Anna and I regard each other. Her expression suggests that she, too, is considering the weekend's possibilities.

"What do you think?" I ask in a low voice.

"I don't know. What do *you* think?"

"Well . . . I think this is a very big house, and it would be very empty with just you, me, and Tracy rattling around in it."

"Hmm," Anna says.

"Hmm," I reply. "We'll have to consider our options carefully, of course—"

"Of *course*."

"—but perhaps we could figure out something to keep us from growing too lonely."

"A sleepover?" Anna says.

"Sure. Why not?"

She smiles, and her eyes brighten, the way they do when we make plans together. I smile back.

CHAPTER FORTY

VONZELLE IS NOT A COCKATOO

People love the "Buckhead Hillbillies" video that Vonzelle, Roger, and I made. Well, that's not entirely true. Some people love it. Some people hate it. More people than both these groups combined have never seen it, nor ever will. *C'est la vie.*

Vonzelle and I share a computer in the media center and check out the latest posts. So far, it's been viewed 923 times and there are sixty-nine comments. *So far.*

An example of a happy comment:

"THE BEVERLY HILLBILLIES" IS MY FAVORITE SHOW OF ALL TIME!!!! BEST. THEME. SONG. EVAH!!!!

An example of a less happy (and completely wacko) comment:

–ARE YOU A PEDOPHILE? HAVE YOU NO CONSCIOUS. DO YOU ENJOY MISGUIDING THE YOUTH? THE BEVERLY HILLBILLIES IS A CLASSIC AND SHOULD NOT BE DEFILED. ANYWAY, WHY IS "TED" CLAMPETT SOMETIMES A GIRL AND SOMETIMES THAT MAN? I AM EAGERLY WAITING YOUR REPLY.

Vonzelle snorts. "She spelled *conscience* wrong," she points out.

"How do you know she's a 'she'?" I ask. "And why does she think we're *pedophiles*? What is pedophile-ish about our video?"

She holds her hands out, palms out. "Because of the Cozy Coupe?"

"That makes no sense."

"She's right about the double identity of Ted Clampett, though."

"He's a shape-shifter," I say, not wanting to admit that I'm a little disturbed at the overlap. I wish I'd planned it better. "Girl to man, man to girl."

"You better tell Angry Pedophile Woman that. She's eagerly waiting your reply, you know."

"Nuh-uh, she's eagerly waiting *your* reply. Maybe you guys can be pen pals."

"That would be so great," Vonzelle says.

"Maybe she can be one of your bridesmaids when you get married."

"Do you think? Seriously? Oh my God, that would *rock*."

I giggle. I love that she plays along with my nonsense so easily. I recall what Anna said yesterday about Vonzelle being "different," and I blurt, "You know I'm not friends with you because you're black, right?"

Whoa. That puts a screaming wrench in the conversation. Vonzelle's eyebrows go sky high, and she says, "Gee, I'm black? Wow. I hadn't noticed."

Uh-oh. "That's what I'm saying. I don't think of you as black. I just think of you as Vonzelle."

"Then why are you talking about it?"

She makes a point. I wish I'd kept my mouth shut—only, part of me needs to make sure she knows there isn't some Vonzelle-as-dashiki thing going on here. Or maybe I need to make sure *I* know?

"Carly?" she says in a voice that's frighteningly patient.

"Um . . . yes?"

"I *assume* you're friends with me because I'm fabulous, just as I'm friends with you because you're fabulous."

I nod quickly. "That *is* why I'm friends with you. And I do think you're fabulous."

"I don't want to be a prop."

"You're not a prop. God."

"'Cause if I'm a prop, I'm out of here."

"You're not a prop. I was just worried that *you* maybe thought I thought you were."

She shakes her head as if I have little hope of surviving till adulthood.

I surprise myself by taking hold of her hands. I lock eyes with her and say, "You *are* fabulous. You are a fabulously fabulous *you*, and I am a fabulously fabulous *me*, and we need never talk of it again."

She makes an overly earnest expression to match what must be my own overly earnest expression. "Okay. But I thought we'd gotten past that black girl/honky girl foolishness the night we delivered stockings."

"Ah. That's, um, because you're so much smarter than I am."

"True. Can we stop holding hands now?"

I let go of her abruptly, which makes both of us giggle, and which makes Mrs. Radisson, the media specialist, come over from her desk and shush us.

"Sorry, Mrs. Radisson," Vonzelle says as I quickly close out of YouTube and hit escape to bring up the screen saver.

"The media center is for quiet studying," Mrs. Radisson warns.

We nod earnestly.

"What were you looking at?" she asks, jerking her chin at the Holy Redeemer logo which is floating like dandelion fluff over the screen.

"Nothing," I say.

"History research," Vonzelle says. "The English cockatoo."

The English cockatoo?

Mrs. Radisson narrows her eyes, but I keep a straight face. The English cockatoo. Yes. Excellent research topic.

"I don't want to get the two of you in trouble," Mrs. Radisson says, "but I *will* write you up if I catch you abusing the computer."

Don't giggle, I tell myself. *Don't you dare.*

Vonzelle presses her thigh against mine.

"Yes, ma'am," I say.

She gives us one last look, then strides away.

"The English cockatoo?!" I whisper.

"Shut up, computer abuser." Vonzelle suppresses a laugh. "We are so bad."

"Aren't we? But hey, could be worse. We could be boyfriend stealers like Anna."

"What?" she says. "Where did *that* come from?"

"Uh . . ." I say, unsure of the answer. After a moment's reflection, I realize the boyfriend-stealer comment is linked to my Vonzelle-is-black embarrassment. They both stemmed from yesterday's talk with Anna.

"*Is* she a boyfriend stealer?" Vonzelle asks.

"No. One of her friends told her she is, though."

"Nice friend."

"Tell me about it. Anna's taking it too personally, though." I shrug. "Oh, well. Saturday's sleepover will cheer her up. You're bringing all six seasons of *Gilmore Girls?*"

"All *seven* seasons," she says. She taps her pen against the surface of the computer desk. "I have a better idea for cheering Anna up, though."

"Yeah? What's that?"

"I think we should help her not fail PE."

"Why are you so fixated on Anna and PE?"

"I am not *fixated* on her. I'm just worried about her."

"Well, why are you worried about her?"

"Because she seems so depressed all the time, like she's slipping through the cracks. I have a cousin who slipped through the cracks—started smoking and sneaking out and all that—and she became, like, the class slut. Before that, she was so sweet."

"Anna's not 'slipping through the cracks,'" I say. "And if anyone should be worrying about her, it should be me."

"So are you?" Vonzelle asks.

"Am I what?"

She rolls her eyes.

"Vonzelle, you are an only child," I inform her. "You have no idea what it's like to have a sister."

"And you have no idea what it's like *not* to have a sister."

"Huh?"

"Onlies are lonely, Carly. When I was little, I asked for a baby sister every Christmas."

"Aw, that's so cute."

"Cute and *sad*. For real, can you imagine not having Anna being in your life? Even though she gets on your nerves sometimes?"

"Sometimes? Try all the time."

She eyeballs me. "Get over yourself. Anna needs your help, and you need to step up. That's what sisters do."

"I've been helping her my whole entire life. Don't I ever get to be done?"

"Nope."

"Why not?"

"You just don't. And how can you claim you've been stepping up your whole life when you're not stepping up now?"

Huh. I'm stumped, because I *have* stepped up for Anna. I know I have. Like with the Percolator—I totally stepped up when he thought Anna had a porn fetish.

So what's changed? Why don't I want to step up for her now, with the Wanker? Why have I gotten stingy when the stakes are even higher?

You know why, an annoying voice singsongs in my brain.

No, I don't, I tell the annoying voice, using the same annoying singsong. Is it normal to have a singsong argument in my own head?

Why do you care if it's normal or not? the voice says. *You aren't normal, and you never will be, so just shut up. For your whole life, you've been the Almighty Big Sister. First to learn to swim, first to use a tampon, first to start high school. And all the crap that comes with being a freshman? You dealt with it by yourself, while Anna was still a kid making a family tree on poster board. You even helped her with her dinky family tree. You resented it, maybe, but you got off on being the One Who Knew It All.*

(To be fair, you sometimes liked *helping her. You weren't always stingy.)*

Then Anna started high school, and you were all, "Yay! We'll be equals now!" Only, you didn't want Anna to be your equal. You wanted to keep being Carly Almighty. So when Anna needed to be saved from Headmaster Perkins, who was there, ready to jump in and save her?

Bingo! Because by saving her, you could pretend she was still little Anna, even though anyone with eyes could see that she'd outgrown "little" just as indisputably as she'd outgrown poster board.

Bottom line? Anna isn't a kid anymore. She's got curves. She's got sex appeal. Guys think she's hot, and girls are crazy jealous of her. They want to see her taken down.

And guess what? You do, too.

That's what's changed.

That's why you don't want to step up for her with the Wanker.

Vonzelle is staring at me. "Carly? You look like you've just eaten salt."

"Do you think I *want* Anna to fail?" I ask.

"Do you?"

No. Yes. Maybe.

"But if I help her, or try to help her . . . isn't that, like, disempowering her or something? Shouldn't she have to fend for herself?"

"I don't know. Should she?"

"You're not helping."

"*Ohhh.* Sorry. But if I help you, won't I be disempowering you?"

I glower.

She shrugs. "I call 'em like I see 'em."

Grasping the edge of the computer desk, I pull my roller chair forward an inch, then push it backward an inch. Forward and backward, forward and backward.

"I don't *not* wish her well," I say slowly.

"Wow. I'm overwhelmed," Vonzelle says. She puts her hand on my chair to stop my rolling. "Just say, for the sake of argument, that you weren't so balled up inside yourself. Does that mean you *do* wish her well?"

"Of course," I say. And it's true. Because if there is a part of me that wants to see Anna go down, well, then that's a part I want to say no to. I get to choose, right? Don't I get to choose what kind of person I want to be?

Grumpily, I say, "Fine. What's your idea?"

Vonzelle is pleased. "I think you should go to the Wanker and ask him to let Anna redo her dive. Easy as that."

"Yeah, sure. Easy as that."

"'Cause Anna's never going to ask him. You know she's not."

"What makes you think Anna would be able to do the dive even if she *did* get a second chance? She couldn't do it the first time."

"Yeah, because the Wanker's technique was all about high pressure, and obviously high pressure doesn't work with Anna. But *we* could help her, you and me. We could be calm and patient and all the things Coach Wanker isn't."

I gaze out the window that overlooks the lawn. It's gray and drizzly outside, making it especially cozy here in the media center.

"Remember that swim class Coach Wanker told us about?" Vonzelle goes on. "For Holy Redeemer employees? Well, my mama's in that class—"

"She is?"

"—and the teacher is Coach Boden, who's the polar opposite of the Wanker. I know he'd let us come and use the high board if we asked. We could teach Anna ourselves."

"Your mom takes swimming lessons?" I repeat. "But . . . you're a great swimmer."

"Because my mom started me early. She didn't want me growing up scared of the water."

"Anna's scared of the water," I say.

"Yep," Vonzelle says. She lets it hang there. The space she creates is big enough for me to think—again—about how much it would suck to be scared of something like that.

"All right," I say in a martyred tone. I stand up. "Let's go find Coach Boden and the Wanker."

CHAPTER FORTY-ONE
LUST IS A LOADED GUN

Coach Boden says sure, we can use the pool during Thursday's evening swim lesson.

"That's so cool," I tell him. Now that I've committed to Vonzelle's plan, I'm pumped up by the possibility it might work. "We'll come this Thursday—*if* Coach Schranker says he's willing to give her a second chance. Do you know where he is?"

"Probably in the weight room," Coach Boden says. He gives me a stern look. "You tell him I'm all for it, you hear?"

"Yes, sir," I say, thinking that if we'd gotten Coach Boden for PE, none of this would have even been an issue.

"Thanks, Coach," Vonzelle says.

"Anytime. Say 'hey' to your mom for me, Vonzelle."

We find Coach Schranker doing bench presses. He's not teaching a class. He's just doing his own personal bodybuilding.

"Um, Coach Schranker?" I say. "Can I talk to you for a second?"

He glances at me from under the bar, which is loaded with black weights the size of car tires. "What is it?" he says tersely. He strains as he pushes the bar up.

"It's about my sister. And . . . the, um, high dive."

He clangs the bar into the support stand, but keeps his fingers gripped around it. He doesn't sit up. Perhaps he's resting, or pondering, or just admiring his biceps, which *are* pretty spectacular. He's got serious armpit hair, though.

Eventually he ducks under the bar, swings his legs around, and regards me, his hands planted on his thighs. He's wearing an I've-swallowed-too-many-eggs expression.

"You know, Carly, I've felt bad about that since the day it happened." He doesn't make eye contact with Vonzelle, which is creepy. "It's just . . . I refuse to give anyone special treatment. It doesn't do anyone any good, I can tell you that right now."

"Uh-huh," I say.

"That's the problem with society today. People expect special treatment, and then, when they get it, they can't understand why they don't get any respect. Respect has to be *earned*. You can understand that, can't you?"

I scratch my head. I'm not asking him to respect Anna; I'm asking him to let her do the stupid dive again.

"Coach Boden says we can use the pool on Thursday night, during the staff's swimming lesson. Vonzelle and I will help her—you don't have to do a thing."

He folds his arms over his Captain Awesome chest and gazes at the far end of the weight room. I get the sense it's for my benefit, like maybe I'm supposed to think, *Coach Schranker is struggling with big issues. Coach Schranker is deep.* I'm reminded of Cole's faraway stares when he plays his guitar, and I'm struck with a disloyal thought. Does Cole make that expression when he's playing by himself?

Coach Schranker pulls his focus back to me. "She'll have to do it in front of me in order to receive a passing grade. I can't take her word for it, or yours."

Of course not, because we might lie even though Coach Boden and the whole swim class will be there to bear witness.

"Okay," I say.

"And I want you to know—I want you to tell Anna this—that I'm making an allowance on this one occasion, because I believe in second chances. But just because Anna . . . just because she . . ."

I furrow my brow. He's stammering, and I don't have the slightest clue what he's trying to spit out.

He pulls back his shoulders. "Anna is an attractive young lady," he says stiffly. "No doubt she uses that to her advantage—but not with me. Do you understand?"

Something hard and cold kicks in, and it takes extreme willpower to cover what I'm feeling. "Thank you so much, Coach Schranker."

When we're away from the weight room, I say furiously, "I can't believe that man. I can't *believe* him."

Vonzelle nods, but in a way that suggests she can . . . and does.

"Anna's *fourteen*," I say.

"I know."

"He shouldn't be noticing what an *attractive young lady* she is. That's sick! And then punishing her for it?"

"I know," Vonzelle says again.

"Bad Attitude Cindy has bigger boobs than Anna, and he didn't punish her."

"'Cause Cindy did the dive." We exit the gymnasium and head toward Butler Hall. "But I don't think Cindy's boobs are bigger. Not anymore."

I consider.

"Holy crud," I say at last. "If Anna keeps growing like this, I swear she's going to *pop*."

CHAPTER FORTY-TWO
"FOREVER" CAN BE COMPLICATED

I find Anna during her lunch period—she's sitting with the band kids, which is strange, because she's not a band rat—and convince her to go along with our plan. Is she happy about it? *No.* Am I able to persuade her by reminding her that otherwise she'll have to take the whole class over? *Yes.*

"And . . . it was Vonzelle's idea?" she says, twisting her shoulders away from the others at her table so they can't overhear. Not that they're listening. They're talking about the drummer from our rival high school and how he supposedly smokes chive cigarettes. Or clove cigarettes. Something.

"Yeah," I say.

"Weird," she says softly.

So we're on for this Thursday evening. I'll tell Mom we're staying late for a community-service meeting, because there's no reason to get her and Dad involved till we know the outcome. I'll remind Anna to bring her hair dryer so she doesn't blow our cover.

As I head for pickup at the end of the day, I'm riding high. I'm walking with a bounce and humming to myself and feeling just plain good when Peyton's voice intrudes into my reverie.

"Carly! Hold up!" she calls.

I turn and spot Peyton a couple of yards behind me. She's with Lydia, and the two of them wave enthusiastically. I wave back, thinking, *That's odd*. They're not really wavers, those two, and anyway, Peyton and I have drifted out of each other's orbit recently. Drifted all the way into different solar systems, I'd have said . . . and yet there she is. *Waving*.

Peyton leans toward Lydia and says something I can't hear. They both smile at me, and Peyton jogs over.

"God, it's been forever since I've seen you," Peyton says, flushed and pretty as always. "Doesn't it seem like it's been for*ever*?"

"I guess." I tilt my head. "What's up?"

"Nothing," she says, pretending that she's run over and love-bombed me every day of the last month, and that today is no different from any other. "I'll walk you to pickup, 'kay?"

"Okay," I say. "Peyton—do you have sparkles on your lashes?"

"Oh my God, it's changed my life," she says. "It's called Glitter Lash Freak mascara. At first I thought it was too disco, but now I wear it every day. The wand's not like a normal mascara wand. It's more like a stick. And the tube's not like a normal tube, either. It's more . . . skinny-ish. The sparkles themselves are like confetti, and they float in this, like, liquidy clear stuff."

She goes on for a while, then eventually runs out of Lash Freak details. Or maybe she doesn't. Maybe she realizes I'm not quite as into the mascara discussion as she is.

Is it a discussion if only one person is talking?

"It's hard to explain," Peyton says. "But I love it."

"It makes your lashes look wet," I say. "Like you've been crying, only without the actual crying part."

"Yeah!" She smiles sunnily.

"Peyton?"

She's all innocence. "Huh?"

"You want something."

"No, I—"

"What do you want, Peyton?" I laugh to show that I mean this in the most amicable way possible, which I think I do.

After a moment's hesitation, she laughs, too. "Okay. Busted. I hear your parents are going out of town this weekend."

Aaargh, I think. *Anna.* Why in the world did she tell Peyton, when we'd already decided we weren't going to invite Peyton over? Initially, Anna had assumed we would—which made for a weird moment, because *I* assumed Anna knew we wouldn't.

"You guys having a party?" Peyton asks.

"Ha," I say. "You know my dad. We'd be killed."

We reach the brick wall where kids sit and wait for their rides, and I lean against it. Peyton squints her Glitter Lash-ed eyes. It's like she's trying to look inside me.

"Oh," she says. "Okay." She lifts her eyebrows. "Hey—did you hear about Cole and Trista?"

"Is there something new?" I blush when she giggles.

"Well, how much do you already know?"

"That they almost broke up, but didn't. That Cole may or may not be cheating on her with some girl from Northside."

Peyton situates herself against the wall. "Here's what I've heard. He feels penned in by her, and like, he's in *love* with her, but he's not ready for that kind of commitment. And that he did have a fling with some Northside girl, but it didn't mean anything."

She watches my face. "So I'd say he's on the market. Obviously Trista wants more from him than he's able to give, you know? And guys don't put up with that for long."

My insides are jumpy. Peyton used to step hard on my Cole fantasies, just like Vonzelle. But now she's acting like she thinks there's a chance.

"I think you guys would be so good together," she says. "I think the only reason he didn't go out with you instead of Trista in the first place was because you're more . . . *complex* than she is. But he needs complex, don't you think?"

I don't know what I think. Well, yes I do. I'm intoxicated by what she's suggesting. I'm also sweating.

"Maybe you *should* have a party," Peyton says casually. She stretches, reaching her hands high over her head. Her eyes slide to me, and I come to my senses. Visions of parties-gone-bad from scores of teen movies flash through my head.

"I'm not having a party," I say.

"Not the whole grade or anything," Peyton says. "Just me and Lydia . . . and Cole . . . and maybe Roger?"

I feel guilty. I should just tell the truth.

"I've already made plans with Vonzelle," I confess. "She's sleeping over—we're going to have a *Gilmore Girls* marathon."

"Oh," Peyton says in a trying-to-be-neutral tone. "And Vonzelle doesn't want you hanging with other people?"

I press my lips together. I'm being played, I'm being played, I'm being played. But old loyalties complicate the dynamic, because Peyton's been my friend since second grade.

Mom's BMW pulls into the pickup line. It's time for the conversation to be over.

"Vonzelle doesn't care who I hang out with," I say. "She likes all my friends."

"So why *not* have a party? Forget *Gilmore Girls*. You can watch *Gilmore Girls* anytime."

"Peyton, *no*. No party."

"An *intimate gathering*, then. Just me and Cole and Roger and Lydia, like I said. And Vonzelle, of course." She widens her sparkly eyes. "Why not, you know?"

Yes, why not? Especially if Cole and Trista really are . . . having trouble.

"Trista's going to a cheerleading competition," Peyton mentions, "so Cole's going to be on his own, anyway. Hanging out with his buds might be the very best thing for him."

Well. I certainly want to be there for Cole if he's in need.

"*Maybe*," I hear myself say, drawing the word out long.

Peyton squeals and claps her hands.

"But *I'll* tell Cole and Roger," I quickly add. My heart rate picks up—*what have I done?* "You can invite Lydia, but *no one else.* Got it?"

She beams. "Oh my God, we're going to have a blast. I'm getting extensions put in that afternoon—it takes, like, six hours—so I will be so ready to cut loose." She pushes off the wall and heads back across the lawn. "Lydia's going to be so psyched!"

"Wait," I say, wanting to stress how low-key this has to be. She turns around.

Mom honks, and I glance at the car-pool line. Anna's already walking toward her. I hold up a finger to say *I'm coming, I'll be right there.* When I turn back to Peyton, she's gone.

On our way home, Mom stops by Whole Foods for a loaf of ciabatta. Anna and I elect to wait in the car, but as Mom moves to get out, Anna says, "Will you get some Marcona almonds, too?"

Mom purses her lips. "We'll see," she says, and her tone tells me what she's thinking. She's thinking, *Oh, Anna, those almonds are drenched in oil.*

Anna's face goes flat, like it's too much. Like everyone is riding her all the time, even her mother, and like she *could* be falling through the cracks, with just one Marcona almond standing between her and the Home for Unwed Mothers.

I was planning on being annoyed with her for the Peyton thing, but I push it from my mind, deciding what's done is done. Sisters should step up for each other and all that. I say, "Hey, Mom?"

"Yes, Carly?"

"Anna's not chubby. They're called breasts."

Both Anna and Mom are shocked. In the backseat, Anna crosses her arms over her chest.

"Yes, Carly," Mom says. "I realize that."

"I don't think you do."

Mom opens her mouth, then shuts it. She shifts her attention to Anna. "Anna, have I been making you . . . self-conscious about your body?"

"You've been making me feel like crap," Anna says. She blushes.

"Oh," Mom says. "Well." She's silent for a moment, and when she speaks again, her tone is melancholy. "You're both growing up, I suppose."

"And that's *normal*," I point out.

"You're right. I know." She pulls herself together. "I'll try to watch what I say."

She closes the door and crosses the parking lot to Whole Foods. She returns bearing bread, mineral water, and Marcona almonds, and I remember how good it feels to help my sister.

CHAPTER FORTY-THREE
A TRUE SOUTHERN BELLE IS A BULLDOZER DISGUISED AS A POWDER PUFF

Thursday is Anna's learn-to-dive day. In the girls' locker room after school, she changes into her red one-piece. The bottom is nubbly. I put on my boring blue number again, and Vonzelle puts on her same suit. We're stepping back in time.

"Carly," Anna says. Her throat closes in the middle of it, strangling the last syllable.

I put my arm around her. "Don't talk."

"Don't even think," Vonzelle says.

I squeeze her. "Just breathe."

In the echoey pool area, the lunch ladies and the custodians are in the shallow end having a grand old time. They're in the water up to their waists, and I can't help but think how cute they are. Wide bodies, skinny bodies, dark bodies, white bodies. Bazooms bigger than Bad Attitude Cindy's. Chest hair as thick as Dr. al-Fulani's.

"Woo-eee," one very plump woman says as the water laps her ribs. She rises on her toes and laughs.

"Why do I like their class so much more than our PE class?" I ask Vonzelle. We haven't gotten in; we're standing at the edge of the deep end. Anna's being wimpy behind us, and I'm giving her a few minutes of space before getting this show on the road.

"Because they're having fun?" Vonzelle suggests.

"Hi, hon!" Vonzelle's mom calls to Vonzelle, waving from beside Coach Boden. The flesh under her arm wiggles.

"That's exactly it," I say. "I want to have fun one day. I want to wear a bathing suit with a skirt."

"You can wear a bathing suit with a skirt now," Vonzelle says.

"You are so right." I contemplate, imagining myself in an old-lady skirt suit.

"Or not," Vonzelle says.

"Or not." I look over my shoulder. "Anna!"

She trudges forward and sticks her hands under her armpits. "So . . . what do I do?"

"Well, you have *fun,* first of all," I say. "What's the point of doing it if you don't have fun?"

She gazes at me like a lizard. "Did you have fun when you did it?"

"Kind of," I say. "Okay . . . no. But it was fun once I was done."

Anna jerks her chin at the ladder. "Go have some more fun. Show me how it's done."

I shake my head, then turn it into a nod. "Fair enough. But come up with me."

She sighs as if she's being led to the stake. When we get to the platform, she says, "I am really, really scared, in case you didn't notice. What if I break my neck?"

"You won't break your neck."

"What if I go down so far that I hit the bottom of the pool? I *could* break my neck."

"Won't happen. Water's too deep. Coach Wanker's a sadist, but he wouldn't make us do something if there was truly a chance we could get hurt."

Anna is unconvinced. "The people who design roller coasters say that, too, and then the tracks break and the cars go flying off into infinity and people die."

"Luckily, no roller-coaster tracks here." I take a breath. "Do you remember the steps?"

I get the lizard gaze again, eyelids at half-mast and features blank.

"Right," I say. "Let's have a refresher course." I walk her through the steps, emphasizing the most important ones like *not* arching your spine and *not* freaking out in the middle and windmilling your limbs.

"And yes, I'll show you, because that's how much I love you," I say. Do I want to do another back dive off the high dive? No. But if I fall off that board like I own it, then Anna will assume I do . . . or something. And she'll have the courage to do it, too.

I don't talk. I don't think. I just breathe and walk to the end of the board. It bounces with far too much sway. I turn and edge out onto the end. I feel Vonzelle watching me from below, but this isn't the time to look at her. I don't look at Anna, either.

I lift my hands into the air and clasp one over the other. I tilt my head and stare at my knuckles. A tremor runs through me . . . and I fall. I am sideways, I am upside down, I am plunging like an arrow.

Splash.

The night class cheers when I emerge. I grin.

"Wh-hoo!" Vonzelle calls from the edge of the deep end.

"Your turn!" I call up to Anna.

Up on the platform, she does a funny, nervous, bendy thing with her hands, pressing one against the other. "I can't."

"Anna, stop saying that. You *can*." I swim to the middle of the deep end, a yard or two from where she should land. "I'll be right here. Or I can come back up there if you'd rather."

"No," she says. "Stay there." She takes shallow breaths.

"Okay, do it," I say.

She approaches the board.

"You're going to be fine," Vonzelle says, using a matter-of-fact, not-overly-invested voice. She's casual city, as if people do this every day.

Anna steps *onto* the board and walks to the end. There's a stillness in the shallow end that makes me suspect she's got an audience, but I don't turn around. *Casual city, casual city.* I focus all my positive energy and send it to Anna in a stream of light.

"Now turn around," I say. I make figure eights with my legs to stay afloat.

Anna turns around. The board jostles, and she drops and grabs it.

"Nah," I say. "Just stand back up."

"You can do it," Vonzelle says.

Anna stands. I continue feeding her strength and courage and faith.

"Lift your arms," I tell her. "You're almost there."

She raises her hands above her head. She looks up at her knuckles, and this alone is much farther than she ever got with Coach Schranker, who said, *Get off the board, Anna. You're done. You fail.*

"All you have to do is let go," Vonzelle says.

"I'm scared," Anna says.

"I know," I say. "And what do you do when you're scared? You paddle harder. Even if you're not in the water, even if you're in the air, way up high on a diving board. You paddle harder, because the only other choice—"

Oh my God. I don't have to finish my cheesy sermon, because ANNA IS DOING IT! She's falling, and she does not crumple, but sluices clean into the water: first hands, then head, then body, then toes.

"Anna!" I scream when her head pops up. "You did it! You did it, you did it, you did it!"

"Wow," Anna says, seeming dazed. "I did, didn't I?"

The night class whoops and hollers, and Vonzelle looks proud as heck. Almost as proud as me.

CHAPTER FORTY-FOUR
DON'T PAWN THE SILVER

On Friday morning before Mom and Dad leave for New York, we have a family powwow during which they give us a printout of flight deets, hotel deets, and arrival-back-home deets.

"No wild parties," Dad says.

"Ha ha," I say. My stomach twinges just the tiniest amount. Anna is appropriately and convincingly eye-roll-y, though, because as far as she knows—and this is true for Vonzelle, as well—we're still just having our slumber party. I haven't gotten around to telling them the change in plans, exactly.

"No pawning the silver," Dad goes on.

"Ha ha again."

"And Carly, I want that video off the Web before we get back."

I don't answer.

"We've left Tracy some money," Mom says, intuiting that this is not a good time for tension. "You can order pizza if you want."

"Where's Tracy going to sleep?" Anna asks, because even in our big house, there are only three bedrooms. There used to be a fourth, but Mom turned it into a room for storing her fancy wrapping paper and rolls upon rolls of French ribbon.

"With you, of course," Dad says, then chortles at Anna's horror.

But it's an icky joke, because Anna agrees with me about the Tracy-being-strange thing. Tracy never graduated from high school, and she wears really tight jeans and really tight shirts. She's got the roundest, bulgiest eyes I've ever in my life seen. They look like blue marbles lolling about in her eye sockets.

"Tracy will sleep in our bed," Mom says. "I've left out a clean set of sheets."

"And explicit instructions to change the sheets again before we get home," Dad says, with more chortling. He's not a big fan of Tracy himself. He thinks she's shifty, not that he's letting that get in the way of having her "babysit" us. Just last week, for example, Tracy asked for an advance on her salary. She said she needed it for a lawyer, because her cousin had gotten thrown in jail.

"Apparently her cousin attempted to break into Circuit City," Mom told us the night Tracy made her request. "He wanted *woofers* for his truck. I said, 'Tracy, I don't know what a *woofer* is,' and Tracy said they make it so that he can play his music loud enough to make his truck shake."

Dad's laughter started then.

"I asked how he got caught," Mom went on, "and Tracy said, 'Well, he threw a brick at the window, only the window wasn't made out of glass. It was that *Plexi* stuff, and the brick bounced back and hit him smack in the head. The cops found him knocked out cold on the sidewalk.'"

Dad was wheezing by then. "They couldn't arrest him just for *lying* there. How'd they know what the brick was for?"

"Good point," I said. "Maybe *you* should be his lawyer."

Dad about choked on his pork medallion.

"Ted, stop laughing," Mom scolded, though she was laughing, too.

"Maureen, you better fire Tracy before she brings her cousin here for a sting," Dad said, red-faced and guffawing.

But Mom did not fire her. Instead, she said, "Hey, why don't you come spend a weekend with my children?"

"Tracy has our travel information," Mom says now. "She'll be here when you get home from school."

Mrs. Bucco, our three-houses-down neighbor, gives a polite tap on her horn from our driveway. She's taking us to Holy Redeemer today, since Mom and Dad have to get to the airport.

"You girls better get going," Dad says. "Hold down the fort. We'll see you on Sunday."

Mom gives us each a hug. Anna's is full-on; mine is the sideways sort. "Have fun. Be safe. And no doing anything foolish, like trashing the house."

I groan. "Yes, Mom, you really needed to say that, because that's exactly what we were planning to do. We just love trashing houses."

"And no wandering around the neighborhood late at night," she says.

"Yes, and again, thank you for planting that idea," I say, looking at her as if she's lost her mind.

"I want you to be here when we return, that's all."

"That's so cool, because so do I."

Anna stifles a laugh.

"Come on, Anna," I say, grabbing my backpack. At the door, I pause and look back at Mom and Dad. "Have fun," I tell them.

"Bring us souvenirs," Anna adds.

Mom smiles. "Love you, girls."

"Love you, too," we chorus.

CHAPTER FORTY-FIVE

THREE HOT CHICKS

Vonzelle's mom drops her off at our house at four on Saturday. When I open the door to let her in, she says, "Why is there a box of ducks on your front step?"

"*What?!*" I say.

She gestures with the hand not holding her overnight bag. "Look."

My eyes fly to the beat-up cardboard box by the wall of the house. I've never seen this box in my life. It has no top, and when I walk over, I see that inside are three ducks. Three baby ducks, each the size of a cupcake.

"Why is there a box of baby ducks outside my house?" I ask Vonzelle stupidly.

She squats and peels a blue sticky note from the side of the box. "Three hot chicks for three hot chicks," she reads aloud.

One of the ducks quacks.

"They're not chicks," I say. "They're ducks."

A wolf whistle cuts through the air from the direction of the Millers' house.

"Oh, nuh-uh," I say, putting my hands on my hips. I spot Gary peeking over the top of the wall. Or maybe Barry. I raise my voice. "Did you leave these ducks here? You better come get them!"

Gary (or Barry) laughs and disappears.

"Who's the third hot chick?" Vonzelle asks. "Is it me?"

"No," I say, disgusted.

She seems offended.

"You *are* a hot chick," I say, "but how would they know you were going to be here? I think they mean Tracy."

"Tracy, your babysitter?"

"Please don't call her that. But, yes." Last night Tracy took a pizza box out to the trash, and when she didn't come back in after several minutes, I went to check on her. She was chatting with all four Miller boys, whose heads were a row of bowling balls on the wall between our houses. She was wearing tight jeans and a fuzzy sweater, which she'd hiked up so they could see the star above her left hipbone.

"Tracy!" I'd said.

"What?" She smoothed down her sweater and sashayed past me. She winked and said, "Give 'em something to dream about."

"Is Tracy a hot chick?" Vonzelle asks.

I look at her, unwilling to even go there.

I turn back toward the Millers' house and cup my hands around my mouth. "Get over here and get your ducks!"

Laughter spills from behind the wall.

"What's going on?" Anna says, emerging from the house.

Vonzelle hands Anna the note. "You got a delivery."

Anna skims it and looks down at the box. "They're not chicks. They're ducks."

Three heads appear over the wall, followed, after a scramble, by the fourth. All four boys grin. Barry, or maybe Gary, makes kissy sounds and calls, "Hi, Anna!"

Gary, or maybe Barry, yells, "We love hot chicks!"

"They're not chicks!" Anna yells back. "They're *ducks!*"

Why don't any of them say "Hi, Carly?" I wonder, then immediately hate myself for it.

"Where's your babysitter?" Larry asks, waggling his eyebrows. He's *twelve,* and he's waggling his eyebrows.

That's it. I squat, awkwardly grab the box of ducklings, and heave it up. The ducks flap their wings and make sounds of alarm. Two of them are yellow with white chests and tummies; the third has a pale yellow chest with black feathers everywhere else. Except they're not really feathers. They're more just . . . fuzzies. Maybe they turn into feathers later?

"They're so cute," Vonzelle says.

"And now they're going bye-bye." I march over to the wall. Barry smirks down at me. Or Gary. They all look the same, anyway.

"Here are your ducks," I say, lifting my offering. The ducks skitter and squawk, and I feel the soft weight of them hit the more tilted-down side of the box.

"Not my ducks," Gary says. "Yours."

"No, Gary, they're not . . . and where did you get them, anyway?"

"My name's not Gary. It's Barry."

"Yay for you. You didn't steal them from the Duck Pond, did you?" The Duck Pond is over by Garden Hills swimming pool. It's a twenty-minute walk from our house, and Anna and I used to go and feed the ducks stale bread. We used to do that a lot, actually, and then buy toffee crunch bars from the ice-cream truck that trolled the neighborhood. When did we stop going to the Duck Pond?

"We liberated them," Barry says.

"It was easy," Gary says—if he's even Gary. Maybe there isn't a Gary.

Anna comes up behind me. Vonzelle, too.

"They're babies," Anna says. "You didn't take them from their mother, did you?"

One of the Miller boys shrugs.

"That's awful!" Anna says.

My biceps ache, so I lower the box and rest one edge of it on my hip. The ducks flap about, and I glance down. Both of the yellow ducklings have orange bills, I notice, while the black one has a black bill. All of them have teeny webbed feet and bright, inquisitive eyes. The black one looks up at me and quacks, though it's more of a squeak-quack. A squack.

"We got them for Brad's python, but we gave them to you instead," Barry says.

"'Cause you're hot chicks," pipes up the youngest Miller boy, who's about five. "Hot chicks for hot chicks."

"They're *not*—" I close my mouth. Why bother?

"Come on," Vonzelle says, touching my elbow. "We can't give them back to these jerks."

She's right, of course. My stomach is a tight ball as the three of us head for the house.

"I'll call Brad if you want!" Barry yells to our backs. "I'm sure his python is still hungry!"

Inside, I set the box in the hall. I crouch beside it, and Vonzelle and Anna join me. We look at the ducks.

"So what do we do with them?" I ask.

Anna strokes one of the yellow ones. "Oh, you're so soft," she says. "Hi, baby. Don't worry, we're not going to let you be eaten by a python."

"Can you take them back to the Duck Pond or wherever?" Vonzelle asks.

"I don't know. What if they're like baby birds? What if their mom rejects them now that they've been touched by humans?"

Anna jerks her hand away.

"I meant the Miller boys," I tell her. "Obviously they touched them when they caught them."

"Who would do something like that?" Vonzelle asks, though we already know the answer.

"Back to the more pressing concern," I say. "What do we do with them?"

"We could send them to a poor family in China," Anna says. When I look at her, she shrugs. "What?"

"We are not the Heifer Project," I say, "and I highly doubt a flock of baby ducks would survive being shipped from Atlanta to China. If *three* even counts as a flock." I push myself up. "I'm going to call Animal Control, and Anna, why don't you get them some water. I don't know what ducks eat, do you?"

"Algae?" she suggests.

"Bugs?" Vonzelle tries.

The three of us look at one another. The absurdity of the situation creeps in, and Vonzelle giggles. "Where's your babysitter? Would she know what to do?"

This makes Anna and me giggle, and I say, "Yeah, right. She's probably up in my parents' room, going through my mom's makeup."

Vonzelle scoots closer to the box. "So we figure it out on our own. No big deal."

CHAPTER FORTY-SIX
LUCKY DUCK

Nina at Animal Control informs me that no, we can't take the ducklings back to the Duck Pond and drop them off.

"Eventually they can be returned to the pond," she says, "but
based on your description, they're too young to go back yet. It'll be
another couple of weeks before they can fend for themselves."

"Well, can you come get them?"

"Sorry, but we don't provide that service. I can direct you to a
Web site on caring for ducklings, if you'd like."

I wouldn't like that at all. I'd like her to come get the ducks and
care for them herself. "Are you sure you can't take them? What
about the Humane Society? Should I call them?"

"The Humane Society doesn't handle waterfowl." Her tone is de-
void of concern, and I wonder just how often she has to tell people
that "duck rescue" isn't a service that anyone in the city provides.

I'm flummoxed. *I've got people coming over tonight!* I want to tell
her. *Cute people! Cole people!*

Instead, I sigh and say, "Fine. Give me the address of the Web
site."

What I learn isn't much. The first thing we do is move the ducks to my bathtub, where there's less chance of them escaping and where it's easier to clean up their poop, which is sticky and doesn't play well with cardboard. Then we give them names. Bonding is important, the Web site says. Ducks need attention and affection.

The black duck we name "Beans," because it seems to fit him. I say "him," but my research teaches me that we won't know if our ducklings are male or female until they're older. I don't know what that means. Will they suddenly sprout (or fail to sprout) little duck penises? But Beans is a multigender name, as is Dandelion, the larger of the two yellow ducklings. Vonzelle picked his/her name based on his/her sweet yellow chest fuzzies.

Voodoo Baby works either way, too, though we think she's a girl. I wanted to name her Ducky-Wucky, but I was outvoted, and the look Anna shot me dissuaded me from pursuing it. So we named her Voodoo Baby, which was Anna's choice. Voodoo Baby is the smallest of the three, and when she gets scared, which is often, she lifts her bitsy wing nubs, takes tiny steps backward, and tries to hiss. It's like she's trying to put a spell on us.

I tell Anna and Vonzelle not to fill the tub with water, even just an inch. The tub will have to serve as their cage until we build them a better one, and their cage needs to be dry. I find the plastic bucket Tracy uses when she mops and bring it upstairs for them to swim in. I fill it up, and we let each duck have a turn paddling about. Then we put the ducks back in the tub.

"Hey!" Vonzelle cries, jerking back her hand after Beans nips her.

"That means he likes you," I say. "It's how ducks kiss."

"You are so full of it."

"No, it's true."

"For real?" She hesitates, then pets Beans's back. This time when he nips her, she says, "Well, what do you know? I am loved by ducks."

"Actually, I lied. It means he thinks you're a duck. Perhaps you smell swampy."

She swats me.

"Kidding!" I say. "*Kid*ding. But it's time to stop playing with them, anyway. Tracy said she'd take us to Peachtree Battle Shopping Center to get the stuff we need." I tick items off on my fingers. "Materials to build a hutch. Pea gravel for them to poop in. Purina Wild Bird Chow. A bowl for water."

"I'll stay here and get started on our brownies," Anna says. She puts her hands on her thighs and pushes herself up.

"Excellent idea," I say, my heart fluttering at the realization of, *Yikes, she still thinks we're chowing down on brownies while bonding with Rory and Lorelei.* I need to tell her about the change in plans. I need to tell Vonzelle, too.

I work up a supercasual tone and say, "Oh, and, um, Cole and Roger might come by, 'kay?"

They stare at me.

"I mean, they might not." I swallow. "But . . . they might."

"Oh, Carly, yay!" Anna says, and I want to hug her for being such a good sister. "That'll be so fun. I'll put extra chocolate chips in the brownies."

"When did you invite them?" Vonzelle asks. She is less thrilled than Anna. "And why didn't you tell us?"

"I just *did* tell you," I say. I head out of my room and call, "Tracy! We're ready for you to drive us to Peachtree Battle!"

"Two minutes!" Tracy hollers from Mom and Dad's master suite.

"Only I still think you should forget about Cole and go for Roger," Anna says as we go downstairs. "Don't you agree, Vonzelle? Don't you think Roger should be Carly's love boodle?"

"I do," Vonzelle replies, as if I'm not right there with them. "Cole is all wrong for her."

"Could we stop talking about it?" I suggest. But since I'm not part of the "we," they ignore me.

"I keep telling her to wake up and smell the Dutch-grown coffee," Vonzelle says.

"*Ew,*" I say. "I'm not smelling Roger's coffee. That's gross."

Vonzelle leans against the kitchen table. "The happy ending is right there in front of her."

"The happy *beginning*," Anna clarifies. "And I know. I think so, too!"

Yay for Anna and Vonzelle bonding! Wh-hoo! But enough is enough. I elbow in and give a single, sharp clap of my hands.

"Okeydokey!" I say when they jump. "Moving on!"

"Here I am," Tracy says, strutting into the kitchen. I have never been happier to see her.

"Tracy, this is Vonzelle," I say. "Vonzelle, Tracy."

"Nice to meet you," Vonzelle says.

"Likewise," Tracy says.

"Tracy's cousin's in jail," Anna contributes, and my jaw drops. Tracy, however, is unfazed.

"Oh yeah," she says. "He got the good jail, though. Everyone says he's really lucky. On his first day, this big black guy pulled him over—scared the shit out of Jimmy—and was like, 'Don't worry. Everyone here's a Christian. The screwups, they get sent to the state prison, but everyone here knows how to behave.'"

"Huh," Vonzelle says.

Anna giggles.

"Now he's going all preacher on me," Tracy goes on. "Doesn't drink, doesn't swear, doesn't party."

"How could he do any of that in jail, anyway?" I ask.

"That's what I said," Tracy replies. "Says he's studying ministry now. Whatever. He wants me to call him all the time because he's only allowed one call a week, but I'm like, 'Sorry, Jimmy. I don't want no hundred-dollar phone bill.'"

"What did Jimmy say to that?" Vonzelle asks.

"He said, 'It's not my fault I'm in here.' And I said, 'Uh, yeah,

Jimmy, actually it is.'" Tracy looks at me and raises her plucked eyebrows. "You think it'd be okay if we took the Jag?"

"The Jag?"

"To Peachtree Battle. It'd be so crowded in my Pinto."

I am positive, without a single shred of doubt, that it would *not* be okay to take Dad's Jaguar. And yet, as Tracy waits expectantly in her tight green shirt with the shamrock on it, I hear myself say, "Um . . . I guess."

"Nice," Tracy says. She knows right where the key is kept, and she strolls to the ceramic bowl by the phone and snares it, twirling the sterling ring it's attached to on her index finger.

As we cruise through the neighborhood, Tracy treats us to a running commentary about what her cousin would think of Dad's Jag.

"I mean, *dang*, this car's nicer than Jimmy's apartment. You could live in this thing." She experiments with the dashboard controls. "Is there a seat warmer? Jimmy rode in a car with a seat warmer once. Said it was like his own personal butt spa." She pulls onto West Wesley, zooms down the hill, and guns the engine to make it through a yellow light. She kisses her palm and smacks it on the roof of the car.

"Tracy?" I say. We're rapidly approaching the shopping center. "There's the . . . don't miss the . . ."

She careens into the parking lot, and I'm thrown against the door. She laughs. "You think I don't know how to get here? Carly, who do you think runs to the A&P and gets more Greased Lightning when the spray bottle runs out?"

Chuckling to herself, she pulls up in front of Ace Hardware. "How long y'all need? An hour? Two hours?"

"Um, an hour'll be fine," I say. Vonzelle climbs out of the back looking woozy.

"Let's make it two," Tracy says breezily. "I'm going to my girlfriend Pammy's place to show off my wheels. Bye!"

She peels away.

"Oh," I say. "Uh, okay."

"Farewell, Jaguar," Vonzelle says. "It was nice knowing you."

"Oh my God," I say. "Please let her come back with Dad's Jaguar."

"If not, he can always have her Pinto."

"The Pinto. Right. Dad would love the Pinto."

"So," Vonzelle says. "Let's go get pea gravel."

We purchase everything in under an hour. I call Tracy's cell so she can come get us, but she doesn't answer. Great. I call two more times, and then we walk to Cloud Nine and get walk-in appointments for manicures.

"Might as well make use of the time," I say.

"Might as well doll yourself up for Cole, you mean," Vonzelle replies. "For the record, Roger likes girls who are real."

"Cole likes girls who are real," I argue.

"Maybe so, but he *kisses* girls who do their nails. Roger, on the other hand, would kiss you no matter what."

"There's nothing wrong with pretty nails," I say, and it's freaky, because I hear Mom coming through my vocal cords.

"I'm just saying," Vonzelle says.

Kim-Hue calls me to her station while Vonzelle is set up with a nail technician named Sally.

"So? How are things?" Kim-Hue asks. She indicates that I should take off my rings and my watch and put them in the little bowl.

"They're good."

"Your parents?"

"Good."

"And Anna? How is she?"

"She's good, too."

Kim-Hue guides my hands into the bowl of warm water with smooth pebbles at the bottom. She crosses her legs, and I catch a glimpse of her feet. She's wearing sexy high-heeled sling backs, the sort of shoes Trista might wear.

"Nice shoes," I say.

"You like them?"

"Well, yeah. For you, not for me."

She pulls my left hand out and pats it dry. "Why not for you?"

"I'm horrible with high heels." She rubs lotion up and down my forearm. I make an *mmm* sound, because I love this part. "I can't walk in them to save my life, and they hurt my feet. Don't they hurt your feet?"

"They do. It's terrible," Kim-Hue says. "By the end of the day, all I want to do is take them off."

"So why do you wear them? You should wear comfortable shoes, like these." I stretch my leg to show her my black sneaker.

"Oh, I could never wear shoes like that," Kim-Hue says. "I'm too short."

"Too short to wear sneakers?" I don't get it. "I'm short. I wear them."

"Because you are brave. You don't care what anyone thinks— like with your hair."

I blush. "Actually, I'm probably going to turn my hair back to its normal color. It's got to be healthy enough by now to redye, don't you think?"

She studies my hair. In addition to the goldish layer and the red layer, I've got at least two inches of brown roots.

"Maybe mix and match," she says. "Maybe add some chunks of brown, but leave some blond and red, too. It suits you."

"It does?"

Kim-Hue smiles. She slides a heated mitt onto my left hand and goes to work on my right. "You've put on weight since your wilderness adventure."

"I have?"

"You look very pretty. Don't get skinny again."

"But . . ." I don't finish my sentence. First she tells me I'm fat, then she tells me I'm pretty?

"You eat more, perhaps you will grow to be like Anna," Kim-Hue says. She cups both hands in front of her chest, the universal symbol for big bazooms.

"I don't want to be like Anna," I say.

"No?" she says quizzically.

"No," I insist.

"Anna wants to be like you," Kim-Hue says, as if it's fact.

"What are you talking about? No, she doesn't."

"All little sisters want to be like their big sisters," she states. "My little sister, Linh , , , don't you think she wants to be like me?"

"But Linh's not a manicurist. She's going to college." I blush, realizing how that sounds. "Sorry."

Kim-Hue isn't offended. "Little sisters want to be better than their big sisters. Everything the big sister has, the little sister wants— and more."

"That's creepy and disturbing."

Kim-Hue laughs. "But think: Without the big sisters, where would the little sisters be? Nowhere." She pats my right hand to tell me it's time to put it in the hot mitt, and eases my left hand back into the world. The air on my skin is cool.

"Have you chosen your color?" she asks.

I was planning on purple. I was. Yet the word that comes out of my mouth is "pink."

CHAPTER FORTY-SEVEN
TRACY IS SO HILARIOUS

"Where is she?" Vonzelle asks, scanning the parking lot for Tracy. I scan, too. No black Jaguar. "Do you think she came and left?"

"She better not have," I say. Careful of my pearly-pink nails, I put down the bag from Ace Hardware.

Vonzelle is dubious. "Call her."

"Again?"

"Call Anna and see if she's at the house."

I look around. It's full-on twilight, and the scattered cars cast spooky shadows. Where the heck *is* she? She wouldn't truly have abandoned us, would she?

I pull out my cell, open it, and hit speed dial two. I get Mom's overly formal message: *You have reached the Lauderdale residence. Please leave your number, and we'll be happy to call you back.*

"Anna, call me," I say curtly, then flip it shut.

"Voice mail?" Vonzelle asks.

"Voice mail."

Vonzelle puts down the bag with the duck food in it. I'm annoyed with Anna for not answering the phone, I'm anxious that Roger and Cole might get to the house before we do, and I'm absolutely furious at Tracy for not showing up. I'm also worried that Vonzelle is irritated with me for getting us into this.

Irrationally, the possibility of Vonzelle being irritated with me makes *me* irritated at *her*. Plus there's the fact that I haven't yet told her about Peyton and Lydia. That's adding to my stress level, too.

My cell rings, and I think, *Anna, thank God.* But when I flip it back open, the caller ID says *Peyton*.

Well, here we go, I think. I hit the talk button and say, "Peyton?"

Vonzelle's eyebrows shoot up. I angle my body away from her.

"Where are you guys?" Peyton says. There's music and voices behind her. "Are y'all *still* out shopping?"

"Where are *you?*"

"At your house. Duh. Cole and Roger are here, too."

"And Lydia!" I hear in the background.

Peyton giggles. "Oh, yeah. And Lydia. She's wearing a shirt that makes her look like the Chiquita banana lady."

"Nuh-*uh!*" Lydia says. Then more giggles from Peyton, loud enough that I'm sure Vonzelle can hear.

"Is Tracy there?" I ask tensely.

"Yeah, she's here. She is so hilarious."

I don't like the sound of that—*and* I'm pissed that Tracy's there and not here. "How is she hilarious?"

"I don't know. Just, *Oh, look, teenagers drinking wine coolers. Got enough to share?* So I gave her a four-pack, and she disappeared upstairs."

"You have *wine* coolers?"

"Relax," she says in a tone that makes me anything but relaxed. It's a tone that says, *Carly, you're overreacting.* But I'm *not* overreacting. She's living it up in my house while I'm stuck in the Peachtree Battle parking lot. She's being all cool-relaxed-Peyton in front of

Cole, who's no doubt hearing her end of the conversation and thinking how un-cool-and-relaxed I am. But Peyton's not cool. Peyton's a giggler. And *wine* coolers???

"They're, like, four percent alcohol," Peyton says. "Just get here, okay? I want you to see my extensions."

"Let me speak to Anna."

"Got to go—someone's at the door. Bye!"

I close my phone. I turn to Vonzelle, feeling defensive before she says a word. I am a slab of fudge slowly hardening as it cools, only minus any sweetness.

"Peyton's at your house?" Vonzelle asks.

"Anna told her our parents were going to be out of town," I say. "She basically invited herself." I jut my chin. "And then Peyton invited Cole and Roger, pretty much."

"And they're drinking?"

"Apparently." *And so is Tracy.*

Vonzelle appraises me. "You seem really angry."

"Well, I'm not."

She doesn't believe me. Well, fine. I don't believe me, either. I wish I could say that to Vonzelle. I wish I could just open my heart and say, *God, this sucks, I'm sorry.* But I can't. My insides have locked up.

"Is anyone coming to get us?" she asks.

"No, we have to walk." I pick up my bag, and my fingernail grazes one of the pieces of plywood. The polish smears.

I start across the parking lot. Vonzelle doesn't immediately follow, and I'm sure she's wishing she never said she'd spend the night. But I don't know how to make things better. Or maybe I'm too wound up inside to make things better. Either way, "better" is out of my reach.

CHAPTER FORTY-EIGHT
HARD CANDY

It's a long walk home, most of it uphill, and my arms are killing me before we're halfway there. I've got the heaviest and most awkward load, but I don't ask Vonzelle to switch with me, and she doesn't offer. In fact, we don't talk at all. We just walk. We walk the way Mom does on her power walks, only I'm fueled by anger rather than the desire to burn calories. I don't know about Vonzelle.

As we approach my driveway, my anxiety level spikes. There are multiple cars parked along the street, and three lined up in the driveway niche in front of the house. One is Roger's mom's station wagon, which Roger drives when he doesn't take his motorcycle. One is a black BMW convertible. The third is a sky-blue Karmann Ghia that I think belongs to a Holy Roller senior.

Through the windows, I see kids I don't know. My heart thrums.

"Did you invite these people?" Vonzelle says.

"Are you kidding?" I say, giving her a sharp look.

She shoots me an equally sharp look in return. "Well, you invited other people without telling me."

God, I need to stop taking it out on her. "I know," I mutter. "Sorry."

Her expression hardly changes. As I stride toward the front door, I think, *I am going to kill Anna. Anna. Is. Dead.*

Inside is chaos. Music throbs against my eardrums—guess someone found Dad's stereo system with full-house surround sound. Mixed in with the music are raucous people sounds, like laughter and "Dude!"s and a chanted countdown coming from the kitchen.

In the den I find Derek from my math class watching the Sports Network on the flat screen with Chuck, whose Hummer I rode in when we delivered stockings.

"Carly!" Chuck calls. "Big ups on the party, babe!"

"Please take your feet off the coffee table," I say.

He grins, but complies.

"And you have to use coasters. God."

"Coasters?"

I put down my Ace Hardware bag, march into the room, and grab the leather case of coasters from the mantel over the fireplace. I smack two Indian-themed coasters onto the coffee table and set each boy's beer on one.

Where did the beer come from? Wine coolers *and* beer? Crap, crap, crap.

I try to hide my shakiness as I leave the den. Vonzelle and I stare at each other, and we drop our anger. The fact that there is a full-on party happening requires us to join forces.

"Come on," she says. "We better see how bad it is." She puts her duck-food bag next to mine and uses her foot to push both bags against the wall of the entryway.

In the living room we see several junior girls drinking Dad's brandy from his brandy snifters.

"What is *wrong* with y'all?" I say, going over and grabbing the brandy. I put it back on the shelf and leave the room. Seconds later, I hear them burst out laughing.

"More brandy, please, Lola," one of the girls says.

Giggling-bumping sounds tell me Lola's getting it down again, and I curse my stupidity. I should have taken it with me. I should have hidden it.

In the kitchen, I find Anna, Peyton, Cole, Roger, Lydia, and Trista. *Trista?!* What is she doing here? But back to Trista later, because my eyes can't help but return to Peyton. Her blond hair reaches her butt. It used to reach midway down her back, and now she can sit on it. She *is* sitting on it, looking proud.

"What do you think, Carly?" she says. She lifts her butt, frees the ends with a swipe of her hands, and flips her movie-star hair the way a movie star very well might.

"She got extensions," Lydia says. Her irises are glazed, and I think, *Since when did "I'll pray for you" Lydia start drinking?* "Doesn't she look glamorous?"

She does look glamorous . . . but she's got someone else's hair glued to her head. Does no one but me find this unnatural? Not to mention that in India, where the donated hair comes from, I'm pretty sure the women aren't blond. No blond religious pilgrims, which means the monks or whoever must have taken some Indian woman's shaved-off dark hair and processed it to make it Caucasian pale.

"It took for-frickin'-ever," Peyton says. "I have to use this special brush now, and I can't get my hair wet for three days." She giggles and casts her eyes at Cole. "Guess I'll have to get someone to give me a sponge bath."

Ugh. Enough. I glance around the kitchen table and take in the whole of what's going on. Peyton is on one side of Cole, while Trista's on the other. There is a heaping plate of brownies in front of them. Anna, I realize, is wearing my potato-print peace shirt. It's snug and looks way better on her than it ever looked on me.

"Anna?" I say dangerously.

She smiles brightly. Too brightly. "Carly! You're here!"

"You're wearing my shirt." I can't believe that of all the things I could say, this is what comes out of my mouth. But it is.

"Is that all right? I didn't think you'd mind."

Well, I do, I think.

"I'll change if you want," she tacks on.

"No, it's fine," I say shortly. Like I'm really going to tell her in front of Cole and everyone else that she can't borrow a stupid shirt. I shoot beams of fury at her. She looks confused.

"Hey, Carly," Cole says. He grins and lifts his beer in welcome. "Come. Sit."

"No thanks," I say. How can he be so . . . at ease? Does he not get—or *care*—that this is my house and I didn't invite these people and maybe, just maybe, I don't want to "come sit" like an obedient puppy?

"I'm having a Coke," Roger says. I give him the briefest of glances. His Adam's apple jerks. "Want me to get you one?"

I don't respond. My eyes go to Trista, whose body language suggests that she doesn't want to be here any more than I want her here.

"Anna, I need to talk to you," I say.

Anna rises from her chair. She hesitates.

"Now," I say.

Vonzelle says, "I'll go check on the ducks," and leaves the room.

I go to the far end of the kitchen, over by the back door. Anna joins me, gnawing her lip. The kitchen-table crew goes back to whatever drinking game they're playing, and they're noisy enough that we can talk without being overheard.

"What the hell?" I say to her.

"I didn't know what to do."

"I am so mad at you, Anna. I am *so* mad."

She blanches. "At *me*? Why are you mad at me?"

"Don't," I say. I can barely stand to look at her. "God, Anna. Do you know we could be expelled for this?" Holy Redeemer has a strict student conduct policy, and students can be punished even for offenses that occur off school property.

Her shoulders hitch up. "*I* didn't invite all these people. Why are you acting like this is my fault?"

"Why is Trista here?" I say in a low voice.

"I don't *know*," Anna says. She tries to get me to look at her, but I refuse. "Carly, I did *not* invite these people."

"But you invited Peyton, which is the same thing."

"No, I didn't," she says.

"*Fine*. But you told her Mom and Dad were going out of town, which is the same thing."

She looks scared. Caught out. "I didn't tell Peyton anything. I swear."

"Why are you lying? Stop being such a baby and just own up to it."

"Carly—"

"No, seriously, Anna. You tell me I'm not allowed to call you my little sister since you're such a *big girl* now." I say "a big girl" in a tone loaded with sarcasm, and hurt registers in her eyes.

"But guess what?" I go on. "Just because your boobs are all grown up doesn't mean *you* are. And for the record, you look like—" I press my lips together, because I want to say *a slut*. I want to call my sister a slut. "You look like trash in my shirt. It's way too tight."

The way she draws back makes my gut cramp. But I remind myself that she brought it on herself. I can't maintain eye contact, so I glance back at the kitchen table. Peyton is in high flirt mode, with rosy cheeks and butt-length hair that she flips and flips. Trista doesn't like it. I don't, either.

"Screw you," Anna says, all at once tremblingly angry. She goes straight to the Sub-Zero and gets a wine cooler. She twists off the top and chugs it, challenging me with her gaze. She downs the whole thing.

"Oh, that's so mature," I hiss. "That's really the way to prove you're grown-up, drinking wine coolers."

She acts as if I'm not there. She gets a second wine cooler, holds the refrigerator door open with her knee while she gets its cap off, and says, "Peyton? Trista? Anyone need another?"

"Heck yeah!" Peyton says. Then she sees my face. She gets concerned—or pretends to be concerned—and comes over. Her hair is longer than her skirt. How can she go to Tuesday-night Bible study and wear a skirt that short?

"What's going on?" she says. The scent of her Hard Candy perfume drips over me like apple-caramel syrup.

"Carly thinks I need a babysitter," Anna says. "She thinks everything she does is right, and everything I do is wrong. Oh, and she thinks I'm trash."

Peyton's eyes widen.

"I didn't say—" I break off, wrapping my arms around my ribs. I am so over both of them. I mean, God. Peyton used to chuck golf balls into the bathtub with me to crack their outer shells, so we could find the vinegar-smelling cores inside. And now she's giving my sister wine coolers and flirting with the boy she *knows* I like?

Anna gulps her wine cooler.

"Is something wrong, Carly?" Peyton says. "Are you all right?"

Just shut up, I tell her in my mind. She is so fake. "I'm fine. Go back to your friends. Have fun."

"Are you having opinions again, Carly?" she says. "Are we breaking Carly's Rules of Life by engaging in *underage drinking*?" She uses air quotes to be funny.

I don't laugh. She rolls her eyes.

"JK. LOL. *Enter*," she says. "God, Carly." She turns to the table. "You guys, Carly's mad. She thinks we're corrupting her sister."

"Naw, man, your sister's awesome," Cole says. His words are slightly slurred. "She's a babe, Carls. She made us brownies."

She's a babe? She made us brownies? And this is supposed to make things better how?!

"We're not corrupting you, don't worry," Peyton says to Anna, putting her arm around her.

"I know," Anna says. She rests her head on Peyton's shoulders because they're wine-cooler buddies now. Yippee for them.

My glance chances upon Trista, who's holding Cole's arm and not smiling. She's not eating a brownie, either.

"Where's Tracy?" I ask Anna frostily.

Anna takes a gulp of her second wine cooler.

"She's upstairs in your parents' bedroom," Peyton says. She giggles. "She's drunk."

I leave the kitchen, half aware of Roger following me. In the dining room, some guy is standing on our ten-foot-long mahogany table, reaching for the teardrop pendant at the bottom of the Waterford chandelier.

"Get off the table," Roger says in disgust.

The guy sees us. "Heyyyy," he says. "You're Roger, right? I know you."

"Oh my God," I say.

"Get off the table," Roger commands.

"Dude," the guy says, holding up his hands. He hops off the table, trips, and laughs. "Ow. That hurt like *shit.*"

A senior named Travis barges through the front door. "Keg's here!" he heralds.

A keg? I lean on the dining-room table. I try to breathe.

"No keg," Roger says. Out of the corner of my eye, I see him stride to the entry hall and turn Travis around. "Wrong house, buddy."

"But—"

"Wrong house," Roger repeats. He's a foot taller than Travis, and he pushes Travis out the door.

"I've got to sit down," I say to myself. "I've got to get out of here."

"*Yes!*" someone crows in the kitchen, and there's the scuffling of chairs being pushed back. Peyton runs through the dining room with Anna. They're flushed. They're each holding a brown leather boot, and, laughing hysterically, they dash upstairs.

"Don't worry, Tris," Cole says, emerging from the kitchen. "I'll get them." He grins at me and shakes his head. "They stole Trista's boots."

"Why?" I say dumbly.

"Now, that's the mystery, isn't it?" Cole says, amused. He saunters through the dining room.

Roger comes to me. "You okay?"

I shake my head.

He looks at me. I don't look at him.

"Want me to kick everyone out?"

I say nothing.

"I'm going to kick everyone out," he states. A second or two ticks by. "Carly?"

"I'm going to have some alone time," I say. I'm pretty much having an out-of-body experience. I climb the stairs mechanically. At the far end of the hall, I see Vonzelle pounding on the door to Mom and Dad's suite.

"Tracy!" she calls. "*Tra*-cy!"

I go to my room and lock the door. I sit on the edge of my bed. I gaze at nothing. After a few moments, I rise, walk around the bed, and go into my bathroom.

"Hi, ducks," I say, kneeling by the tub. "Beans. Dandelion. Voodoo Baby."

Beans quacks, and I stroke his little head. His eyes are bright black seeds.

Voodoo Baby cautiously approaches. She pulls her wings back, but she doesn't hiss. She steps an inch closer, and I realize she *wants* attention, she just doesn't know how to ask for it without coming across all voodoo-freaky. Poor little thing.

"Come here, Voodoo." I cup her in my hand, and her tiny wings flap crazily. "It's okay," I tell her. "You're okay. You're a duck, and you're okay."

I keep my hands firmly around her body. I feel her heartbeat. I notice oily flakes beneath her fluff-feathers, and I push the feathers around to check it out.

"You need a bath," I say. "You're all scaly."

I put Voodoo Baby back in the tub and grab the plastic bucket. I fill it with water from the sink, making sure it's neither too hot nor too cool, and try to lose myself in the chore-ness of it. Because ducks need water. Ducks need to bob about and do happy duck things. Anna can get wasted and stupid, see if I care. I'm going to let Voodoo Baby take a dip.

"Come on," I say. I lower her into the water, and she flaps her wings and paddles about. She swims from one side of the bucket to the other, and she is *happy*. She is. The pleasure I feel is fierce—and not exactly pleasurable, to tell the truth—but this dumb duck is happy, so there.

I watch her for a bit. Then I stretch out on my blue fluffy bath mat and stare at the ceiling. I drape my right hand over the top of the bucket and dangle my fingers in the water to let Voodoo Baby know I'm still here. A few moments later, I feel an exploratory nibble. Tears well in my eyes.

I lie like that for a long time . . . but not long enough. Someone raps on my bedroom door, and I hear Roger call, "Carly? You in there?"

Can I not answer? Can I just hide with the ducks all night and let everyone fend for themselves?

"Carly, Chuck peed in your living room."

I scramble to my feet. "What?!"

"He peed. On the wall."

I hurry from the bathroom and open my door. From downstairs, I hear some guy say, "Chuck! *Dude!*"

"I thought you were going to kick everyone out!" I say to Roger.

"I didn't know if you wanted me to."

"Obviously!" I snap. I push past him and storm downstairs. I stride into the living room, and there is *pee* on the wall, and Chuck is zipping up his frickin' pants.

"Sorry, man," he slurs. "Where's the john?"

His friends think this is the best show in town. Derek is doubled over with hilarity.

"Get out of my house," I say. My voice is shrill.

Drunk Chuck comes over to me and slings his arm around me. "Aw, baby, don't be like that."

I shove him off. "The party is *over*. Everybody leave."

Nobody leaves.

"Now!" I bark. "Get. Out. *Now!*" They stare at me like I'm a talking puppy, a curiosity, and I throw back my head, close my eyes, and SCREAM.

I hear commotion. I hear some guy say, "Dude, bitch needs her meds."

"Give her some Midol, man," another guy says. "She is majorly on the rag."

"You heard her," Roger says in his deep voice. Usually it's a gentle deep voice. Now it's an intimidating deep voice. *"Out."*

When I open my eyes, Roger is shoving Chuck toward the front door. I watch mutely as he herds Derek and the junior guys out. Then the brandy girls, one of whom keeps trying to persuade Roger that she *can't* leave because she lost her *ear*ring and it's her *favorite*.

"Bye," Roger says. "*Vaarwel.* Don't come back."

"Where's Peyton?" I ask him. "Where's Vonzelle?"

"Someone puked in the kitchen. Vonzelle's cleaning it up."

I absorb this, and I wish I could feel grateful. Instead, I say, "What about Peyton? Where's Peyton—and for that matter, where's Cole?"

Roger looks at me the way he always does when I mention Cole. Like I'm letting him down.

"No," I say, my hands curling into fists. "You can't make me feel like I'm the jerk here."

He walks over to me, closer and closer until he's *right there.* He looks directly into my eyes. "Carly . . ."

My heart is all of a sudden pounding.

"Do you remember when you said sixties music was an acquired taste?"

"No." *Maybe.*

"Well, maybe I'm an acquired taste, too."

I swallow. I kind of can't believe he's saying this.

"I don't play the guitar," he goes on. "I don't have soulful eyes, and I'm not good at cool remarks."

My palms are sweating, and he *does* have soulful eyes. Soulful brown eyes that are making my body respond in an extremely unexpected manner. "Roger . . ."

"When you figure it out, I'm here," he says. "I will always be here."

His words strip me bare, and what's underneath scares the heck out of me. Roger must see a bit of this, because his expression changes. It goes from solemn to surprised, from surprised to hopeful—and his hope is so raw I can't take it.

"If Peyton's with Cole, I'm going to kill her," I say. "She *knows* how much I like Cole. She *knows* he's mine."

It's like I've punched him. I have to leave, I have to stop seeing his wounded eyes, so I turn on my heel and jog upstairs. I look in my room—no Peyton. I go to Anna's room. The door is closed, and my breath grows shallow. I twist the knob and burst in, and Cole is in bed with Peyton, only it isn't Peyton—it's Anna. Anna is with Cole. Anna is with Cole, and Cole is on top of her. His lips are on hers and his hand is under her shirt, except it's not her shirt. It's my shirt. His hand is under my shirt, which is on my sister.

Cole startles at the sound that comes out of me. Anna looks up, blinks, and gives a confused, swollen-lipped smile.

"Hi, Carly," she says. She giggles.

"Get out of my house," I tell Cole.

"Carly, babe, relax."

"Get out of my house and out of my life," I say furiously.

He slides off Anna and off her bed. He looks at me, not her, and rakes his hand through his hair. "There's no reason to tell Trista, you know."

I don't reply.

"Carly?" Anna says.

I start to cry, and I don't want anyone to see, so I go into the hall. My sobs rip through me. I can taste the salt of my snot.

"Carly, what's wrong?" Vonzelle calls. She's at the bottom of the stairs. She starts up at a jog, but I can't handle human contact right now. I retreat to my room, close the door, and go to be with my ducks, who love me. Who don't betray me. Who would *never* kiss the asshole boy I thought I liked.

In my bathroom, I drop to my knees. "Hey, guys," I say through my tears. "Humans suck—did you know that? Take it from me, be glad you're ducks."

In the tub, Dandelion looks at me. Beans cocks his head and quacks.

"Yeah," I say. I scoot on my knees toward the bucket, where Voodoo Baby's been living the good life. "You hear that, Voodoo Baby? Be glad you're a duck, even if you have to eat bugs."

Voodoo Baby doesn't respond, because Voodoo Baby is floating sideways on the surface of the water. *Oh my God.* Nausea churns my stomach, because ducks don't float sideways on the surface of the water. Ducks don't slosh when someone grabs the bucket and shakes it.

Dimly, I register the sound of my bedroom door being opened. "Carly?" Vonzelle says.

I nudge Voodoo Baby's tiny body. Her body moves, but not in the right way. It moves in the wrongest way possible, and my eyes fill so that I can hardly see. I have a hard time breathing, too.

Vonzelle's feet appear beside me. "Carly, what happened?"

Then Anna's feet join the party. Hers are bare. Bare, naked feet with ugly pink polish.

"I killed Voodoo Baby," I tell them, lifting my head. Tears streak down my face, but my voice is distant and weird. I focus on Anna, who's swaying. "No, I take that back. *You* killed Voodoo Baby."

She starts crying.

"Oh, and I hate you," I add. "I really, really do."

"Don't say that," she says, drunk and beautiful and sobbing. "You can't hate me. You're my *sister.*"

There are things called tears running down my face, but they're something apart from me. I gaze at her dispassionately, and it scares her. I'm neither glad nor un-glad. I'm nothing.

"Carly?" she whispers.

"I used to be your sister," I say slowly. "But see, here's something interesting. Can I tell you something interesting?"

"Carly," Vonzelle says, meaning *stop it* and *don't* and *this isn't you.*

Anna's a gasping mess. She really is such a mess, and when she reaches to touch me, I shake her off.

"I no longer want the job," I say.

CHAPTER FORTY-NINE
BYE-BYE BIRDIE

I wrap Voodoo Baby's weightless body in a washcloth. I walk past Vonzelle and Anna, angling my body so that I don't touch either of them. There is to be no touching. I can hear Vonzelle's words, Anna's hysterics—how *sloppy* she is, how embarrassingly out of control—but all of that is outside of me. I'm outside of me, too.

I go downstairs, down the hall, through the entryway. Out the door. Cold air tries to chill me, but fails, because I'm already cold to the core. As I walk, one phrase loops continuously in my brain: *Anna sucks, Anna sucks, Anna sucks.*

By the time I reach the Duck Pond, I've begun—ironically—to thaw. My body's still cold, but my heart can't help but pump, and the *blood* inside me is warm. Deadness, it seems, can't last in a still-alive body. That sucks, too.

Other thoughts filter in, such as the realization that actually, Cole sucks. Not instead of Anna, because Anna also sucks. But *Cole has a girlfriend, or had a girlfriend, and he cheated on her. And not with me.*

Clearly, I am as sucky as they come.

I bury Voodoo Baby on the shore of the pond. The other ducks are sleeping, but they'll wake up. Voodoo Baby won't. I imagine her paddling about in the bucket. Paddling and happy, and then not so happy. Wanting to paddle harder, but unable to. Wanting out, but unable to get out. No duckling-size lifesaver tossed her way.

A fresh wave of crying racks my body.

"I'm sorry, Voodoo Baby," I say. The sobs ripping out of me are grotesque, and I'm as ugly as Anna, I'm sure of it.

No, uglier.

At some point, the sobs change to gulps, the gulps change to hitchy, sniffly inhales. I'm all cried out. I sit there for a while, and then I rise from the shore, say good-bye to Voodoo Baby, and start for home. To my surprise, I want to *be* home. It's late, and it's dark, and I've come back to myself enough to know that I'm an idiot to be wandering the streets alone, because there are so many bad people in the world, even in wealthy Atlanta neighborhoods. There's so much badness, period.

As I approach my house, I see that there are no longer cars lining the street. Pete's Volvo is gone. The yellow Karmann Ghia is gone. The only car left is Roger's mom's station wagon.

Roger. My stomach plummets.

I enter the house through the front door, and Vonzelle almost immediately appears.

"Carly," she says. "Thank God." She hugs me full on.

I hug her back, close enough that our boobs squish together.

"Vonzelle . . ."

She twists her head over her shoulder. "She's here! She's safe!"

I glance toward the kitchen.

"Roger?" I say. My voice trembles, and Vonzelle's eyebrows go up.

I hear the back door open and shut.

Did he leave?

"Where *were* you?" Vonzelle demands, pulling my attention to her. "You scared the crap out of us."

"To bury Voodoo Baby," I say. "I left her alone in the water."

(*I* am *paddling. Then paddle harder!*)

My eyes burn, but I'm all dried up of tears. "I left her too long."

Vonzelle doesn't judge. She just looks sad.

I take a shuddery breath. I look around and say, "You cleaned up."

"Me and Roger," she says. She pauses. "He scrubbed Chuck's pee off the wall."

"Are you serious?"

"You don't think *I* was going to do it, do you?"

Outside, I hear Roger's station wagon start up. He scrubbed Chuck's pee off the wall for me, and now he's leaving. Why?

Because he's now disillusioned with me the way I'm disillusioned with Cole?

Vonzelle's cell phone rings. She fishes it out of her pocket. "Hey, Roger," she says. My pulse picks up. I also feel ill.

"Yeah," she says. "Okay, sure." She listens. "No problem. Bye."

She hangs up.

"What did he say?"

"He's glad you're okay."

"Did he . . . ask to talk to me?" I know the answer already. I just have to ask.

Vonzelle shakes her head. My lungs do something wrong and painful.

"Let's go upstairs," she says softly. "It's been a long night."

As I follow her to my room, I know there's something else I need to ask. I don't want to, but I make myself.

"So, um, where's Anna? Is she . . . okay?"

"She went to bed," Vonzelle says. Her eyes slide toward me. "She was kind of a wreck. She couldn't stop crying, and she wanted to go after you. But I didn't let her."

"Why not?" I say, thinking, *Anna could have stood a dose of anxious neighborhood wandering. It could have done her some good.*

"She was drunk, Carly."

Oh, I think. *Yeah.*

Vonzelle touches my arm. She lets her fingers linger, and then drops her hand.

CHAPTER FIFTY
DUCK, DUCK, GOOSE

I let Vonzelle have my bed. I sleep in the big claw-footed bath-tub with Beans and Dandelion. At first they don't know what to make of this, but eventually Beans gets up the nerve to investi-gate. He waddles up to me, cocking his head. I hold still. He pit-pats from one webbed foot to another. If he tries to nip me, I'll let him.

Instead, he settles himself in the crook of my arm. Soon, Dan-delion crowds in, too.

I'm sorry about your sister, I say in my mind. Do they know? Do they miss her?

They're just ducks.

My throat hurts.

Beans tucks his beak under his wing. Dandelion does the same thing. They breathe in sync, and it seems miraculous, their fragile chests rising and falling in harmony. I'm pretty sure they're asleep, and within seconds, I am, too.

———

In the morning, I feed Beans and Dandelion and give them water. Vonzelle's in my bed, not yet awake, and her mouth hangs open like a little kid's. I go into the hall, where I stand for several moments outside Anna's door. I think about how strange emotions are, because they're real, and they can be crazy-strong, but there's an ebb and flow to them that doesn't have a lot to do with personal choice. At least, that's how it works for me.

My fury at Anna, which last night crashed down and did its worst, has now retreated. I still ache inside, which proves the bad stuff happened. And I'm sure my anger will come again. But right now I'm barefoot on the damp stretch of sand left in its wake.

My love for Anna is stronger than my hate.

My love for Cole is gone, because if a guy turns out to be a jerk and not the person you thought he was, then you never were in love with him anyway. Not the real him.

I knock on Anna's door. She doesn't answer, so I twist the knob and go in. I'm hit with the memory of Anna and Cole glancing up at me in surprise, and God, it hurts.

"Anna?" I say, peering into the murky early-morning light.

She's not in her bed. I flip on the lights to make certain, but no, she's not there. *Huh.*

I go back into the hall. The door to my parents' master suite is closed, but I'm sure Anna's not in there with Tracy. Maybe she's downstairs? Maybe she crashed on a sofa, or maybe she's awake and having a Pop-Tart.

I go downstairs and peek into the living room. No Anna. Also, no pee stains. I still can't believe Chuck peed on the wall.

I go down the hall and look in the TV room, where Derek had his way with the flat screen. Two sofas, five throw pillows, one chrome-and-glass coffee table. No Anna.

I cut through the dining room, where the crystals of the Waterford chandelier cast flecks of light onto the wall. I enter the kitchen and say, "Anna?"

She's not there.

My skin starts to tingle. I head back through the lower level of the house, taking a closer look in all the rooms I've already searched. I don't find her this time, either. I spot Vonzelle at the top of the staircase and say, "Where's Anna?"

"She's not in her room?"

"She's not in her room *or* down here."

"Is it possible she's with Tracy?" Vonzelle asks dubiously.

I doubt it, but there's nothing to do but check. I take the stairs two at a time, and Vonzelle and I have to bam on the door to Mom and Dad's suite for a full five minutes before Tracy unlocks the dead bolt. She squints at us. She smells like sour wine coolers.

"What?" she says.

"Is Anna with you?" I demand.

"Is Anna with me?" she repeats, not seeming to understand the question. I interpret her confusion to mean, *Why would she be?* Either that, or *Who's Anna again?*

I push past her and check the bathroom, the bedroom, even Mom and Dad's huge walk-in closet.

"She's not here," Vonzelle says.

"Then where *is* she?" I cry. I dash back down the upstairs hallway. I lean over the railing and call, "Anna! An-na!"

"Why is she yelling?" I hear Tracy complain. "Crap, my head hurts."

"We can't find Anna," Vonzelle tells her.

"Huh? Why not?"

As Vonzelle explains, I check Anna's room again, as well as her bathroom. I check my room again, and my bathroom. She's not there. She's not anywhere. I even check the horrid, nasty basement that no one ever goes into because it's so mildewy and gross.

No Anna.

I hurry up the basement stairs and burst into the kitchen, where Vonzelle and Tracy stand by the island. Tracy's face is pale, like she's finally absorbed the fact that losing your employers' kid is not a good thing.

"Did you find her?" she asks.

I shake my head. "She's gone."

CHAPTER FIFTY-ONE

BEST SEAT IN THE HOUSE

Tracy hyperventilates, blabbering about how Mom and Dad will be here in an hour.

I hyperventilate, too. I replay my last words to Anna, when I told her I no longer wanted to be her sister. Who says something like that? Who is that heartless?

"She must have gone out," I say.

"Where?" Tracy says.

"And why hasn't she come back?" Vonzelle adds.

"I don't know—because she was drunk?" I say. "Maybe she passed out or something."

"She better not have," Tracy says. "If you're going to pass out, you got to do it somewhere safe, where no one can get at you."

Oh God, I think.

"And if you're hired to look after someone's kids, you should look after their frickin' kids," Vonzelle snaps. "Not get wasted on wine coolers in their parents' bedroom."

This shuts Tracy up. She turns a little green.

"I'm going to go look for her," I say.

"I'll come with you," Vonzelle says.

"No." I shove my feet into my black sneakers. "Somebody should be here if she comes back."

"I'm not 'somebody'?" Tracy says. "I'm nobody?"

I cross through the dining room and yank open the front door, Vonzelle and Tracy following on my heels.

"Should I call the police?" Tracy calls after me.

The police. Crap. Please don't let us need the police.

I stride down the driveway. Each second ticking by is one more second without my sister

bruised and bloodied joggers

drugged-out burglars with guns

a world without my sister

"Anna!" I call. The morning light is gray; no one is out except me. "Anna!"

If Dad were here, he'd know what to do. But Dad's not here. Dad left us in the care of Wine Cooler Tracy, so maybe he doesn't know everything after all.

I fast-walk down Woodward Way, calling out to my sister. Ten minutes and two blocks later, I still haven't found her. Should I go back home? Should I tell Tracy to call the police?

Fear is all there is inside me, and it's pinched and clenched in a cold, tight wad. I can't even breathe right. How can I think if I can't even breathe?

I stop. I close my eyes and try to *slow down* so that maybe I can let something else in besides my panic.

Please, God, I pray. *Please and please and please.*

I open my eyes and keep walking, silently saying *please* with every step.

Up ahead, a construction truck is parked half on the street and half on someone's lawn. The owners of the house are adding on some sort of addition. The construction's been going on for over a year. I spot a Porta Potti behind the construction truck, and sticking out from behind the Porta Potti is a foot. *A human foot.* A *naked* foot, connected to a leg. I grow so light-headed I see flashes.

"Anna?" I say. I run over. "Anna!"

Her body is curled in fetal position behind the Porta Potti, and I think, *Oh holy crap she's DEAD. My sister's dead my life is over my sister's dead.*

I shake her roughly. "Anna!"

She stirs. Her eyelids flutter.

"Carly?" she says. Her hair is matted on the side she's been lying on, and there's puke on her shirt. Or rather, *my* shirt.

I fling my arms around her. I hug her tighter than I've ever hugged anyone in my life.

"Ow, you're strangling me."

"You little *shit*," I say, squeezing harder. I'm smearing her nasty vomit all over both of us. "What the hell were you thinking?"

"I don't know," she says into my neck.

I release her. I drink her in. "You. Little. Shit."

"Stop calling me that." She hesitates, and then adds, "You big shit."

"Did you *want* to get raped?" I demand. "Did you *want* some random guy molesting you?"

She rolls her eyes, then presses her fingertips to her forehead. "Yeah, Carly. That's exactly what I wanted."

Her attitude brings my anger coursing back. "I guess so. And that's why you threw yourself into bed with Cole, huh?"

Tears fill her eyes. "Sometimes, Carly," she says deliberately, "you make me feel like nothing."

Sometimes, you make *me make you feel like nothing,* I think.

I press my lips together. The only thing to look at other than Anna is the Porta Potti, so I look at the Porta Potti. It's blue. It has white trim and a vent at the top.

"I can't be perfect like you," she goes on.

"You think I'm perfect? Please."

"Sometimes . . ." She doesn't continue.

"Sometimes what?"

"You're going to think I'm saying this to be mean, but I'm not."

My stomach knots up.

"Sometimes you treat me like Dad does, and I feel like I'm drowning." Her voice quavers at the end, and now tears well in *my* eyes, even though she has *no right* to put this on me. Am I just going to cry and cry for the rest of my life?

"I don't want you to drown," I say. *Do I really treat her like Dad does?*

"There's something else I need to tell you," she says.

"Great."

"I didn't invite Peyton to the party."

"*Jesus,* Anna," I say. "*Fine.* I'm technically the one who said the words 'Do you want to come?' But *you're* the one who told her Mom and Dad were going out of town. If you hadn't, she wouldn't have known, and I wouldn't have had to invite her." As I hear myself, I realize how lame that sounds. Did I *have* to invite her? No. *I* made my lips move. *I* spoke the words.

"I didn't tell Peyton about Mom and Dad going to New York," Anna insists.

I groan. Why is she denying it? What's to be gained at this point? She kissed Cole, I killed Voodoo Baby, we're both smeared with puke.

"Well, *I* didn't tell her," I say. "If I didn't tell her and you didn't tell her, then who did?"

"Carly, Peyton's mom teaches Mom's Nia class."

Oh.

"They see each other at the gym every day."

Oh again. I go back to studying the Porta Potti, which is really blue. And bright. It's a much brighter blue than I'd think. Is the goal to provide a cheerful place to pee? Or maybe it's blue to make people think of water, so that they *can* pee even though they're crammed into a teeny little pee house smack out in the world?

I turn to Anna, and it is a STRUGGLE, but I let go of (some of) my anger and (some of) my defensiveness and my need to always, always be right.

"I'm sorry," I say.

"Well, I am, too," she says quietly. I think she's going to leave it at that, but then an additional avalanche of words lands on top of me. "And Cole's a tool. And I was drunk, which was stupid, and I got puke on your shirt, and I'll wash it, I promise, and if it doesn't come out, I'll make you a new one. And I'm not exactly blaming *you*, but the only reason I got drunk in the first place was—"

"I know," I say. Heat rises in my cheeks. "You didn't look trashy. I was wrong to say that." I swallow. "You're not trash."

She nods.

"And you didn't kill Voodoo Baby," I say. It's awful, the pressure in my chest. "I did. I forgot about her."

"You didn't mean to," she says.

I shake my head. *No, I didn't mean to.*

Her features loosen, as if the worst of it's over now that we've both apologized.

"But back to Cole," I say.

Wariness returns to her eyes.

"You were drunk," I say. "Fine. But that doesn't excuse what you did, and you know it."

"Please don't yell at me," she whispers.

"Please don't pretend to be all weak and wounded," I snap.

She flinches.

"There are rules about how people treat each other," I say with what I think is amazing control. I'm about to continue when I see Anna roll her eyes.

Bam, back comes the anger.

Bam, back comes Cole on top of Anna. Anna smiling blearily. Anna all rumpled and lip-swollen.

"There *are*," I repeat. "There are *rules* about what you do and don't do."

"You and your rules," she mutters.

Screw you, I think.

Yes, I'm glad she's alive. Yes, I've maybe got too many rules. *But she climbed into bed with Cole.*

"You don't fool around with the guy your sister likes," I say, throwing my words at her like stones. I *want* them to sting. "And that's not 'my' rule. It's a decent human being rule. Except actually, it's more than that. It's a *sister's* rule, and you know it."

She bows her head.

"Sisters have to look out for each other," I go on. Only, why is my voice suddenly wobbling? "*We* have to look out for each other, Anna. You and me. Because if we don't . . ." My throat closes. "God, Anna, who will?"

She cries. *I* cry. We are a puddle of ridiculous-ness behind a Porta Potti, but I don't care. Or, I *do* care. I care so much that our ridiculous-ness is absolutely without importance.

"I'm so sorry," Anna says raggedly.

I nod and keep crying, but I also attempt a smile. Our eyes lock, and everything stupid is washed away by our flood of tears.

What's left is love.

I know we'll close back up; I know we'll be big and little shits again. But for this bit of space and time, we flow into each other like water. And this blending of our souls . . . it's breathtaking. It's part of the grandness that, to me, means God.

Thank you, I say silently.

Several moments pass, and then Anna changes the subject. I think she does it because . . . Oh, I don't know. Because humans can only be translucent for short chunks of time, maybe.

"Roger's a lot nicer than Cole," she says.

"Tell me about it."

"He tried to stop Cole from taking me upstairs."

"He did?" I wasn't expecting this. "What do you mean?"

"He tried to stop him. He said, 'That's Carly's sister. Show some respect.'"

It's a punch in the gut. It's awful and lovely and awful again.

"I don't get why you don't like him," Anna says.

"I *do* like him."

"Yeah, but I mean *like* him like him."

"Yeah, well, I think I *do* like him like him." As I say it, I realize it's true. Roger, who lets me be me, and who likes what he sees whether I'm wearing dashikis or nail polish or his own huge jacket. Roger, who isn't someone I squelch my beliefs for. Who isn't someone I have to impress.

Roger, who has not just soulful eyes, but soulful everything.

Anna gets excited, and then her hangover kicks in and she winces. "*Ow.* My head." She squints. "So are you going to tell him? Are you going to go for it?"

I think about how he left without saying good-bye. Under my breath I say, "Going, going, gone."

"Huh?"

I shake my head. "It's too late."

"No way," Anna says. "Not with Roger. I'm sure if you just—"

"Please," I say. I need her to drop it, and after searching my face, she does. She takes my hand and squeezes. I squeeze back. We're holding hands behind a bright blue Porta Potti, and I can't think of any place I'd rather be.

Except one.

I pull Anna to her feet. "Come on, let's go home."

CHAPTER FIFTY-TWO

WHAT HAPPENS IN VEGAS
STAYS IN VEGAS

"I'm not a good babysitter," Tracy proclaims. Anna's gone to take a shower, and Tracy, Vonzelle, and I are sitting in the TV room eating bagels. I've changed shirts and am puke-free. I feel cleaner, and not just from fresh clothes.

"You pretty much suck as a babysitter," I say. "But, hey. We're all still alive."

Tracy cradles her head in her palms. "Oh, crud."

A black limo pulls up in front of the house. When Tracy sees it, she turns ashen. It's Mom and Dad's car service.

"I'll go pack now," she says, rising from the sofa.

"Okay," I say. "But don't worry. I'm not going to tell."

"You're not?"

I shrug. "Ehh. No one was hit in the head with a brick. No one got sent to jail."

She stands there, looking bewildered.

"Go pack," I instruct her, and she scurries out of the room.

Next comes the commotion of arrivals and departures as Mom and Dad reclaim the house and Tracy and Vonzelle take off.

"Stay cool," Vonzelle whispers as she hugs me good-bye.

Stay cool. I almost laugh. "Yeah, I'll do that. You stay cool, too."

She does laugh. "It's going to be okay, Carly. I swear."

I don't know about that, but I nod and tell her I'll see her to-morrow.

Anna comes downstairs smelling like her sugar-cookie body wash, and Dad gives her a far more exuberant welcome than he gave me. I got, "You didn't burn the house down, I see." She gets, "Anna!" and a big hug, as if he hasn't seen her in months. Then he holds her shoulders and gives her a once-over. She's wearing a baby-blue tank top, the straps of which don't fully overlap the straps of her pink bra.

"Is it possible you've *grown* in the two days we've been gone?" he asks.

She smiles a pained smile. I decide exuberant Dad-welcomes aren't all they're cracked up to be.

Hours later, after Mom and Dad have taken time to unwind, Dad summons me to the living room.

"Carly!" he yells. "I need to talk to you!"

Oh no. Does he know about the party? Does he know I let my sister sleep behind a Porta Potti? Am I totally busted? I'm hit with a nause-ating swill of adrenaline, and sweat pops out under my armpits.

Chill, I tell myself as I put down my book and scooch off my bed. Maybe he just wants to talk about the ducks, which he's *not* excited about. Anna did her sweet, darling-daughter thing, twining her arms around his waist and saying, "*Please* can we keep them? Please, Daddy? Their poop makes very good fertilizer, you know."

He hemmed and hawed, because he has a hard time saying no to Anna. He never has any trouble telling me no, however. Maybe that's what this is about. Maybe he wants to get me alone so he can dash our duck hopes without having to witness Anna's disappointment.

Or maybe he knows about the party.

No. Stop it. He doesn't know anything. How could he know anything? The trick is to stay cool, like Vonzelle said. *Walk into a room like you own it,* I coach myself as I go downstairs.

But I stop a few feet shy of the living room, and I don't go in, even though Dad's waiting. I don't go in because I've been struck by a realization: I don't *want* to walk into a room like I own it. That's so . . . alpha dog, and I don't want to be an alpha dog.

Do I want to own my own self? Sure. But I have absolutely no need to own the whole room. In fact, I'd prefer not to.

So I straighten my spine and own myself.

"What's up?" I say, taking a seat on the sofa opposite Dad's.

His expression is hard to interpret. He seems relaxed, yet definitely in alpha-dog mode, the way he's scrutinizing me.

"Did you remove that video?" he asks.

My eyebrows go up. *This* is what he called me down about? The Buckhead Hillbillies video?

"No," I say. Not rudely, just stating the facts.

"Carly, I told you to take it down," he says, and now his expression is easy to read. His anger was waiting there all along. "It's offensive."

Stay calm, I tell myself. *He gets to have his opinion, you get to have yours.* Working to keep any defensiveness from my tone, I say, "I don't think it's offensive. What makes it offensive?"

"You know exactly what makes it offensive."

"No, Dad, I honestly don't." I can guess what *he* thinks makes it offensive—the implication that wealth is stupid and that having money doesn't make you better than anyone else—but even that I'm not sure of. Either way, why should he get to cast the ruling vote? If Dad finds something offensive, does that make it universally offensive?

He regards me as if I'm deliberately provoking him. "The Buckhead Hillbillies? When we and all our friends live in Buckhead?"

"It's a farce! Sheesh!"

"Carly, I want it gone," Dad says tersely. "Stop arguing and do what I ask."

I dig my fingernails into my palms. "But, Dad . . . you *aren't* asking. You never asked. You *ordered.*"

"And you out-and-out disobeyed me. How do you think that makes me feel?"

"Well—"

"It doesn't make me feel inclined to let you keep those ducks, I'll tell you that," he says. "Either the video goes or the ducks go— and I'll let *you* inform your sister of your decision."

The breath is knocked out of me. He's blackmailing me into doing what he wants! He thinks this is how fathers should act, and I don't know if I can hold strong against him. I want to—I want very much to own myself—but tears prick my eyes, dammit, and I panic, because I can't let him see me cry. And that means I can't challenge him, because if I do, I *will* cry.

So? the innermost me says. *If you cry, you cry. You're allowed to cry.*

"There's no law that says I have to take it down," I say in a quivery voice, "and you make me feel about this small"—I demonstrate with my thumb and forefinger—"when you order me around."

Ah, crap. Saying it out loud *does* make me cry . . . and not just one tear or two, but a whole river of them. Here we go again, just minus the Porta Potti.

But I don't like feeling small. It's not nice to make people feel small. I don't want to make anyone feel small ever again.

As I cry, *Dad* tears up. He turns away, blinking repeatedly. His face contorts as if he's fighting against himself.

"Dad?" I say.

He shakes his head. He holds up his hand to ward me off.

I'm stunned, and scared, because I have *never* seen Dad cry.

"*Dad?*"

"Carly . . ." His voice is clogged. "I don't mean . . . I don't mean to make you . . ." He can't say it. This scares me even more, that there is something in this world my father can't do.

He meets my gaze. His eyes are wet. "Don't you know how proud I am of you?"

No, I think, and my tears flow harder. He's *proud* of me? Why has he never told me?

"You think for yourself," he says. "You don't care when people laugh at you."

When people laugh at me?! When have people laughed at me? Even in this moment when I *know* he's trying, he manages to mess it up.

"But, Carly, it's one thing to be strong when people laugh at you." He swallows. "It's another to turn around and laugh at others."

I don't understand. He's looking at me as if I've wounded him, callously and intentionally. But . . . how? With my stupid video?

I try to see it from his perspective.

I pasted his face onto Jed Clampett's body. I called the video "The Ballad of Ted Clampett." Of course he thinks I was laughing at him—*because I was*. I didn't realize I actually hurt his feelings, though. It never occurred to me that I, his often ridiculous daughter, had that power.

A hole opens inside of me.

"I'm so sorry," I say. I hurt my dad, and I'm bawling, and I sound like Anna. Like a little little kid. "I'm so sorry! I'm so *sorry!*"

He beckons me, and I go to him. He presses me to his chest.

"I'm sorry, too," he says. His voice breaks, and my tears are hot and never-ending. His Italian-cut dress shirt is a goner.

"Carly?"

"Wh-what?"

"I would like to ask you a question."

"Okay." I'm doing that hitching, snuffly sort of breathing that feels strangely good. "Go"—snuffle-hitch—"ahead."

"Would you please take down the video you made?"

"No problem." I pull back enough to see him. "Anyway, I think all your law partners have seen it by now, don't you?"

He shoots me a look, and I laugh. It comes out thick and mucus-y. He tries, but fails, to suppress a Dad-style chuckle.

"So now *I* have a question for *you*," I say. "Can we keep the ducks?"

He shakes his head like he's a fool. It gives me hope.

"Please?"

"I suppose," he says. "But only until they're old enough to survive on their own."

I nod.

"And you're going to have to build that hutch for them. They can't keep living in your bathtub."

"I will, don't worry." I don't know *how* I will, but I will. I'll pull directions off the Web or something.

"Just tell me one thing," he says bluntly. He's back to the constipated Dad I know and love. "I don't want to hear the whole story, because I doubt my heart could take it. But, Carly. Please tell me you didn't *pay* for those ducks."

His words prompt a fresh batch of tears, but they're the burbly, feel-good kind. "Don't worry, Dad. I got a very good deal."

CHAPTER FIFTY-THREE
THE NON-IRONIC LOVE BOODLE

On Monday, Coach Schranker has our whole PE class file into the pool area to watch Anna do her dive. He's making her do it publicly, just as he said he would. What a wanker.

Anna comes out of the locker-room in her red bathing suit. She wraps her arms around her ribs and stands hunch-shouldered. The rest of us are dressed out in our PE shirts and shorts, and I'm sure she's embarrassed to be the only one in a swimsuit.

"All right, Anna," Coach Schranker says, using his no-nonsense voice. "Let's see it."

Anna looks at us. I give her a big thumbs-up.

Vonzelle says, "You can do it, Anna."

"It's easy, I swear," Peyton chimes in.

Whatever, I think. Peyton's acting like Saturday night never happened, and while I'm not about to join in and pretend to be best buds again, I choose not to call her on it. I do stifle a laugh when Vonzelle rolls her eyes, though. Peyton huffs and flips her butt-long extensions.

"Let's go," Coach Schranker says.

Anna walks slowly to the bottom of the ladder that leads to the high dive. She puts her hand on the railing. She stops and looks back.

"Anna," Coach Schranker warns.

She locks eyes with mine, and the message she's transmitting is, *Please come here. I need you.*

I hurry over. The air smells even more chlorine-y by the boards.

"Anna, you can do it."

"I don't know," she says. Her tone makes my gut twist. "I'm scared."

I try to stay calm. "I know. But you have to do it anyway." I swallow. "You *have* to, Anna."

She wraps her bare foot around the back of her other leg. Gazing at me from under her long lashes, she says, "Well . . . I'd kind of feel better if maybe you did something scary, too."

Wait a second. What is she up to?

"I called Roger last night," she says.

"What?!"

"I told him you need help building the duck hutch. And, um, that you like him."

"Anna!"

"Oh, come on," Anna pleads. "You said yourself that you do. Can't you please be the right girl who finally ends up with the right guy?"

"You've been spending *way* too much time with Vonzelle," I say, thinking, *Oh my God, she told him I like him? What did he say? She wouldn't be telling me if it was bad, would she?*

"But Vonzelle agrees," Anna says. "We want you to have your happy beginning."

I turn to glare at Vonzelle, who waves. She then gives an unsubtle jerk of her chin to direct my attention to the bleachers. I look where she wants me to, and my pulse quickens, because sure enough, there's Roger, leaning over the bleacher railing and resting his weight on his forearms. He's wearing a flannel shirt and his usual unflappable expression. Except he *is* flappable. I saw it when he proclaimed his feelings for me . . . and again when I proceeded to rip his heart out and stomp all over it.

But he's *here*, looking strong and kind and handsome. *So* handsome, because it comes from his sweet soul, which is ten thousand times sexier than a stupid guitar.

Whoa, my body says. Not "whoa" as in stop, but "whoa" as in . . . *whoa*.

I turn quickly back to Anna, blushing so hard I can feel heat radiating off me.

"He came to cheer me on," Anna says, all innocence.

"Uh-huh," I say. I might faint. I really might faint.

"Ladies, this isn't social hour," Coach Schranker says from the side of the pool. "Do it or don't, Anna. Pass or fail."

"Roger's your ironic love boodle," Anna says softly.

I concentrate on breathing.

"Promise you'll talk to him, or I won't do the dive."

Coach Schranker strides over. "Am I going to have to start counting again?"

Anna keeps her focus on me. She arches her eyebrows.

"Fine," I say dizzily.

She grins.

"I think we've wasted enough time here," Coach Schranker says, and damn if his eyes don't dip to Anna's chest. What a serious, serious wanker. "I've gone out of my way to give you a second chance, Anna, and I must say, I'm very disappointed."

"Don't be," Anna says. She climbs confidently up the ladder, strides to the end of the board, and turns around. She lifts her hands above her head, looks up, and falls.

"She . . . she did it," Coach Schranker says, flabbergasted.

"She did it!" I cry. I've got so many emotions churning inside of me that I can hardly function—but she did it, she *did* it, *she did it!*

"Wh-hoo!" Bad Attitude Cindy calls out. Other girls join in. "Way to go, Anna!" "Beautiful!" "You rock!"

I rush to the side of the pool. When she surfaces, I squat and slap her a high five that turns into a wet handclasp.

"Anna! I'm so proud of you!" I exclaim giddily. She spits out a little water and smiles.

"*Gefeliciteerd*," someone says in a deep voice behind me.

Still gripping Anna's hand, I glance over my shoulder. It's Roger, of course, saying some Dutch thing that no one understands, but which is clearly congratulatory.

I'm dimly aware of Anna telling him thanks. I'm far more aware of his eyes on mine. He might have come to support Anna, but really, he's here because of me. His expression tells me that without words, as does the up-and-down jerk of his Adam's apple. He's flappable all over again.

I'm slammed with nervousness. Still, I manage a timid smile which means *yes* and *I'm sorry* and *you are a beautiful, gorgeous boy.*

Relief transforms his features, followed by solid, sturdy joy. My heart leaps, and I lose my balance. Or maybe Anna accidentally tugs me. All I know is I'm falling backward. *Oh, crap.*

And then Roger lunges forward and extends his hand—

which I grab—

and it's big and strong and holds me tight—

and yet I'm too far gone, I'm toppling into the pool. I'm *in* the pool, my PE clothes drenched, and Roger falls in with me, his fingers clasping mine. He comes up spluttering like a surprised, flannel-wearing Loch Ness monster, and I laugh. Anna squeals, and water goes up my nose. I can't stop laughing.

The Wanker blows his whistle. "Carly! Out of the pool!"

I ignore him and grin at Vonzelle, issuing a challenge with my eyes.

"Not a chance," she says. Then she makes an *oh, fine* face and jumps in, splashing the girls on the side.

Bad Attitude Cindy launches herself into the air next, yelling, "Cow-a-bunga!"

Anne Heather and Tatiana shriek, and then *they* leap in. Lydia shields herself with her hands and cries, "You're getting me wet!"

"Too bad!" Jodie says, giving her a shove. Lydia yelps and clutches Jodie's arm, and they both plunge in together.

The Wanker blows and blows his whistle. "Girls! Out! Now!"

Jackie, Hailey, and Margot interpret that to mean "Girls! In! Now!," and they jump in holding hands. Peyton is the only girl left on the pool deck. She steps away from the water, anxiously gathering her extensions into a ponytail and holding them off her back. I'm almost sorry for her, my once-upon-a-time friend who's unable to get wet for fear her hair will fall out. It's too bad for her. I'd rather have real-ness any day.

Roger pulls me toward him in the deep end. We're treading water, because even he isn't tall enough to stand.

"I'm going to kiss you now," he tells me.

"You are?" I say, giggling and also struck with a sudden zing of nerves. "Better do it quick before the Wanker calls the National Guard."

He draws me close. My heart flutters like crazy.

"I've got to warn you, I'll probably taste like chlorine," I say.

"*Sakkerloot*," he says. He presses his lips to mine, and we both go under.

And then? We paddle harder and come back up, because that's all we *can* do. Anna and Vonzelle are whooping. The Wanker is furiously blowing his whistle.

Roger and I smile foolishly at each other. We keep paddling and try again.

BIG DUCKY KISSES TO:

All the quacks at Dutton who take care of me with such skill and enthusiasm: Stephanie Owens Lurie, Steve Meltzer, Scottie Bowditch, Eileen Kreit, Irene Vandervoort, Rosanne Lauer, and Lisa Yoskowitz, as well as every single sales and marketing peep out there, because I know how hard y'all rock. I mean *work*. Oh, let's be honest, I mean both.

A special Dutton-thanks to Allison Verost, for casting the deciding vote to allow "Git R Done" to stay in—and for being an absolutely fabulous publicist (who just happens to have absolutely fabulous hair).

My Atlanta buds who help me with Atlanta details whenever I need them: Gini, Julianne, and Mags.

Jeanette Meyer for talking to me about sisters.

Sarah Mlynowski and E. Lockhart for their most excellent early reads of this book. Sweetie-dudes, I don't know what I'd do without you. Y'all helped me make this novel *sooooooooooo*—takes deep breath—*ooooooooooo* much better. And plus, y'all are just cute, and you make me laugh, and if you were ducklings, I would throw you the yummiest bread crumbs ever, and they wouldn't ever be stale. ☺

Bob! Yo yo yo! Couldn't have done it without you.

My huggable agent, Barry Goldblatt, whose outward ferocity hides his squishy-marshmallow-Peep interior, and who keeps me safe in the shelter of his wing.

My family in general (every one of you, always), but especially:

*my mom, who's the best mama duck IN THE WORLD;

*Le Grande Fromage for all the life lessons he's passed on, and which I've absorbed, though not always in the form he intended;

*and Susan White, Mary Ellen Evangelista, and Eden Knox for being my dear sisters. Love you ~~guys~~ ladies!!!

My in-house flock of duckies: Jack, Al, Jamie, and Mirabelle. Y'all inspire me, delight me, put up with me, and is loving me. I is loving you right back, forever.

And finally, Julie. *Oh, Julie.* Julie Strauss-Gabel, that is—an editor so extraordinary she can turn duck poop into gold. Thanks for pushing me so frickin' hard. Thanks for caring. Thanks for being you.